Return to Me

James Oliver French

Kaituhi Press
Christchurch, New Zealand

Printed by CreateSpace

ISBN:13: 978-0-473-29466-3 (Paperback)

Edited by Michelle Browne (Magpie Editing)
Cover by James Oliver French

*I dedicate this book to all LGBT couples in loving relationships,
because you prove to the world that our love
is no different from anybody else's.*

Chapter One

I'm not the most gregarious guy, so it took a whole lot of convincing from my roommate Lee for me to come along with him to the party tonight. After I finally gave in, he thought it might be best if we had a couple of socially lubricating drinks in our dorm room before heading out, so that I wouldn't be too socially awkward. What a dick! As I stare across the heaving hordes of partying students, I ask myself, "Why was I so hesitant?" This party is off the hook and I'm wasted … such a good feeling.

A girl trips and falls onto me, spilling her drink all over my new shirt. I catch her and she stares deep into my eyes like I'm her savior.

"I'm sorry, but I'm gay," I try to shout over the noise of the crowd.

She slurs, "Hey, Ray. I'm Kirsty." She belches and almost vomits, but swallows it back down. Not sexy!

"No, I'm gay," I shout even louder in her ear.

"You're what?" she yells, cupping a hand to her ear.

1

"Never mind," I say and walk off, much to her annoyance. I need to get my shirt dry, and our little conversation was clearly going nowhere.

I squeeze my way through the crowds, and it takes two laps through the house to find the bathroom. I finally have a good look at the damage to my shirt. That dumb bimbo was drinking some vile concoction and it's stained the fabric deep red. I take my t-shirt off and try to rinse it under running water. The world starts spinning and I wobble on my feet. I have to grab hold of the hand basin to steady myself. Wowzers, I'm drunk. Most of whatever she was drinking washes out, but it leaves behind a bright pink smudge that looks like it's here to stay. Now my shirt is not only stained, but also drenched. Smart move, Todd. What was it again that everybody always says about alcohol and making unwise decisions?

The bathroom door swings open, and a hot guy with a short military-style haircut, wearing dark blue jeans and a black singlet, walks in while undoing his zipper. He pulls out his johnson before he realizes that he's got company, and startles when he notices me. I take a step back in surprise too. My eyes drop straight to his crotch and he stares at my bare torso.

"Sorry, man. Didn't know anybody was in here," he apologizes.

He zips up his pants, leaves the room and closes the door behind him in a hurry.

I just saw another guy's dick. Score! I mean, I've seen other guys naked before, obviously. But if I'm going to be honest, mostly in porn videos, almost never in real life. I hope he didn't catch me staring.

I do my best to wring out every drop of water from my t-shirt, then put it back on. It used to cling to my body and make me feel sexy, but now it's creased and baggy. I look like a homeless person. Ah well, who cares! I'm here to have a good time, right?

Lee finds me lurking in the hallway and drags me into the crowds.

"Where are we going?" I say, ducking out the path of a flying wad of toilet paper.

"To dance off the alcohol. You'll thank me tomorrow." He smiles and leads me into the belly of the house, where the lights are down low and the music is pumping.

Within minutes, Lee has his tongue down the throat of some girl he just met. I know he's going to regret taking her home with him tonight, which he inevitably always does. Probably safer if I don't go back to our room until tomorrow morning. I'd rather not have to try sleep through the sounds of them doing the nasty.

For a long time I don't notice the guy staring at me from across the room. He winks, and I smile back bashfully. I'm not used to getting attention from the hottest guy in the room … or any guy, for that matter. Wait a second … he's the one who flashed me in the bathroom! Standing there in his black singlet, showing off his muscled arms, and swaying to the music: just oozing cool. I cross the dance floor, never breaking eye contact with my handsome admirer.

"Hey," I say.

"Hey, I'm Kyle."

We shake hands. He's got a strong grip. I wonder how it would feel wrapped around my dick. Whoa! Where did that come from? Is this the alcohol talking? I'm still a virgin! The furthest I've ever gone was heavy petting. I'm a good Christian boy, after all. In high school, my boyfriend and I pledged "no sex before marriage" chastity vows. We even gave each other those stupid promise rings that everyone was wearing a few years back.

"I'm Todd."

"I'm a big fan of the comics," he shouts in my ear.

Kyle points at my stained t-shirt with a picture of the Wolverine from X-Men on it. I've never met anyone my age who's even heard about the comic books, let alone been a fan of them. Most people my age are fans of the movies, which don't even come near to portraying the true depth of the characters and meaningful story arcs. They're only interested in the cool mutant powers.

"It's ruined, though." I rub at the pink stain.

"I have to apologize for barging in on you in the bathroom earlier."

"There's no need," I assure him, putting my hands on his hips. He smiles and we draw closer together.

We dance for over an hour without saying a word to one another. It's too noisy to have a conversation anyway. The packed room means that we can grind up against each other without being inappropriate in public, same as all the other couples in the room. I can feel the bulge of his erection rubbing against mine through my jeans. Our lips connect and almost magnetically lock together. Our tongues dance while our bodies merge into one. His kiss electrifies me.

I glance around the room filled with other couples kissing and drunk singles staring with envious eyes at their hooked-up friends. Kyle touches my cheeks with his fingertips and guides my lips back to his. Goosebumps spread across my skin as he touches me. It's as if nothing exists in the room except the two of us.

Bright light explodes all around us and illuminates the entire room. There's a deafening silence as the music stops abruptly. Everyone in the room shields their eyes and looks around, filled with indignation.

"Okay, kids, it's time to wrap this up," booms the stern voice of a police officer. Several members of the riot squad show up behind him.

Girls start screaming and rushing for the doors. There must have been a hell of a lot of underage drinking going on, because I've never seen so many people swarming for the nearest exit in my entire life. It doesn't dawn on me immediately, but I'm on the honor roll and need to get out of Dodge, pronto. Getting arrested at a party isn't going to look great on my med school application.

Kyle whispers in my ear, "If I lose you in the crowd—" just as a line of girls pushes their way between us and through the crowd. Kyle is pulled away as we're swept apart by the sea of people.

"Meet you where?" The pandemonium going on around us drowns out my words.

I lose sight of him and then he's gone. I stand there in disbelief.

"Move, asshole!" A girl snaps at me as she shoves past. I recognize her from earlier. Kirsty is dragging a skinny nerd by the hand, a guy so drunk he can barely keep his eyes open. She's found her prey, and boy is she going to be disappointed when he passes out on top of her tonight. I guess that's what we're at college for—to live and learn, right?

I follow the masses out onto the street and decide to take a shortcut through a nearby park. Now I see why the police were called out. A bunch of imbeciles had started throwing bottles at the neighbors' houses and trashed one of the cars parked on the street. Our night of drunken debauchery has officially drawn to a close. It's been fun, but now it's time to go home.

Then I remember—I don't want to see Lee having sex ever again. Once was enough to scar me for life. I'll take a walk home and go the scenic route. That should help kill a few hours and burn off what's left of the alcohol in my system.

As I walk through the park, I wonder if I'll ever see Kyle again. I feel so alive right now. There isn't a cloud in the night sky, and the park bench looks like an inviting place to lie down for a moment to marvel at the canopy of stars. It's a bit more uncomfortable than I imagined it would be, but the view is spectacular.

I get a strange shiver down my leg that gives me a fright. There's something moving in my pants. I leap to my feet and push out the contents of my pocket. Out falls a phone. It's an iPhone, and I'm definitely an Android guy, so where did this come from? I pick up the phone. The call is coming from an unknown number.

"HELLO, Todd SPEAKING!" I shout into the phone. My ears are still cottony from the loud music at the party. I repeat myself, more quietly than before. "Um … hello, Todd speaking."

"Hey, sexy man."

I know exactly whose voice it is, but I still have to check. "Is this … Kyle?"

"You're talking on my phone," he chuckles to himself. "Look, I've borrowed a phone from a very kind gentleman who I just became acquainted with here on the corner of I'm-Lost and Middle-of-Nowhere, so how about you come meet me some place we both know? Outside the zoo in twenty?"

"I think I can find it."

"If you get lost, use the GPS on my phone."

"See you in twenty," I say eagerly.

Now where is the zoo? I orient myself and start running as fast as my Converse shoes will carry me.

I make it to the zoo, but I'm out of breath and sweating like a pig. Compounded with the ruined shirt and drunk dancing all night, there couldn't possibly be a single attractive thing about my appearance. There Kyle is, leaning up against a guardrail, waiting patiently for me.

"How … did you … manage to get here so fast?" I say in between desperate gasps for air.

Kyle laughs at me and says, "Taxied. I hate cardio. Are you okay? Please don't have a heart attack."

"Just give me a minute," I say, my hands on my knees and head between my legs.

Kyle ambles over and puts his arm around me. "Let's go on a little adventure together. Ever been on a safari?"

I don't know what to expect. Tonight has gone nothing like I'd planned. One thing is for certain, though—there is no way I'm going to be able to climb over those twenty-foot-high, spiked walls in my inebriated state.

Kyle takes his keychain out of his pocket and uses one of the keys to unlock the side-entrance gate.

"This way, sir," he says with a bad French accent as he gestures to me to walk inside the zoo.

"Are we going to get in trouble?" I hesitate as I walk through the gate.

"Nah, the security guard who does the night shift is pretty hopeless. He isn't going to bother us." He can see the unease in my expression. "Trust me." His voice is reassuring, but it's not easy for me to challenge the rules like this.

He peers into the security office. An old guy in uniform is sound asleep, leaning back in his chair with his hat over his face and feet up on the desk.

It's dark inside the zoo, the only illumination coming from emergency strip lighting that runs along the boundary of each of the enclosures. Listening to animal and bird sounds at night is completely different from during the day. There's a creepy, mysterious peacefulness. We jump onto a golf cart covered in zoo advertising and Kyle starts the engine. He keeps the lights dimmed so that our eyes can adjust to the dark. We cruise along the empty paths, which during the day would be surging with throngs of tourists.

We stop when we come to a garden in the very center of the zoo. He kills the engine and we dismount the cart. I run across the grass lawn and Kyle playfully tackles me to the ground. The soft grass cushions our fall, and I once again find myself in his strong arms. We kiss and he slowly runs his hands through my hair. I can't believe what I've been missing out on all these years.

We slump onto our backs. Too amped up to fall asleep, and too tired to say a single word, we communicate with each other through touch. This feeling of another person's skin against mine is so foreign. I have no control over where his hands travel across my body. His fingertips graze over the sparse hair on my belly. It tickles like having a feather dust over my skin. I catch his hands and our fingers link together. We stare into each other's eyes.

I'm not sure how much time passes before we realize that the sun has started to rise above the horizon.

"Shit!" Kyle curses. He springs to his feet. "We'd better get out of here before the next shift changes over."

We run past the security office on our way out the zoo, and I see that the guard is still snoring his head off. As the sun starts to make its slow ascent it feels peculiar walking down empty streets devoid of pedestrians and traffic. Kyle takes my hand and slow dances with me down the street. This boy just can't stop making me smile.

He whispers in my ear, "Would you like to come home with me?"

Without a moment's hesitation, I answer, "Can we get a

taxi? 'Cause my feet are killing me."

We both laugh and he reaches into my pocket to find his phone. I had forgotten it was there this whole time. While he's fixated on the phone, I check him out from head to toe, taking in every little detail, from his dimpled cheeks down to the way his jeans hang loosely below his belt line, showing off his underwear. He's perfect.

We arrive at Kyle's apartment building, which is in a shabbier part of town. He's on a major bus route, though, so it's a short ride to the main university campus. I notice his hand jitter as he puts the key in the door. He must be nervous about bringing me home. That makes me feel so very special. I've never done anything like this before, so I can't decide if I'm excited or anxious. Probably both.

We step into the tiniest apartment I have ever seen. 'Mini-malist' doesn't begin to describe the place. There's only enough space for a couch and a television in the living room, and the open plan kitchen has a single workbench with an oven, sink and microwave. Everything is spotlessly clean and tidy.

"Can I make you a cup of tea?" he asks.

"I'd love one," I reply with a raspy voice from having to shout all night at the party.

Kyle fills two cups with water and puts them into the microwave to heat up.

"The shower is through there if you want to go first." He points to one of two doors leading out of the room. I assume the other door must lead to his bedroom. I still can't believe how tiny it is.

"You have a nice place," I say as I walk into the bathroom.

I shut the door behind me, then wish I hadn't. Did I just literally and figuratively close the door on him? Would it be weird now if I opened it again? No point psychoanalyzing myself. I need to get out of these disgusting, sticky clothes and back to Kyle. The shower pressure is amazing. Every tiny drop of water massages my tired body and washes away the alcohol, sweat and party smells from my skin.

I step out of the shower feeling like a new man. With a towel wrapped around my waist, I head back into the living room. Kyle isn't there, but his bedroom light is on. I enter his room, which just fits a double bed and bedside drawers. There's a fresh cup of tea waiting on my side. Kyle lies sprawled out on the bed, fast asleep. I'm not sure what to do. Should I wake him?

"Kyle?" I say, hoping he'll stir.

Kyle rouses with a snort. "Sorry, I closed my eyes for a second." He rubs his tired eyes and stumbles like a zombie off to the bathroom. He leaves the door open. From where I'm sitting on the end of the bed, I can see the mirror on the wall of the bathroom and part of his reflection. In a complete daze, he undresses and then steps out of view into the running shower.

I don't want to climb into his bed before he asks me to, even though the invitation is implied. Two minutes later, the shower turns off and Kyle walks back into the bedroom with a towel around his waist. I gape at his amazing abs and defined chest. I notice that he has a small tattoo of a bird on the right side of his chest, over his heart. Kyle drops the towel onto the floor and I avert my eyes like the polite prude I was raised to be. He scoots into bed and lays his head on the pillow with his eyes closed.

"You not getting in?" he asks with a yawn.

"I'll get the lights." I hit the light switch on the wall near the door. The apartment goes pitch black. I can't see a thing.

I drop my towel and search for the edge of the bed with outstretched hands. I find the bed and slip in under the warm blankets, only to find Kyle snoring softly beside me. As my head hits the pillow, I'm out like a light.

Chapter Two

It's lunchtime on Monday, and I can't get Kyle off my mind. I sat through every lecture in a dreamlike stupor, playing back the events of Saturday night. When I woke up yesterday, he had a full breakfast ready and waiting for me to eat in bed. It was so romantic, although we never went any further than kissing. It took a lot of restraint, but I just didn't feel ready to take things to the next level, and he never pressured me to do anything else. We exchanged phone numbers when I left after breakfast, but I haven't heard anything from him since then.

All day I've been checking my phone with obsessive-compulsive regularity, hoping, wishing, *praying* he'll text me. I consult Google on my phone and open the first few search results that appear. The advice I read from various agony aunties is disheartening. They all say the same thing—"*Wait for the guy to text you back*". Now, this works great in theory, except I'm pretty sure that it's directed at straight people. Because if two gay guys were to follow this advice, it would create an infinite circle of waiting. I finally find a gay search result, which is even less helpful, as it takes me straight to a porn site. Not what I was hoping to find, but a couple of the guys look pretty hot, so I'll spend a few minutes exploring.

My phone vibrates, sending a surge of adrenaline coursing through my veins.

It's my mom—*"Hi honey. Just checking in on you. Love mom xox."*

What a let-down! At first I can't stop my fingers from bashing out a text, telling her all about the weekend and meeting Kyle, but a feeling of dread sweeps through me. I don't want to jinx things this early on, so I delete the message and send my standard—*"All is well in the world of Todd"* response.

This is ridiculous. If I'm going to get anything accomplished today, I'd better suck it up and send a text—*"Hi Kyle. Bn thinkin bout the party on Sat. Had a gr8 time with u. Wud u lk to hang out sumtime? Todd."*

I read the message about a hundred times. He's going to think I'm illiterate if I use textspeak. *Delete.* I try again—*"Hi Kyle. Been thinking about the party on Saturday. Had a great time. Would you like to hang out again? Todd."*

My finger moves towards the send button in slow motion while my mind screams *STOP!* He's going to read *"been thinking about"* and know that I've been obsessing about him all day, or he'll see *"like to hang out"* and think that I just want to be friends. *Delete. Delete. Delete.* And again—*"Hi Kyle. Would you like to come to the cinema with me on Thursday? Todd."*

Short, sweet and to the point. *Send.* There's a buzz in my hand two minutes later. It's a message from Kyle—*"It's a date.*

I've been thinking about you all day ;-)"

I resist the urge to reply. There's so much more I want to say to him. But as confusing as the advice columns were in their approaches to sending the first text, they all consistently said that after the arrangements are confirmed, play it cool and commence radio silence.

How am I going to survive until Thursday?

My wish is answered when I get a call from Kyle later in the day.

"Hey, Todd. It's Kyle here."

"Hey, you. How are things going?" I try to sound chilled out, but my hands are already slick with sweat.

"There's this thing tonight that I wondered if maybe you would like to … you know … if you might be interested in coming along to—"

"Yeah, sure. What thing?" So much for playing it cool.

"Tryouts for the wrestling team."

"You think you have a chance?"

Kyle laughs and says, "Maybe with the right people supporting me."

"Can I get back to you?" I have nothing planned tonight, but I don't want him to know that.

"Oh?" I can hear the disappointment in his voice. "Of course."

"Awesome! Text me the details."

"Will do. Hopefully see you later."

I wait fifteen minutes and text him back with an affirmative for tonight. He replies with a smiley face and I let out a tiny squeal of excitement.

Now I can call my mom and tell her all about him. She'll be so excited for me. When I came out of the closet to my parents as a teenager, they were as loving and accepting as a young gay guy could wish for. Mind you, my family probably had their suspicions long before I said anything. The simultaneous My Little Pony and GI Joe requests for Christmas must have confused the hell out of them. For me, being gay was completely normal. No one, not even the people at the church I went to, treated me any differently than the straight kids. I had dreams, just like all of them, of meeting someone amazing, falling in love, getting married and living happily ever after. I'm grateful because it saved me from having to be secretive. And secrets have a nasty habit of coming back to bite you when you least expect it.

Sounds of cheering and whistles blowing guide me into the student rec center. I'm late, as usual, and the event is already well underway. There are two large wrestling mats, both with manhandling going on in each of the central circles. Guys dressed in one-piece wrestling singlets and headgear wander around everywhere, reminding me of Borat in his mankini. Sometimes I marvel at how immature I can be. There's a decent crowd that turned out tonight, and I'm forced to find a seat halfway up the stands.

All I can say is WOW! I've never seen so much visible penis line in all my life. I don't get this sport. It just looks like homoerotic roughhousing to me. Two guys mounting each other and wrestling for dominance—isn't that what gay guys call foreplay? And those singlets? Not that I'm complaining, but the guy—and he could only have been a guy—who made up the rules about having to wear spandex must have been gay. And all these dumb, buff straight guys fell for his nefarious plot to bring a homo fantasy to reality. "Bravo," I say to him. "Well played."

The coach yells out, "Kyle, you're up next!" A muscled guy in a navy wrestling singlet stands up and approaches the mat. His opponent, dressed in red, meets him in the central circle. I wouldn't have recognized Kyle with his mouth guard and headgear. His package looks enormous in that ridiculous outfit.

The referee says something to Kyle and the guy in red before leaving the mat. Both wrestlers stand opposite each other, shifting the weight between their feet. The whistle blows and they grab each other in a headlock. Kyle's opponent bulldozes into him and catches his leg, sweeping him up into the air. The crowd gasps in unison as Kyle lands on his back at an awkward angle, bringing the other guy down with him. That's going to hurt. Kyle swings his body over the other guy and lands on top of him, pressing him flat against the floor. The guy in red pushes himself back up onto his knees with Kyle still attached to his back. He stumbles, and they both fall out of the circle and onto the mat. The referee blows his whistle and they both return to the circle.

The next part of the match gives me instant wood. Kyle's opponent gets down on all fours, facing away from Kyle, who assumes a doggy-style position directly behind him. I don't know how Kyle maintains his flaccid composure, because I couldn't participate in this sport. There's a whole lot of choking, headlocks and intimate clutching. This sport makes no sense to me.

The whistle blows a few more times, and then the match is over. Kyle shakes the other guy's hand and heads over to the team benches. He walks with a bad limp and his left shoulder is hunched. It's the first time that I notice he's hurt, and I won't deny that I'm concerned about his wellbeing. His coach looks happy and the other guys congratulate Kyle. I guess he must have won. The team physiotherapist runs over and examines Kyle's shoulder. It looks like he's in a lot of pain as the physiotherapist and one of his teammates help lift Kyle onto a stretcher and carry him away.

Half an hour passes by, and Kyle hasn't re-emerged from the bowels of the sports center. The last match finished ages ago, and I'm sitting here in the empty stands, playing with my phone. I sent him a text fifteen minutes ago, but he hasn't responded to that either. I hope he's all right and not on his way to the hospital. I'm tired of waiting and need to put my mind at ease. I take a deep breath, put my brave pants on, and go searching for him.

I walk through the doors that Kyle went through earlier and follow the signs to the team locker rooms. This leads me downstairs and into a rabbit warren of crisscrossing hallways.

A guy in a tracksuit passes me and asks, "Are you lost?"

"A little. I'm looking for Kyle. Do you know where—?"

"Ah, yeah. He was in the medical bay last time I saw him." The guy points me in the right direction and I thank him.

With directions in hand, the medical bay isn't that hard to find. I walk in on Kyle saying thanks to the doctor, who smiles at me as he leaves the room. Kyle's now wearing track pants and a t-shirt. Such a pity; I liked seeing him in the wrestling outfit.

"Hey, Todd! Did you see me out there?" He must be on some strong painkillers, because he's way more animated than I was expecting him to be.

"You were great," I enthuse.

"You don't have a clue how wrestling works, do you?" Am I an open book to this guy? He has me completely figured out.

"Nope. But I do want to know your secret for not … you know … getting turned on while you're fighting. Those guys are hot!"

Kyle laughs at me. "They're *all* straight, you fool."

"Whatever works for you," I laugh with him. "Do you need a hand with your bag? I'll walk you home."

"Look at you coming to my rescue." He hops off the bench and grits his teeth in pain as his feet hit the floor.

"Where does it hurt?"

"Everywhere."

Pete, the captain of the wrestling team, pops his head into the medical bay to check on Kyle. "Someone order an ambulance?"

Kyle tries to laugh, but he's in too much pain. Pete saunters in and gives Kyle a supportive pat on the back. "You did well tonight. I hope the coaches see the potential that I see in you. Be great to finally have you on the team, bro."

"Thanks, Pete." The two guys fist-bump.

Pete gives me the once-over. "This your boyfriend? Hey, bro, I'm Pete."

"I don't know," says Kyle. He looks at me and winks. "Maybe?"

I blush.

"His name is Todd," Kyle answers for me. "I think we just embarrassed him."

Pete shakes my hand with the most powerful grip I've ever felt in my life.

"Nice to meet you, Pete," I say.

"Right. I'm out of here. Catch you homos later." Pete dashes off, and it's just me and Kyle left on our own.

"Come on," I say. "Let's get you home."

We arrive at the bus stop just in time to catch the next ride home, and find ourselves a seat near the back.

"Why do you live so far off campus?" I ask.

"Bit of a long story. I'm paying my own way through college and couldn't afford the dormitory fees."

"Is that why you work at the zoo?"

"Most Saturdays," he says, "but most of my costs are covered by the scholarship."

"You got a scholarship?"

"Don't sound so surprised. I was class valedictorian."

I'm unsure if he's having me on or being dead serious, but I'll take his word for it.

"You always been good at sports too?" I ask him.

"Competitive swimming in junior high, and then really got

into my wrestling later on. You play any sports?"

"Is chess a sport?"

He laughs at me. "No, chess is not a sport."

"Oh good, 'cause I don't play that either."

He smiles at my lame joke. The bus slows down and pulls over.

"This is our stop," says Kyle.

I grab his bags and we step down onto the sidewalk. I remember where we are now. Kyle's apartment building isn't far from here.

"You from Los Angeles?" asks Kyle.

"Denver. Moved here for college," I reply.

"I have family in Denver."

"You been there?"

"No," Kyle shakes his head. "Sorry."

"Maybe one day I'll get to take you on a tour of the city."

Kyle smiles at me.

I continue. "Where do you call home?"

"This is home now," sighs Kyle. "My parents moved around a lot when I was growing up. Dad was never any good at holding down a job for long."

Kyle blows out a puff of air. "By the way, I didn't mention this before, but if I seemed uninterested in having sex the other night when you stayed over." He pauses and considers his next few words. "It's because I'm still a virgin," he says.

It explains so much. "Me too."

"I hoped you might say that," says Kyle with a devilish grin. "You ever fooled around with another guy?"

"I had a long-term boyfriend through high school. We

jerked off together now and then watching porn."

"But you guys never had sex?"

"No." I want to tell him about the vow of chastity, but that kind of thing sounds weird to people who haven't been brought up in the church. "I guess we weren't attracted to each other like that. So—what's your reason?"

"Reason for what? Still being a virgin?"

I nod.

"I guess I've known since I hit puberty that I liked guys and not girls, but … I don't know … I guess until I left home, I wasn't ready to admit to myself that I was gay."

"And since you got to college?" I ask, my curiosity getting the better of me.

Kyle blushes. "Never had 'sex' sex, but I have had a bit of fun. That's what college is for, right?"

"How did your parents take the news?"

"Not well." He casts his eyes down at the sidewalk and furrows his brow. "It was just before I left for college. My mother erupted in tears and my father threw a chair across the room at me."

I look at Kyle in horror. He doesn't make eye contact.

"They told me they never wanted to see me again, and that I was a total waste of all the love and resources they had invested in me. I couldn't convince them. They didn't want to listen. So I took my bags and left. That was two years ago. I haven't heard from then since, and they won't answer any of my calls or emails."

I step in front of Kyle and he looks up at me. His lip is trembling and his eyes are watering.

"I'm sorry. I think the pain killers are making me all emotional," he says.

I throw my arms around him and hug him as tightly as I can.

"I didn't do anything wrong," he splutters as the tears begin to flow.

"I'm so sorry." I don't know what else to say. What would make a difference? I've upset him now, and I wish I hadn't said anything.

Kyle wipes the tears from his eyes and we carry on walking. I hold his hand to reassure him that I'm not going anywhere. He lifts my hand and plants a single kiss on it.

"Can't pick your parents, but you can choose who to spend your life with, right?" My words seem to comfort Kyle.

We reach the entrance to his apartment building. I turn to him and say, "Thank you for inviting me tonight."

"No. Thank you for being there to support me. You have no idea how much I appreciate it." He brushes aside the locks of hair that have fallen over my forehead.

"Can I kiss you goodnight?" I ask.

"Yes," he answers with a grin.

I lean in and kiss him softly. We break for a moment to gaze into each other's eyes. Nothing has ever made my heart pound as much as having this guy in my arms.

Kyle looks at the ground sheepishly and says, "Would you like to come upstairs?"

"I'd like that."

"Come on, then." He limps on ahead of me and I follow close behind.

Kyle drops his sports bag on the floor in the living room and tries to pull off his shirt. He winces in pain.

"You okay?" I ask.

"Not really."

"Let me help." He raises his arms as best he can and I lift the t-shirt up over his head. I run a hand down his chest and stomach. The bruises from tonight's matches are already starting to show. I envy his olive skin, which looks tanned compared with my pale complexion.

Kyle's lips touch mine. I wasn't expecting that. We kiss each other gently. I help him remove his shoes and socks and steer him to the bathroom. The shower takes a few minutes to warm up, and we stand stark naked together. I pull him under the hot water and watch it ripple across his flawless, toned body. I lather up the sponge and spin him around. Tenderly, I scrub him from head to toe. The soapy water is sleek against his skin. We both can't help getting turned on by the whole experience.

Soon we're both rock hard. I take his shaft in my hand. His penis feels so different to my own—thicker, more veiny, and uncut. His hand wraps around my dick. He fumbles at first, unsure what to do with a circumcised member, but he soon gets the hang of it. We stand under the cascading water, kissing and touching one another. I always thought that people had sex in the shower because there's less of a mess. I never imagined in my wildest dreams that it was because it feels so unbelievably good gliding wet skin against wet skin. I could do this all day.

Almost without warning, the hot water runs out. The icy surprise is an instant boner killer, and we leap out of the shower.

"Do you have any massage oil?" I ask him.

"Would sweet almond oil work?"

"Let's give it a try."

He grabs the bottle of almond oil from the bathroom cabinet and we move into the bedroom. Kyle drops his towel and lies face down on the bed in front of me. I remove my towel and climb onto the bed beside him. I fill the palm of my hand with oil and begin to gently massage it into Kyle's back and shoulders. He whimpers whenever I hit a spot that hurts, and I'm careful to avoid putting too much pressure on those areas again.

"So what's your favorite color?" I ask.

He snickers. "We're playing this game, are we?"

"Yip. I want to know everything about you."

"Hmm. Let me think ... blue. Yours?"

"Teal."

Kyle peers back over his shoulder at me and snorts. "If we're getting fancy, then I'm changing mine to cobalt."

"Favorite food?"

"That's easy," he says with a huge yawn. "A big, juicy piece of meat."

I know he's talking about beef, but I imagine him chewing on a very different piece of meat. My hands slowly work the oil down his back.

"Favorite song?"

"'Good Life' by ..." He yawns even wider than before.

"Excuse me. By Tim Myers."

The name doesn't sound familiar. "I've never heard it before."

Kyle utters his reply in a barely audible whisper. "You should listen to it sometime. It's beautiful."

My fingertips skim over Kyle's slightly fuzzy butt and slide down the back of his legs. He falls asleep as I massage him, but I don't stop what I'm doing. I'm enjoying examining every square inch of his beautiful body too much to stop just yet. My heart is racing, my dick is throbbing, and the guy of my dreams is sleeping in front of me. Sometimes life can be so incredibly amazing, and yet so unfair at the very same time. I consider for a moment whether it might be inappropriate to jack the beanstalk while rubbing his body, and sensibly decide to abandon that fantasy. Instead, I shoot into the bathroom to knock one out. After tonight's scintillating entertainment I don't even last two minutes.

Chapter Three

I spend half the afternoon trying to decide what to wear on my date with Kyle tonight. Lee ran out of patience hours ago and went to the gym to escape watching me go into diva meltdown mode. As if that ever happens! The movie starts at nine, and I'm only half-dressed. There's a knock on the door.

"Just a second," I shout, and make a last minute decision to go with a v-neck t-shirt that makes my shoulders look a lot more defined than they really are.

I open the door. It's Kyle, with red roses that must have cost him a small fortune.

"Hey you," I say.

"Nice shirt," he replies, using it as an excuse to check me out.

He places his hand on my shoulder and guides me towards him for a kiss. His cologne smells incredible—hints of bergamot and cedar.

"These are for you," he says and passes the flowers to me. This is so romantic. Who buys flowers anymore? Should I skip the romancing and straight-up ask him to marry me?

"That's so sweet of you," I say.

Now to find a vessel to hold them in. I start hunting around the room, but the closest thing I have to a vase is a Fleshjack case, and I don't want to frighten him away by pulling out a sex toy this early on in our relationship.

"Would you be offended if I left them in the bathroom sink for the meanwhile?" I ask.

"Of course not," says Kyle. "We should really get moving, though, or we're going to be late."

I grab my wallet, phone, and a jacket just in case it gets cold later, and we head out on our big date.

We thought that half an hour would be ample time to stand in line, get tickets and be seated long before the previews started rolling. Unfortunately, it turns out that tonight is opening night of some cheesy teenage love story about a couple of kids dying of cancer. The queue to buy tickets is mental: at least two hundred teenage girls, all wanting soda and popcorn, and on top of that, they all want to pay individually. At this rate, we might just get to see the midnight screening.

"Shall we go somewhere else?" says Kyle.

"What do you have in mind?"

"Want to go to the zoo again?"

My eyes light up. "Yes!"

This time we stop by the security office on our way into the zoo to say hello to the old guy who works with Kyle. He's asleep, as Kyle predicted, and we leave him to his dreams.

"Walk or drive?" he says to me.

"Let's take a leisurely stroll and pretend we're on a safari," I suggest.

It doesn't take long for our eyes to adjust to the dim lighting. Kyle leads me down the path to the "African Encounters" enclosures. My parents went to South Africa on their honeymoon and spent a few weeks in the Kruger National Park. We always planned to go back as a family, but the logistics never worked out in our favor. Dad always said that seeing animals caged up in the zoo was criminal, but I'm grateful having the opportunity to see these creatures, even if they aren't roaming the open savanna.

"What are you studying again?" I ask.

"I don't think I told you," he says. "Guys don't exactly go weak at the knees when I tell them I'm going to be an accountant."

I giggle. "My dad's an accountant."

That brings a smile to Kyle's face. "You're studying psychology, right?"

"That's right."

"What made you decide to do that?"

"I don't know exactly. I think it's because I'm one of the lucky ones. Life has pretty much been an easy ride so far. But then I see how many people suffer on a daily basis in the name of survival and ... well, I suppose that's the reason why I've always wanted to be a doctor. I want to help spread some hope around."

"Wait, I'm confused. You want to be a doctor, but you're studying psychology?"

"Psychology is my backup plan. I'm going to apply for a position in a medical program once I've finished my clinical psychology degree."

"Right. I see. So you're totally risk-averse?" he says as he drapes an arm around me.

"Are you calling me boring?" I tickle him, and he runs away, giggling. I chase him, but he vanishes into the dark.

"Okay, you can come out now!" I call out. All I hear are the chirps, shrieks and howls of the animals.

A ghostly figure rushes through my peripheral vision and tackles me from the side. I get the fright of my life and scramble to my feet. Kyle can't stop laughing at my cat-like reflexes.

"Oh man, that was funny. You should have seen your face!" he says.

My hands are shaking. "I'm glad you had fun. You scared me shitless."

"Come here. I'm sorry. I didn't mean to scare you."

He hugs me and rubs his nose against mine. The electricity that courses through my veins from his touch makes me instantly forget the fear. His soft lips meet mine, and they taste so good. Every kiss we share is better than the one before.

"Let's go find a place to sit, or I'll end up kissing you standing here like this all night," he says.

We find that same old spot in the center of the zoo and lie down on the grass alongside each other. Kyle rolls over onto his stomach and props himself up on his elbows. The view from down here couldn't be any more stunning—his handsome face framed by a sky full of stars.

"So how come I've never seen you at one of the LGBT student mixers?" he asks.

"Not really my scene."

"What? You don't like hanging out with gay people?"

"I don't see why we need to have exclusive clubs and events. I helped out last year with the LGBT student committee, but it was depressing. It felt kind of like a club for kids who no one else wanted to be friends with."

"Isn't that the whole point?"

"That made me sound like such a douche. I'm sorry. I'm kind of nervous."

"Nervous?"

"About this. Being here with you."

"What do you have to be nervous about?" he says.

"Well, I really like you, and ..."

"And?"

"Hypothetically speaking ... if you and I were a property ... would you be interested in signing the lease, or are you just squatting until the right location becomes available?"

Kyle leans over me and peers down with a quizzical look.

"Are you asking me out?"

"Only if the answer is 'yes'?"

"What am I getting myself into?" he says and laughs. "You're weird, Todd Chambers. Of course I want to be your boyfriend."

He seals it with a kiss.

Chapter Four

Perhaps staying up all night last night talking wasn't the best idea. I had an 8 AM lecture this morning, which I missed, along with the lecture at 10 AM ... and 2 PM. I just can't get enough of Kyle.

There's hardly any time to tidy up my room and get chores done before he comes over tonight. I also forgot to speak to Lee about having the room to myself, but I'm sure he'll be cool with it. I've lost count of how many times he's asked me to study a bit later at the library so he can entertain a young lady in our room.

Lee walks through the door with a satchel slung over his shoulder.

"Sup," says Lee.

I sidle up to him. "What are you doing tonight?"

He narrows his eyes at me. "Nothing. Where were you last night?"

"I had a date."

"I already know that part." He taps his fingers on his desk

and waits for me to give him the gory details, but I'm as tight-lipped as a CIA operative under enemy interrogation. "Is he coming over tonight?"

"That's the plan."

"You want some privacy, right?" he asks while he boots up his laptop. Great! He gets my drift. "Okay, let me see if I can find somewhere to sleep tonight."

He whips out his phone and starts texting. I cross my fingers and toes that one of his friends with benefits is free. The funny/sad thing about these girls is that when one of them calls herself his "girlfriend", Lee almost never corrects them. If only they knew how much of a manwhore he is, he'd be singing soprano by the end of the week.

I make a quick trip to the store to collect essential supplies. When I return, I see that Lee has very sweetly left a ribbed condom sitting on my pillow. For the first time, I consider the possibility that tonight could be the night that I lose my virginity. The thought paralyzes me with fear. Kyle is also a virgin, so at least he won't have high expectations. Or maybe he'll have huge expectations of a porn-star quality performance because he doesn't know any better! What if I'm terrible in the sack? Tonight could ruin sex for both of us for the rest of our lives. There's a knock on the door, and my anxiety turns into outright panic.

I open the door to Kyle's smiling face and the panic melts away.

"Good evening, handsome," I say, mimicking his infectious grin.

He lifts a pack of beers. "I brought beverages."

I'm not much of a drinker, but I'd guzzle gasoline if he asked me to.

Kyle eyes the condom packet still sitting on my pillow. "Expecting company?"

I almost die of embarrassment.

"My roommate wanted me to be prepared," I reply.

"That's my sexy Boy Scout."

He edges closer and pulls me in for a kiss. Our kiss lingers, and it amazes me that a guy can have such sweet and tender lips, and still be so damn masculine at the same time.

"Beer?" he asks.

"Yes, please."

He cracks open a beer and passes one to me. The cold, bitter flavor is comforting and soon settles my nerves.

"I got a couple of DVDs for us to watch," I say, heading over to my desk to grab the boxes. "Are you a thriller or a horror fan?"

I hold up both DVDs and he quickly scans the titles. He looks a little disheartened.

"I'm more of a comedy guy," he says.

Crap. I guess I shouldn't have assumed anything. "We could download something?"

Kyle smiles and nods. "That sounds cool."

He jumps onto my bed. I lean over the desk, flicking through a list of movies until I find one that sounds funny. I turn around to confirm the choice of film with Kyle and catch him staring at my butt.

"Are you happy with this one?" I ask.

"Yes, very," he answers, that adorable smile plastered all over his face.

The download starts. It's going to take a minute or two for the movie to buffer. In the meantime, I kill the lights and hop onto the bed beside Kyle. He puts his arm around my shoulders and I snuggle into him as the movie begins. My heart thumps, and I don't even bother to hide the growing tent in my shorts. Kyle is completely immersed in the film and doesn't seem to notice my response to his close proximity. Soon I find myself engrossed in the hilarity on screen. Before I know it, the credits are rolling.

I get up off the bed and head over to the refrigerator.

"Would you like another beer?"

"You read my mind."

I pass him another cold one. The conversation dries up and both of us chug our beers, too apprehensive to make the next move. After what feels like an eternity, Kyle pats the bed beside him and confidently says, "Come sit here."

I sit a couple of inches away from him on the edge of the bed.

"I really like you," he says.

"I really like—"

He puts a finger to my lips. "Hush ... I wasn't finished yet." He continues, "If you're ready ... I'd like you to be my first."

His words echo in my head for a few seconds.

"You mean ... sexually?"

"I always wanted my first time to be with someone special. And I think you're pretty neat."

I don't know how to respond to that with words, so I place a hand on his thigh and give him a gentle squeeze. His lips part ever so slightly, and I know he wants to kiss me again.

Our lips connect and passion ignites inside of me. I've never been so scared and so excited at the same time in my short life. We fall back onto the bed, and our tongues entwine as he kisses me more deeply. I unbutton my shirt, and he pulls his t-shirt off too. He rolls on top of me, and we press our half-naked bodies together. I can feel his erection straining to break free of his jeans as we grind into one another. He starts nibbling on my earlobe and neck, which sends tingles down my spine.

He plants tender kisses on my chest and runs circles with his tongue around my nipples. With a gentle breath, he makes them go rock hard. As his tongue dances over my skin, the most exquisite feelings race through my body. He moves lower now, and with the same technique, teases the groove running from each hip towards my crotch. The ecstasy has me on edge already.

He unbuttons my jeans, and with a single pull, they're sitting around my ankles. I lie there, exposed, in nothing but my bulging underwear. Kyle sucks seductively on the damp spot starting to appear. He runs his mouth along my swollen member, squeezing it between his lips. His tongue flicks across each side of my groin, and he pulls my underwear open just enough to expose my balls. As his tongue flicks across my skin, I let out a gentle moan. Kyle pulls off my underwear, allowing my penis to stand at attention.

He wraps his hand around the base of my shaft. "Have you ever measured how big it is?" he asks.

I laugh at him, and he starts to swirl his tongue around the head while simultaneously stroking the shaft. His other hand tickles my balls, setting off a symphony of sensations that drive up the intensity. The muscles in my butt and abs start to contract, and I know that I'm getting close. It's never happened this fast before.

He runs a finger across my hole and his touch drives me over the edge. I can't hold back any longer, and my orgasm erupts. Kyle chokes momentarily as the first pulse hits the back of his throat. He greedily swallows every drop. I gasp, and my whole body contracts rhythmically for half a minute. As the calm sets in and the orgasm fades, I lie there in a daze.

"That was AMAZING!" I say, panting.

He watches me tenderly and my heart flutters.

"My turn," I announce with a smirk.

Kyle pulls off his jeans. He's not wearing any underwear, and I marvel at his large dick, framed by full public hair. He lies back on the bed and folds his arms behind his head.

"I meant to ask you before, what's the tattoo of?" I say, pointing at the bird on his chest.

"It's a hummingbird," he says, brushing his hand gently over the tattoo. The corners of his mouth turn down. The tattoo has special significance, but I get the feeling that it's not a good time to ask what it means.

I crouch low to get a good look at him. As a circumcised guy, I've never seen an uncut penis in real life up close like this, and I find it fascinating. The way the foreskin wrinkles together at the end reminds me of an old-fashioned money-bag with the purse strings pulled tight. It's peculiar, even though it's the way every guy's tool is supposed to be.

"Are you just going to stare at it?" Kyle chortles.

It's literally a stretch to fit his erection inside my mouth. I want to get it all in so badly, but my jaw aches from being stretched so far wide open.

"Babe ... Todd, stop." Kyle lifts my head and looks me in the eyes. "You don't need to swallow it all at once. Maybe try it like this?" He pulls his foreskin back to reveal a glistening mushroom head. Why didn't I think of that? I knew I was doing something wrong. I try a different technique that makes Kyle squirm in delight. I guess it must be true what they say about uncut guys being extra sensitive.

"Fuck yeah, that's it!" Kyle groans in delight and pulls my hair gently like he's reining in a horse.

I copy what he did earlier to me, jerking him off with one hand while going down on him. Every swirl of my tongue makes him twitch in satisfaction.

He grips my hair tighter and starts pumping my mouth, pushing his dick further and stretching my jaw to the limits. I start to gag, and he releases his hold on my head.

"My bad." He laughs at me. "You okay?"

"Yeah. I think you hit my gag—"

"Good." He pushes my head back down and impales my mouth. Rude! But kind of hot, so I'm not complaining, just moaning.

I can hear his breathing getting shallow, and his body starts to tense. But then he suddenly pulls my head away from

38

his crotch.

"Okay, you better stop," he says, squeezing his eyes shut and tensing up for a second.

"Why?"

"I want to save it for later." He winks and pulls me in for another wet kiss.

"How are we going to do this?"

I look down at my shriveled dick, which is in refractory hiding, and see only one possibility.

"You go first. I'll be the bottom," I say, in a tone much braver than I feel about the prospect of losing my anal virginity.

"Do you think we need to use condoms?" he asks.

"You've never had sex before, right?"

He shakes his head. "Just oral."

"We could do it bareback, then. Can't catch anything if we're both virgins, right?" For once, I'm grateful that I've been so chaste in the past.

"I don't think you can get HIV or hep C, but you can definitely catch the clap ... and chlamydia."

"Oh," I say, feeling a bit dispirited.

Kyle chuckles. "If I did have either of those, I think you'd already be infected by now."

My heart starts galloping in my chest. I throw caution to the wind. "Let's do it."

Kyle gets the naughtiest glint in his eyes. "You sure?"

I run my hands up his thighs. "I hear it feels better, too."

"I guess we're about to find out," he says with an eager grin. "Do you have any lube?"

"As a matter of fact, I do."

My brief excursion earlier today also included swinging by the drugstore and becoming the proud owner of a large pump bottle dispenser of personal lubricant. I chose to swallow my pride and ask the pharmacist what she recommended for anal sex. She was surprisingly nonchalant about discussing the ins and outs with me.

I reach into my bedside drawer and pull out the expert-endorsed lube dispenser.

"How do you want me?" I ask.

"I don't know." He studies the label on the lube bottle. "What do you think you would like?"

"Lying on my stomach?"

"Yeah, let's try that."

I flip over onto my stomach and slip a pillow under my hips, which lifts up my butt.

"You have a fucking sexy ass," he says as he kneads my buttcheeks. *Thanks*, I think to myself.

He massages my hole with his thumb, and my dick springs back to life. I feel a cold sensation as he squirts out a blob of lube. He works a finger into my butt. My hole clenches down hard and holds his finger in a viselike grip.

"Man, you're tight!" exclaims Kyle. "Can I have my finger back?"

"No," I say, and squeeze harder, which paradoxically makes everything start to relax.

I close my eyes and remind myself to breathe. He slides a second finger inside and I'm surprised by how good it feels. This could be easier than I expected.

I feel his dick slap against my butt. He rubs the head around the entrance, and I lift my ass to tempt him to enter me. He squirts more lube into his hand and makes sure he's well-oiled. Kyle grips his dick at the base of the shaft and lines the head up with my hole. His penis slides everywhere except inside me. I thought there was no such thing as using too much lube. We've inadvertently discovered an edge case.

By some miracle, the stars align and he manages to hit the target, only it feels like someone just shoved a fist up my ass. I let out a yelp, and his dick pops out. Kyle lets out an exasperated sigh.

I lie there, patiently enjoying all the attention, but Kyle's efforts are proving fruitless. He keeps stopping to jerk himself off, but his poor penis has deflated to a shadow of its former glorious self. It looks like he's trying to shove a marshmallow through a keyhole. Losing your virginity shouldn't be this hard.

"There's no rush," I reassure him.

"I can't even stay hard now." He tries one last time, then throws himself on the bed in defeat.

I hate seeing him grow so frustrated. "Can I make a suggestion?" I say.

"What's that?"

"Roll onto your back."

He eyes me with suspicion, but complies with my command. I throw his legs up in the air and pin his knees to his shoulders, resting my full bodyweight on top of him. My penis nudges his hole, and that sexy smile of his returns.

"You going to fuck me?"

I reach for the lube to grease myself up and slide a finger inside him. It meets almost no resistance, so I slide in a second, and then a third finger. This is beyond any fantasy I've ever had.

"I'm ready," he says.

I push just the tip inside him and his butt squeezes shut.

"Just keep breathing," I whisper in his ear, and we begin to kiss.

Our kissing grows more intense, and we start to explore each other's mouths with our tongues. I'm halfway inside him. His eyes are still closed, concentrating hard on keeping himself relaxed. I kiss his neck and nibble his ear. Kyle grabs my hips and pulls me in right up to the hilt. His mouth drops open and his eyes widen like saucers.

"Holy shit," he gasps.

I lie there for a few minutes, and we kiss and cuddle while he accommodates to this new sensation. I love the warmth of being inside him, our bodies merged as one in this primal embrace. I take my time building momentum, rhythmically withdrawing and plunging myself ever so slightly deeper inside him each time. It doesn't take long before my groin and thighs are slapping hard against his butt, pounding his virgin hole.

Kyle jerks himself off in a frenzy. His eyes roll back in ecstasy as I glide out and thrust back in.

"Are you getting close?" I ask with the tiniest amount of desperation in my voice. I can't keep going much longer.

Kyle's breathing quickens and his chest heaves. "Oh fuck. I'm gonna … I'm gonna!"

I lock eyes with Kyle as he reaches orgasm. He throws his head back and grips onto my arms as he shoots and hits the wall behind his head. The next few spurts cover his chest in a sticky mess.

My body quivers. I didn't want to reach the tipping point so soon, but I can't hold back. I blow my load, except it feels like an explosion. My whole body rocks and spasms. Nothing in the world compares to this feeling of reaching climax deep inside him. I tremble in delight as my orgasm slowly peters out.

"Holy fuck, that was incredible!" he shouts out breathlessly.

I slump onto the bed beside him, spent. We lie there, panting and staring up at the ceiling.

"I've never had an orgasm like that," says Kyle.

"You're telling me? That was amazing."

I pass him the t-shirt lying beside me to clean up the mess.

"Thanks," he says.

Kyle wipes away the evidence of our lovemaking before realizing whose shirt I gave him. "Shit. That was my shirt."

"You can borrow one of mine."

"That means I'll have to see you again after tonight to return it."

"You bet your sexy ass you'll return it. I know where you live."

"If I lose this bet, do you win my sexy ass again?" he asks with a cheeky inflection in his voice.

I laugh at his joke. We lie there in post-coital bliss, steeping in this strange, new feeling.

"I'm so happy right now," I say.

"I'm glad you were my first."

"Technically, I'm still half a virgin," I say cheekily.

"For now," Kyle prophesizes.

We put an arm around each other, and I stare into his beautiful brown eyes.

"Is it too soon to say that I think I love you?" I ask, terrified.

"Not at all. Say it," he replies, relishing the moment.

"I love you, Kyle."

"I love you too, Todd."

"You want to do that again?" Kyle asks with a devilish grin.

Ten minutes later, we do it all over again.

Chapter Five

"Babe, have you seen my wrestling singlets?" Kyle calls out from his bedroom.

I know where his singlets are, but I'm enjoying watching him hunt all over the apartment in desperation. His place is the size of a matchbox. How can it be that hard for him to keep track of stuff?

"No, sorry. Haven't seen them."

Kyle found out last week that he made it onto the wrestling team. After two years of being a reserve, he's finally earned a chance to represent the university. Although we've only been together for a few weeks, I feel so overwhelmingly proud of his achievement. I just wish I could go along to support him, but the coach was explicit that no partners are allowed to attend. He wanted his team focused on nothing but winning. The coach did have a point. Every time I've seen Kyle in that tight spandex singlet, all I can think about is getting him naked. I'm certain that all the other girlfriends—we're the only gay couple on the team—have equally sordid intentions that would result in very little sleep, and a definite sub-optimal performance on the mat the next day.

Kyle marches out the bedroom wearing nothing but a towel wrapped around his waist. He just got out of the shower, and still has beads of water all over his body. I wish that gravity or some invisible force would make his towel fall down so that I can check out his tight butt again. I can't get enough of it. Kyle is my bottom bitch, and he knows how to drive me crazy by tempting me with that hot body of his.

"Shit! Where did I put them?" Kyle stops to think, and the light bulb goes off in his head. "They're still at the Laundromat from yesterday! There's no way they'll still be there." He starts to panic, and I decide that this is my opportunity to save the day.

"No, they probably won't be," I say. A sad look falls on his face. "But just maybe someone's amazing boyfriend stopped by on the way home last night and collected them."

His face beams. "Are you serious? You are the best freaking boyfriend ever!" He assaults my face with kisses.

"They're in my bag," I add.

The kisses stop abruptly.

"You serious? You're a dick!" he shouts as he races across the room to pull his gear out of my bag. "You know that?"

"I know that," I chuckle to myself. "Hey, don't I get a reward blowjob or something?"

"Eat me!"

Was worth a try.

Kyle gets himself dressed and finishes packing his bags mere moments before he receives a text saying that his taxi has arrived.

"Sure you got everything?" I call out to him.

"Are you trying to freak me out?" He shoots me a dirty look as he drags his luggage through from the bedroom.

"Do you need a hand?"

"No, I can manage. But I'd like a bit of lovin' before I go."

I give him a massive hug and kiss.

"Good luck with the tournament," I say.

"Thanks. I'm a bit nervous."

"You'll do great. I just know it."

He gives me the tightest squeeze and another slow, amorous kiss before disappearing out the door. I miss him already, and he's still on the same street as me. Without a doubt, it's going to be a long weekend without him.

While I'm left all by my lonesome, I figure it's a great opportunity for some self-exploration and self-improvement. I've been reading a few psychology books recently about relationships, and one piece of advice that stands out above all else is the importance of maintaining your own interests. Too many couples get comfortable, and in time, their fascinating identities merge into a singular, boring entity that's nowhere near as interesting as when they first met. It's all those hobbies and goals that attracted your partner to you in the first place. When a couple does everything together, they end up having no interesting stories to share, or any time apart to miss each other.

I sit down and try to list all of my endearing interests. This list is far too short. So, like the diligent geek that I am, I compile a checklist of goals that I would like to achieve in the coming months—start going to the gym, might even try out a gayrobics class, and go back to the student LGBT group meetings and give those guys a second chance.

I haven't set foot in a real gym since I finished high school, and the prospect actually terrifies me. Seeing all those tanned, muscled guys built like tanks is intimidating for a lanky guy like me. I signed up online at a 24-hour fitness club just down the street. Seeing as my access card arrived in the mail this morning, I have no excuse for delaying going another day.

It's a quick walk down the street to the gym. However, the facade of the building is misleading. I thought I had signed up for a poky gym that only had a handful of members. When I walk through the front door and turn the corner, I discover that the place is gigantic. There's an army of fitness fanatics pounding the cardio equipment to one side, and a swarm of guys pumping iron on the floor above. I take a big gulp and keep moving forward, even though I'm totally out of my element.

I stand in front of the mirror and inspect my gym shorts and singlet. This uniform looks so out of place on a geek like me. No way am I going to use the locker room until I have a bit more muscle … and confidence. You'd think that in a venue filled with Adonises, a gay boy like me would be like a kid in a candy store, but it's not like that at all. Half of me is scared shitless that if I gaze a second longer than I should, I'll end up with a black eye. The other half of me is desperate to fit in with all these straight guys and just be one of the boys working out at the gym.

The difficulty lies in the fact that there are so many mirrors. Mirrors everywhere. Where do I look? No matter which direction you stare in, there is someone who you'll make eye contact with. The only safe place for your eyes is down at the ground, but then you just look like a sad loser.

"Hey bud, could you give me a spot?" says a skinny guy sitting on the bench press beside me.

"I'm sorry, a what?" I have no idea what he's asking me.

The skinny guy laughs. "Newbie, huh?"

I nod. He lies down on the bench press and says, "Spotter stands behind the person pushing the weights and makes sure they don't drop it on their head. Think you can do that?"

Sounds easy enough.

"If it looks like I'm gonna drop the bar, catch it."

"Sure," I say, and assume the position behind the bench press.

The skinny guy is pushing twice the weights that I would have dared to put on the bar. I watch him heave and push like he's about to have an aneurysm, but he manages to finish ten reps.

"Yes!" he exclaims, scribbling something in a little notepad. I notice that most of the guys seem to use them. Must be to keep track of progress. No way will I ever be dedicated enough to do that.

"My name's Felix."

"Todd." We shake hands. "Well, I better get on with my workout. Catch you around, Felix."

"Yeah, sure, bud."

I wander over to the water cooler, where I become sandwiched in line between two beasts whose testosterone I can almost taste, they smell so ripe. I hold my breath and try to ignore their conversation about the pussy they got the night before. It's as if I'm not even standing there. And to be clear, I have nothing against vaginas—we all came out of one—but listening to dumb straight boys talk about it like a tradable commodity grosses me out. I don't think I'm thirsty anymore.

Someone taps me on the shoulder. I turn around, and it's Felix.

"You want to be my workout buddy today? It helps having someone there when you're starting out, just in case."

"Yeah, sure."

"Sweet. Ever done skull crushers?"

I have no idea what he's talking about.

Felix laughs and says, "That's all right. I'll turn you into a machine before you know it."

After three sets of skull crushers, which came very close to living up to their name, and a set of pullups, he shows me the proper technique for doing a bicep curl. I had no idea that pumping iron was so technical.

"Where did you learn how to work out?" I ask.

"Got a diploma in personal training right after finishing high school."

"Oh?" I say, surprised because he's pretty scrawny for a gym bunny. "So you train people professionally?"

Felix waves his hand through the air like he's swatting a fly. "Nah. I'm at med school. Personal training helped me discover that I really enjoy human anatomy ... so I decided to become a doctor."

"How far are you into the degree?" I ask as Felix grunts out his last bicep curl.

"Third year. So about a hundred still to go. What you studying?"

"Psychology. Got one more year."

"Oh cool, bud. You gonna be a counselor or something like that? I like the idea of becoming a psychiatrist, myself."

I pick up the dumbbells that Felix was lifting and almost dislocate my shoulder.

"Those might be a little heavy for you," he says, passing me weights from the rack I assumed were for girls. How embarrassing! "We all gotta start somewhere, right?"

His words of encouragement are empowering, and I battle my way through a full set.

"I was ... thinking of ... going to med school too," I say between reps.

"That's awesome! Maybe one day we'll end up working together on the wards."

"Have to get accepted first." Sometimes I can be such a downer.

"You'll get in. You didn't think you could do a pull up either, and you managed two."

When I think about it like that, he's right. Life throws enough curve balls our way; there's no need to start dreaming up additional obstacles in my path to success.

Felix looks up at the clock. "I think I've punished you enough for one day. Let's hit the sauna."

What could be more uncomfortable than working out amongst towers of physical perfection? The answer is lying half-naked in a hot, sweaty mess surrounded by them.

"You've never had a sauna before either, have you?" Felix laughs at me. "Trust me. You're going to need it, or your body will be aching all over tomorrow."

I follow Felix with tremendous apprehension. The bright colors from the workout area flow through into the locker room. It looks like no expense was spared on top-of-the-range lockers, benches and other fittings. There's a handful of guys of various ages, shapes and sizes going about changing, undressing, or walking around in towels headed for the showers. I catch a glimpse of a naked guy with the most perfect physique I've ever seen. I tell myself to stop staring at his bubble-butt, but it's easier said than done.

"Do you have a towel?" asks Felix.

"No, I wasn't planning on needing one."

"That's okay." He opens a storage cupboard labeled "Staff Only" stacked with towels. He tosses one to me, and we move to the showers.

We have a quick rinse in the public shower area and head into the sauna. By the grace of God, the room is empty. The hot, dry air catches me in the back of the throat as we walk through the door. There are several levels of benches surrounding an open, artificial coal fireplace in the center of the room. We lie back on the benches closest to the heat and close our eyes. I can feel the sweat start to run down my forehead almost instantly. In the silence I begin to drift off to sleep.

"Can I ask you a personal question?" says Felix, which interrupts the quiet and brings me back into focus.

"Sure."

"Are you gay?"

I've been openly gay for almost half my life, and this is the first time in ages that I've felt like someone just exposed one of my dirty little secrets. Making new friends stresses me out sometimes.

"It's okay if you are," he continues. "I don't mind talking about mangina with my gay friends."

I splutter and laugh.

"He did have a nice ass." Felix cracks open his eyes and winks at me. "You know ... the guy you were staring at in the locker room."

"You saw me?"

Felix laughs. "Bud, the way it works in the gym is like this. The fat people stare at the thin people. The thin people stare at the muscled people. The muscled people stare at themselves. The trainers laugh at all of them. You can be guaranteed that the hottest person in the gym is never going to notice you ogling them, because they'll be so busy checking themselves out." He closes his eyes and relaxes back on the bench again. "Just saying, don't hold back."

I chuckle at his words of wisdom. "So you're ..." I don't want to put a word in his mouth.

"Straight. Kissed a guy as a dare once, but all that stubble didn't really do it for me."

My body feels so heavy that I can't even summon the energy to wipe away the sweat that's running down my cheek and tickling my face.

"Got a girlfriend?"

"Fiancée. Her name is Georgina, and she's my darling angel." His voice drips with syrupy sweetness.

"Congratulations, then."

"Thanks, bud. You got a man in your life?"

"His name's Kyle. Been going out for a couple of months."

"Honeymoon period, huh? You guys must be having so much sex."

"Not really. We're waiting for marriage," I say, completely deadpan, but I can only maintain the serious expression for a few seconds before I crack.

"Dickhead!" he sneers.

We both laugh uproariously as a saggy old man with moobs hanging down to his belly button walks through the door. He gives us a disapproving look for disturbing the solitude. We settle back on the bench and allow our bodies to melt in the sweltering heat.

"This time tomorrow?" Felix asks before we go our separate ways from the gym.

"Sure, if I can move any of my limbs. I'm already starting to hurt."

"Two ibuprofen and a concrete pill. You'll be fine."

"Thanks, doc!" I wave him goodbye and make my way back home. I'm looking forward to my next gym workout already.

Chapter Six

I'm lying in bed, studying personality theory, when there's a knock at the door.

"Who is it?" I call out, not wanting to get up from my comfortable position.

"It's Kyle," replies a voice from the hallway outside my room.

I leap out of bed and whip open the door. Kyle's lips instantly smother mine and he envelops me in his arms. I whimper as he crushes my sore muscles, still aching from the gym.

I pull him into the room and he drops his luggage on the floor. He lifts my shirt over my head and caresses my bare skin

"All I could think about the entire weekend was coming home and having my way with you," he says.

"I didn't think you were back until tomorrow."

"Surprise." He kisses me again and removes his shirt. The sight of his toned chest makes me drool, but I fight it.

"No. Stop. We can't. Lee's going to be back any minute now," I say, holding him at arm's length.

He pushes me back and I fall onto my bed. Kyle climbs on top of me and straddles my hips.

Kyle whispers in my ear, "Let's give him a show."

His wish is answered as Lee barges into the room, carrying a box of pizza. He stops and looks at the two of us, semi-naked, fooling around on the bed. Without flinching, Lee sits on his bed and holds out the box of pizza. "Want a slice?"

"Kyle, this is my roommate Lee," I say, fumbling with my t-shirt.

"Nice to meet you," says Kyle, reaching over for a slice. "Don't mind if I do."

"I didn't interrupt you two at a bad time?" asks Lee.

He's trying to be funny, right? Kyle and I look at each other. We both shake our heads, acting all innocent.

"Anyway. I just popped by to collect my beers. It was nice to meet you, Kyle," says Lee. He hops onto his feet and pulls a pack of beers out from under his bed. "I'll be home around eleven. You boys have the room to yourselves until then. Be safe."

Lee departs with his beers and pizza in hand.

"Well that wasn't awkward," Kyle says sarcastically.

The two of us laugh and cuddle on my bed.

"How did you and Lee end up as roommates?" asks Kyle.

"We met the day we both moved in."

"So you didn't know him from before? Lucky he was cool with you being gay."

I laugh. "Funny you should say that. It was literally the

second thing he asked me."

"What? If you were gay?"

"Yeah. He'd been stalking me on social networking sites, and pretty much knew my whole life story before we met."

"Creepy."

"Maybe if it were anybody else, but Lee's harmless. So all my fears about sharing a room with a total stranger, and how he might react to sleeping in the same room as a gay guy, were all a complete waste of emotional energy. He didn't give a shit."

"Silly boy," says Kyle.

He rests his elbow on my chest and I wince in pain.

Kyle pulls away. "What's wrong?"

"I went to the gym. It hurts ... everywhere."

"You managed that all by yourself?"

"Met a really cool guy who knew heaps about bodybuilding. He helped me out."

"Aw, my little nerd made a friend. I'm so proud of you." He squeezes my cheeks like a proud parent. "If you're prepared to beg for it, I've been told I give a great massage," he says with a naughty smile.

I put on my best psycho jealous boyfriend face. "Oh yeah, who says that?"

Kyle leans in and lovingly smooches me.

"Ooh, I got something for you," he jumps off the bed and leaves me mid-kiss, lying there with my eyes closed, mouth pouting like a goldfish.

Kyle rummages through his luggage and extracts a trophy of a tiny bronze wrestler.

"I came third in my division." He hands it to me. "I want you to have this."

I take the trophy and cradle it in my hands.

I shake my head and try to pass it back to him. "I can't take this."

"I want you to have it."

I give Kyle a hug and kiss. "Thank you."

He brushes my hair over my ear.

"That's the sweetest thing anyone has ever given me," I say, my heart overflowing with joy.

"Now, how about that massage?" says Kyle.

I lie down on my bed and close my eyes. I'm like putty in this beautiful man's hands.

Chapter Seven

Kyle and I lie naked on the floor of his apartment, chests heaving and bodies wet with perspiration. The sex just keeps getting better and better.

"Can we have arguments more often? Make-up sex is incredible!" I say breathlessly, still coming down from my orgasmic high.

Kyle punches me lightly on the shoulder and smiles.

"You trying to start another fight?" I say.

"Maybe."

He taps me on the shoulder again with his fist. I launch myself on top of Kyle and tickle him relentlessly. He giggles and squeals like a girl, barely putting up a fight. He knows who's boss in our bedroom.

"Stop, stop. I can't take any more," he begs.

I pin his wrists on either side of his head and lay my body down on top of his. I gently bite his lip, his ear lobe, and slip the tip of my tongue in his ear.

"That tickles," he says, wriggling about.

I flick my tongue behind his ear, and lightly kiss his neck. "I can't help myself. I want to eat you up," I say.

"I hate to ruin a perfect moment, but what's the time?" asks Kyle.

Damn! We have to be at Felix's by 7 PM. I look up at the clock on the wall—6:55 PM. Dammit!

"This was your fault," I say, leaping to my feet and racing into the bathroom to turn on the shower.

"Oh please! You're always running late," he says dismissively.

Kyle saunters up behind me. He puts his hands around my waist and kisses my back. I feel a stirring down below, and know where this is going to lead if I don't put a stop to it.

I shrug him off. "Don't. Or we'll be even later."

I step into the shower and Kyle starts brushing his teeth.

"I'm looking forward to finally meeting your other boyfriend," says Kyle with a mouth full of toothpaste foam.

"Stop being insecure. Felix has a girlfriend."

"I'm not insecure. Someone will have to look after you when I'm gone."

"You're going nowhere," I say, rinsing the last bit of soap from my body before stepping out of the shower.

"The good die young. You, unfortunately, are going to live forever," says Kyle, prodding my chest with his index finger.

I sneer at him. "Get in the shower. We're already late." I slap Kyle's cute butt and he gives me a naughty grin.

We miss the next bus across town and arrive at Felix's apartment shortly before 8 PM. This isn't a great way to make a good first impression with his girlfriend Georgina.

"What if he's pissed off that we're late? He's never going to invite me to anything again," I say, anxiously twiddling my fingers.

"Take a deep breath and relax," says Kyle. "They're not going to give a shit."

All of a sudden I really need to go to the bathroom. Apparently I have a nervous bladder too.

I hit the downstairs buzzer. Felix answers almost immediately—"Hello?"

"Hey, Felix. It's Kyle and Todd."

"Come up." Have my fears been confirmed by his curt response? I hope not.

We take the elevator up to the apartment. Kyle rests against the handrail opposite me. He cocks his head to one side and eyes me up from bottom to top.

"What are you doing?" I ask.

"Nothing. Just trying to get an image of you ingrained in my mind forever."

"Pfft. Take a photo, it'll last longer."

"Who needs a picture when I've got it all up here to dream about on cold, lonely nights?" he says, tapping on his temple. The boy's a charmer, that's for sure.

The elevator doors open and we scuttle down the hallway to Felix's apartment.

"Oh crap, I forgot the alcohol," I say as if it's an absolute tragedy.

Kyle slips his fingers between mine and holds my hand. "You worry too much. It'll be fine. There will be plenty to share." He pecks me on the cheek.

Felix rips open the door. He's got a scowl on his face and he's still dressed in gym gear.

"Hey, I'm Felix," he says abrasively and shakes Kyle's hand. "Come in."

We walk into his apartment. It's luxurious compared with my dorm room, but still fairly cramped. There are platters of nibbles on the kitchen counter, a large bowl of punch, and a stack of red plastic cups, but otherwise the place is completely empty. Did everyone else stand him up?

"Nice place," I say. "But where is everybody?"

"They'll be here at nine," says Felix, opening the refrigerator to check on the status of the vodka jello shots.

Kyle chuckles. "You see what he did? Everybody knows that you're ALWAYS running late."

I look at Felix, who nods. "Pretty much."

I give them both a death stare. "Where's Georgina?" I ask, trying to change the subject.

Felix rolls his eyes and points his head in the direction of the bedroom. He shields his mouth and whispers, "It's that time of the month."

Kyle and I give each other an awkward sideways glance.

"Have you two been fighting?" I say.

"She won't get off my fucking case. All afternoon, she's been a total bitch," mutters Felix, only just loud enough for us to hear him.

"Have you asked her what's wrong?" says Kyle.

Felix looks up to think. He smacks his hand on the kitchen counter and sighs. "Fuck!" He hadn't thought of asking the obvious question.

"Could I use the restroom?" I ask.

"Sure, but you'll have to somehow get past Satan's Bride," says Felix. "I'd introduce you, but she's not speaking to me at the moment."

I leave the two boys in the kitchen and traipse up to the bedroom door. I knock, but there's no answer, so I turn the door handle and walk in.

"Georgina?" I say in a soft voice.

There's someone whimpering in the bathroom. I knock on the door.

"Busy," Georgina calls out, her voice cracking.

"Georgina, it's Felix's friend, Todd."

"I'll just be a minute," she says.

I hear her sniff, blow her nose, and finally the toilet flushes. She opens the door. "All yours."

"Are you all right?" I ask.

Her face crumples, but she manages to maintain her composure. "No. Not really."

"What happened?"

"It's all good. I'm just being silly. Our guests will be here any minute ... well you're already here ... and look at the state of me." She fakes a smile, but it instantly makes her look beautiful again. "I'm sorry," she says, extending her hand, "how rude of me. I didn't even introduce myself. I'm Georgina."

"Todd."

"Oh. You're Todd," she says with a bigger smile. "Felix

has told me all about you. It's so nice to finally meet you."

"Likewise."

"I'm sorry you had to see me like this. It's been a shit day, and Felix has been a total jerk all afternoon ..." Her voice trails off.

"Do you want me to drop a weight on his foot next time we're working out at the gym?"

She laughs. "Make sure it's a heavy one."

What I consider to be heavy would probably just bounce off without inflicting much harm, but she doesn't need to know that.

"I don't want you to think I'm a total drama queen. I'm not usually like this."

I smile and say nothing, giving her an opening to share her thoughts.

"Anyone in your family got dementia?" she asks.

"No," I say, rather confused by where this conversation is going. "Nobody in my family."

"You're lucky."

I put my cold reading skills to good use. "Is that why you're upset?"

She stares at the ceiling and sniffs back the tears.

"I went to visit my grandma at the rest home this morning. She's been living in la-la land for a few years now. She doesn't know what day of the week it is, but she always recognizes me." She chokes up. "Until today. I walked in the room and said, 'Hey grandma,' like I always do. She just stared at me. Then she asked if I knew where she could get a cup of tea, because she was thirsty."

I put an arm around Georgina, which she turns into a hug. "I sat there for half an hour and it was like I was having a blinking contest with a stranger. My grandma's gone. There's just a mindless old woman left behind."

"I can't imagine what that feels like," I say in my most comforting voice.

"Well, that's my melodrama," she says with a sniff and a smile.

"You're not being melodramatic. You have every right to be upset."

"You're so much easier to talk to than Felix. He's got the emotional radar of a robot."

"Nah, he's just your typical straight boy. If you don't spell things out for them, they get all confused and think it's their fault you're not feeling good."

"That sounds like Felix, always making it all about himself."

We both have a chuckle right when Felix walks into the room.

"You trying to steal my new best friend?" Felix gives Georgina the evil eye.

She drapes herself over my shoulder and says, "Too late. He's all mine."

Felix looks at both of us with suspicion, but I can tell he's thrilled to see that Georgina is in a better mood.

"You look stunning, babes," he says, admiring her pretty dress.

She blushes and sways the fabric of her dress slightly. "I must look a sight with these puffy eyes."

"Nah," says Felix. "You look beautiful."

He gives her a kiss on the lips and slips past both of us into the bathroom. "Okay. It's my turn to look pretty. See you in ten."

Felix's med school friends descend on the apartment en masse, and pretty soon every room is jam-packed with people. Drinks are flowing, and we're all having a good time. I haven't been able to wrench Kyle away from Felix all night. Felix is the only other person here who studied something else before med school. The others have no general knowledge outside of medicine, and poor Kyle was struggling to make small talk with anyone else. I've been in my element, though. Heard so much great advice about admissions procedures, how to score brownie points with the interview panel, and what study materials to get my hands on. The more I have to drink, the harder it becomes to stop myself from watching my boy. That's an understatement. We've been having hardcore eye-sex all night.

I look intently at Kyle for like the millionth time tonight. He bites his bottom lip and winks at me. I'm hanging out near the punch bowl with my new best bud, Georgina. We've also been inseparable tonight.

"How did you and Felix meet?" I ask, starting to slur my words ever so slightly. This punch is good shit.

"He hasn't told you?"

I shake my head. "No".

"He'll be mad at me if I tell you," she says.

"Why is that?"

"Because it makes him sound like a total dick, which he's not. I promise."

The corner of my mouth tilts up in a half-smile.

"Okay, fine," she begins, scooting closer to me. "It happened like this. Felix devised this awesome strategy to score himself a future hottie."

"Future hottie?"

"Hello!" she says, pointing at herself.

Okay, I get it now.

"He had this plan to find the fattest, prettiest girl in the club ... which was me ... I weighed a few more ... hundred and fifty pounds back then ... and he said he'd go out with me if he could be my personal trainer."

I try to swallow and laugh at the same time, which causes me to cough and splutter on my drink.

"What a dick!"

She puts her fingers to my lips to shush me.

"No. No. You see you didn't understand what I was trying to say. He's my prince charming. No other boy ever looked at me the way he did. He saw a princess."

I still think it makes him sound like an asshole.

"After that he took me to this dingy little Irish bar where we played pool and talked all night. I think I might have spewed all over him."

"What a beautiful story," I say rather sarcastically. "Would you excuse me? I need to use the little boys' room."

By the grace of God, the bathroom is free. I shut my eyes and siphon the python. I feel myself tipping to one side and quickly open my eyes to correct my balance. I'm way drunker than I realized. I zip up and turn around to find myself in Kyle's arms. He kisses me with tongue and cups my crotch.

"I've wanted to do that all evening," he says, walking back out.

"What? Is that all I get? Tease!" I shout as he slips out of view.

I wash my hands and join the others in the kitchen. Everyone is gathering up their odds and sods.

"What's happening?" I ask.

"Time to get our booty shake on," yells Georgina. She gets a "Hell yeah!" from the other girls.

"We should call for a taxi," I say to Kyle.

"Good luck getting a taxi at this time of night. We're walking," says Georgina.

Chapter Eight

So here we are, elegantly wasted, en-route to some club the girls suggested we go to. The whole way they haven't stopped bitching and moaning about how sore their feet are. What did they think was going to happen if they walked two miles in six-inch heels? I say it with feeling—what exactly do straight boys find attractive about drunk girls?

As we turn the corner and head down the main street that leads to the club, we see a queue of impatiently waiting club kids snaking from the entrance right around the next block. We join the back of the line, and right on cue, one of the girls starts complaining that she needs to go to the restroom.

Kyle laughs at my impatience. "Relax, babe, it's all part of the fun."

I roll my eyes and stare across the street at a much shorter line of hot guys slipping one by one through the doors into another club. My drunk eyes focus on the flaming red neon sign above the door—"*HEAT*".

Gay clubs never really interested me before, but tonight

I'm like a moth drawn hypnotically to a giant bug zapper. Apparently, *Heat* is the club where all the young, cute and twinky guys hang out. There's a couple of other clubs in the neighborhood—*Trap* for the hairy guys; *Base Camp* used to be the main gay hangout, but it got overrun with students who just wanted the cheap drinks; and the seediest of the lot, *Manhandle*, which is basically just a bar with a dimly-lit back room where guys go to hook up.

"I got a better idea," I say. I pinch Kyle on the butt and run across the road, almost getting hit by a passing car.

"Todd? Where are you going?" he calls after me.

I point up at the sign above the gay nightclub. He shakes his head and makes his apologies to our other friends, then runs over to join me.

Felix shouts out across the road, "Hey, can I come too?"

Georgina squeezes hold of Felix's arm. There's no way she's letting her hunky boyfriend near a gay club, even if he is only a one out of six on the Kinsey scale.

I shrug my shoulders and mouth "sorry" to Felix. He affectionately flips me the bird and waves good night.

The bouncer at the gay club sizes us up and says, "You guys have had a few tonight?"

We nod affirmatively.

"And you're aware that this is a homosexual establishment … that means boys will be kissing other boys on the dance floor?"

I giggle and Kyle elbows me.

"Yes, sir. We're a couple actually."

"Sir?" he seems chuffed to be addressed with such respect

by two polite young men. "I see. Okay, you two, just don't make all the single boys envious. I don't want a cat fight."

"Thank you!" we say, stepping into the club.

It's unlike anything we have ever experienced. The straight clubs I have been to simply pale in comparison with the grandiosity of the decor, lighting effects, and double-story dance floor. There are hot young men, as far as the eye can see, and everyone is having a good time.

"I'll get us a drink." Kyle heads towards the bar.

I stand staring out at the scene in front of me in awe. A group of guys walk by and one of them shoots me a wink and smile. I shy away in embarrassment. The music gets my feet tapping, and I start to groove on the spot.

I see Kyle talking to a handsome blonde stranger up at the bar. He's our age, maybe a year or two older, and very well built. Kyle extends his hand and they both shake, and it looks to me like they're exchanging names. The blonde leans across and whispers something in Kyle's ear that makes him blush. The guy keeps touching my boyfriend on the arm and chest. His blatant flirtation makes me rather uncomfortable, and I feel this intrinsic need to defend my man.

Kyle looks across the packed room in my direction, and when he locks eyes with me he points and waves. The handsome blonde follows his line of sight and twiddles his fingers at me. So gay … but so hot.

I head over to the bar to join Kyle and put my arm around his waist. The blonde guy eyes me up and down.

"Hi, I'm Todd. Kyle's boyfriend."

"George, nice to ..." he replies, but I'm too distracted by his perfect, chiseled chin to hear him. "... open relationship?" The last part gets my attention again.

Kyle laughs and answers on our behalf. "No man, we're together."

The blonde guy appears to be confused by the response. "Seriously?" he says with a gasp. "You guys just meet?"

"No," I reply, shaking my head. "We've been together a few months now. What about you?"

"Yeah my boyfriend's right over there." He points at a handsome Latino guy who is kissing some random dude on the dance floor.

"I take it you guys are in an open relationship?" I ask.

"We were open from the beginning. It's less complicated that way." He stares down at his boyfriend, expressionless, and knocks back a large swig of his drink. His matter-of-fact confession creates a rather awkward silence between the three of us. It seems to be a common theme with gay couples. They discard one another so soon after meeting, and claim to be bored with their sex lives. Kyle and I haven't scratched the surface of things we'd like to do together.

George is starting to depress me, and I'm out to have fun, not to be a relationship counselor, so I break the silence. "It was nice to meet you, George."

"You too, man. Good to meet you, Kyle."

We both shake George's hand, and I lead Kyle onto the dance floor.

"It sounded like he needed someone to talk to. We shouldn't have left him hanging like that," Kyle protests.

"Babe, he was after one of two things—some hot action with you, or a threesome with both of us."

Kyle looks aghast. "Really? I thought he was just being friendly."

"Yeah, well, have a gander at how friendly he's being with that guy over there." I look over at George, who now has his tongue in the throat of—and a hand down the pants of—a skinny, overly-preened twink.

Kyle squirms at the sight, then wraps his arms around me. "Guess we made a lucky escape."

"You owe me one," I say loudly into his ear.

I can see the cogs in Kyle's mind start turning. He bites his lip and says, "How about now?"

I'm not a hundred percent sure I understand what he's asking me. He takes my hand and guides it down to the firm bulge in his pants.

Kyle steers me through the crowded dance floor to the restrooms. He pushes me up against the wall and we kiss. With one hand, he takes a coin from his pocket and slides it into the condom dispenser on the wall beside us. Out pops a tiny box containing one serving of safe sex.

We only wait a minute before the door at the end of the corridor opens, then slip into the stall and lock the door behind us. Kyle rips open the condom package and throws away the condom, but keeps the sachet of lubricant. I place the palms of my hands against the wall and lean forward, my butt sticking out.

He wraps his arms around my waist and undoes my belt with the dexterity of a pickpocket. These hidden talents of his keep surprising me. My jeans drop to the floor, and he slides my underwear down to my ankles. He takes a second to admire my hairless bubble butt before I feel his hard-on smacking against my ass cheeks.

I hear the sound of his teeth tearing open the sachet of lube. A finger enters me, and I let out a small gasp. I wasn't nearly ready for the sudden intrusion or cold gel, but it feels good. My dick swells, and my body quivers in response. I feel his penis pressed up against my hole, and I push back slightly to help ease it in. Kyle grinds gently, allowing time for me to relax and accommodate his girth.

I expect the uncomfortable sensation to abate after a couple of minutes. He slides in 'til he's balls deep, resting his whole body against mine, pressing me up against the wall. Kyle turns my head around and kisses me from behind. I welcome the distraction, and quickly the strange fullness changes into something surprisingly pleasant. I grow hard as a rock and my tool begs for attention. I spit in my hand and start to polish the head with my lubricated palm.

Kyle pulls my hips back, and I step my feet further apart to give him better access. He glides his fat dick in and out with slow, steady strokes. I'm completely relaxed, and every thrust sends yet another wave of pleasure through my body. He pulls me upright to kiss again. It's a brief respite before he bends me over and slams even harder.

I'm not sure I can handle much more of this. The intensity takes my breath away, and I feel my whole body flush. The orgasm wells up inside me, and as he thrusts again, I lose control and explode. My legs tremble and almost collapse under me. I shoot one … two … three … four huge loads. Jackson Pollock would be proud of the mess I make on the tiled wall. Some of it lands on my shoes, but I don't care, because I'm in heaven.

I hear Kyle's breathing quicken, and he holds tightly onto my hips. I feel him throb inside me. He releases a deep, animalistic moan as he orgasms. He collapses on my back, and we slump against the wall, trying to catch our breath.

There's a knock at the door, which startles us.

"Occupied," Kyle calls out.

He pulls his softening dick out of my butt just a little too quickly.

"Ouch," I squeal.

"Oops, sorry, babe." He gives me a peck on the cheek.

We make our way home, high on life and buzzing from the hot sex. I'm grateful that it's a Friday night and I still have the whole weekend ahead to recover. Poor Kyle will have work tomorrow night, as usual. I've offered to come along and help him out sometime, but he says that he enjoys working alone. It gives him an evening of solitude and time to contemplate life and other existential crap like that.

We stumble through Kyle's front door. As per our usual routine, by the time our heads hit the pillows, we're both dead to the world.

Chapter Nine

I wake up from my blissful slumber and check the time on my phone. It's 8:30 AM on Saturday morning. Why am I awake so early? Kyle is still comatose on his side of the bed. I close my eyes and tuck the sheets in around me. Then I hear a knock at the door and realize what just disturbed my peaceful sleep. I hope that whoever is there will just go away, but another knock follows.

I creep out of bed so as not to disturb the sexy man sleeping beside me. As I stand upright, a bolt of pain shoots through my skull and I regret drinking so much the night before. Wearing nothing but a pair of brightly-colored boxer briefs, I close the bedroom door behind me and head for the front entrance.

I wipe the sleep from the corners of my puffy, tired eyes and ruffle my hair a little. As I swing the door open, I immediately regret not looking through the peephole first. Standing in front of me are two attractive guys, about the same age as me, hair neatly combed and dressed in suits. There I am, half-naked in underwear that was designed to enhance the bulge in my pants. The two guys stare me right in the eyes without flinching. I recognize one of them, but can't put my finger on where I know him from. I've been confronted by Mormons before, and I have a nasty hunch they're going to make me stand here for the next ten minutes while we chat about some random religious topic. It's the epitome of awkwardness, like they're immune to the weird things that people outside of their cult get up to.

"Who's at the door, babe?" Kyle calls out from the bedroom in a croaky morning voice.

This is going to be fun.

"Sorry, guys, I don't think we're the right target demographic for what you're selling," I say as politely as I can.

The guy who looks familiar says, "We have programs for homosexuals that can help—"

It's then that I recall his name—Samuel Christiansen. We had freshman classes together. At the start of the year we were sort of friendly. I may have even had a tiny crush on him at one point. Always had a thing for Scandinavian-looking guys. But then he discovered that I was gay and never acknowledged my presence again. I didn't know he was an über-Christian either. He kept that one well hidden.

The other Mormon shoots Samuel an irate look and snaps at him, "Shut up, Samuel."

Kyle puts his arms around me and rests his chin on my shoulder.

"I'm sorry, guys," the other Mormon says. "Sorry we bothered you this morning."

"Come back to bed," says Kyle as he drags his hungover body back to the bedroom.

Samuel apologizes, "Sorry, Todd," which takes me by surprise. He remembers my name.

The two of them head off down the hallway with their Bibles under their arms. Samuel's head is hung in shame as the other Mormon admonishes him for speaking out of turn. I feel sorry for him, but unlike being gay, being a Mormon is a choice.

My head is throbbing to the beat of my heart. Definitely need a few more hours of shut-eye.

Chapter Ten

Sweat is running down my chest, my arms are in agony, and the bulging vein on my forehead feels like it's about to burst. I don't know how much more of this I can take.

"One more," bellows Felix.

I flex my biceps and back with all my strength, and pull my chin up to the bar. I lower my legs and Felix smacks my ankles.

"Did I say you could stop?" He holds me by the ankles and pushes my feet up under my butt. "Another one!"

I've never been in so much physical pain in my entire life. This is torture.

I pull with every ounce of strength that's left in my body. My chin edges closer to the bar. I can almost taste the cold steel. But my arms are so pumped that they refuse to flex any further. I tremble and shake, and my sweaty fingers lose their grip on the chin-up bar. I fall and Felix catches me under my armpits.

"Nice work, buddy," he says with a few pats on my back.

Is it wrong that my first thought is of killing Felix? Woe betide us if he ever becomes supreme ruler of the world. He has zero mercy for the weak.

I shake out my arms and give them a rub, trying to get the blood flowing again. I'm proud of my new set of guns.

"Really?" says Felix disapprovingly. "When you're done checking yourself out, join me at the leg press." He throws his gym towel over his shoulder and walks over to the heavy machinery. I still need a couple more minutes to regain my strength.

Felix loads triple his bodyweight on the leg press and lies down to do his first set. I saunter over to join him and lean against the machine.

"So, you and Kyle doing anything special to celebrate six months together?" asks Felix.

"No. Should we?"

"Oh?" he says, surprised. "I pictured you as the sentimental type."

"What's so special about six months?"

"This is when shit starts to get serious. Chicks start talking about weddings, kids, and moving in together one day."

I stare blankly at Felix. "Do I need to remind you that I'm gay?"

"Yeah, yeah. You know what I mean. Same principles apply, don't they?"

I'm not entirely sure about that one. I've heard that every year that a straight couple is together equates to three gay years, but I'm new to this relationship thing. Kyle and I are making up our own rules as we go along.

"You think I should do something special?" I ask.

"Up to you."

Felix starts his set. A beefy guy watches in awe as my friend pushes heavier weights than any of the bodybuilders. I can see him doing some mental arithmetic, counting the weights on the machine, and nodding his head in respect.

"I have to tell you something," I whisper.

"… Ten … eleven … twelve," groans Felix. He hooks the leg press safety catch into place and throws his head back, panting like a worn-out dog.

"You know how Kyle and I have started being a bit more adventurous?"

"Yes?"

"We snuck into a church."

Felix's eyes open wide. "You're going to hell, you know that?"

"It was so hot. We did it in the confessional."

He shakes his head. But I'm not sure if it's disapproval or envy.

"You know, when I suggest to Georgina that we do things like that, she laughs at me."

It's envy.

"Stink, bro. You need to find yourself a man. Then you could be hooking up in clubs, alleyways, parking lots …"

For a minute I think he's actually considering the idea. He scrunches up his face. "Nah. Only room for one dick in my life."

I switch places with Felix.

"You really think I can do this much weight?" I picture

myself going to failure and the machine crushing me to death.

"Come on, champ," he says. "You can do it. Stop being such a pussy."

I grunt my way through six reps.

"Come on, princess," says Felix. "No giving up now. Give me ten."

This is what I imagine childbirth must feel like. Lying on your back, pushing and straining, having someone barking orders in your ear. I make it to my tenth rep, and before Felix has a chance to say "one more," I lock the safety catch in place and put my feet back on the ground.

I gasp for air. "If she doesn't like the idea … of public sex … why not try taking things in the bedroom to the next level?"

"What? Like whips and chains?" asks Felix.

"Well … yeah."

"We've been together for three years. You think we haven't tried that Fifty Shades shit?"

"And?" I ask.

"I didn't like how the handcuffs chafed," he says bluntly.

I'm confused. Did I just hear him right? Was Felix the one wearing the handcuffs?

"Hate when that happens," I snicker.

Felix winks. "Shower time."

The public showers at the gym are not a place I ever expected to feel confident showing my naked body, and yet here I am, soaping myself up to a frothy lather in amongst a crowd of hot, naked guys all doing the same thing. I finally feel like I've been inducted into an ancient society of confident young men. Having said that, I still don't dare let my stare linger on any guy who walks in. It's like being an undercover gay spy in a straight man's world.

"You know, when I first met you I thought you had Asperger's," says Felix, rinsing soap from his eyes.

"Really? And now?" I'm not going to admit to him that I always thought I had a mild case of it myself.

"You've changed. You've really come out of your shell," he says.

I smile and shrug, but don't reply.

I still haven't completely figured Felix out. It's one of the reasons why I like having him as a friend so much. He's not someone I can easily put in a box, and I do so love to methodically psychoanalyze and package everybody I meet into a neatly labeled box based on his or her personality type. Kyle gets so frustrated with me when I do it. He says that my gut instincts about people are misinformed and based on a lifetime of watching from the shadows. I tell him to stick to accounting.

I sit in front of my laptop at Kyle's kitchen counter, waiting for my Mom to answer the video call. Her face fills my entire screen. She's never been able to figure out how far away to sit from the camera.

"Hi honey," she says with a cheerful smile.

"Hey Mom," I reply.

"You caught me on my way out the house."

"Sorry. I won't keep you."

"That's okay, honey. I've got a few minutes."

"I was wondering ... how would you feel about Kyle coming home for Christmas?"

My mom's eyes widen with excitement. "That would be wonderful! So things are getting serious with you two?"

"You could say that."

"Your sister could learn a thing or two from you," says Mom with one eyebrow raised.

My sister Sarah, who is a few years older than me, introduced her boyfriend to my parents last year. My mom was bursting with excitement until she found out that they'd been going out for almost five years. I've decided to jump in early and avoid her wrath.

The door behind me opens and Kyle lurches in, sodden with sweat and exhausted from wrestling practice.

Mom's face moves around the screen as if she's trying to peer over my shoulder. "Is that Kyle?"

I move aside so that I'm not blocking the camera's view of Kyle. He comes over and gives me a kiss on the lips and my mom a big smile.

"Hi, Mrs. Chambers," he says.

"Oh, Kyle. Please call me Pamela. It makes me feel so old when you call me Mrs. Chambers. Where are you boys? Is that Kyle's apartment?"

"It sure is," I say.

"He's just about moved in," says Kyle. "I'm threatening to start charging him rent."

My mom lets out a "proud mom" sigh.

"I was just having a word with Todd about Christmas," says Mom. "Kyle, sweetie, would you like to join us? Todd's father and I can't wait to meet you in person."

I had wanted to ask Kyle in private. I hope he doesn't feel like I've ambushed him into saying yes.

Kyle rests his chin on my shoulder and hugs me from behind. "I'd love to."

"It's settled then. All right, honey. I'm sorry but I have to go. I'm so excited."

"Okay, Mom. Love you. Bye."

"Bye," she says, blowing us both a kiss.

"You've got the sweetest mother," says Kyle.

I shake my head. "You'll see through the façade, just give it time."

Kyle laughs.

"You didn't have any plans for Christmas, did you?" I ask.

"Nope. Was gonna be me on my own, moping around my thirty square feet of happiness."

"Okay, but I warn you … vacations with my family can get pretty intense, so I'm going to limit the visit to a week. That should be long enough to catch up with everyone and escape before we kill each other." I get an ingenious idea. "We could go to my parents' cabin. You'd love it there."

"Sounds good to me."

Kyle strips off his wrestling gear and walks naked into the bathroom.

"You coming?" he calls out. I hear the shower turn on.

He doesn't have to ask me twice.

Chapter Eleven

Exams always seem to come around too soon, and this time I'm woefully unprepared. Since I met Kyle at the beginning of the school year, I've probably invested about half the effort that I used to put into my studies, and that has me feeling anxious. My first exam went terribly. I have a nasty feeling that I went completely off topic in one of the essays, and somehow managed to screw up and use Eysenck and Goldberg's theories interchangeably. I also ran out of time to go back and correct all the incorrect references, so none of it will make any sense to the marker. How could I be so stupid?

I send Kyle a text to let him know that I won't be able to make it to his place for dinner tonight. He texts me back almost instantly—"*Really??!!! WTF?*"

We've hardly seen each other the past two weeks because of our study commitments. We tried studying together for a while, but as soon as one of us got a tad bored, we would always wind up having sex ... repeatedly.

It's 6 PM, and the library is jam-packed. It's like trying to find a parking space at the mall just before Christmas. I wander the rows of desks until I finally find someone packing up to leave. I set up my workspace. For every noise I make—putting stuff down, zipping and unzipping my bag, or cracking open a can of Red Bull—another person looks up with a frown on their face to chastise me for disturbing them. I settle into my seat and pour my energy into studying a forensic psychology textbook, the topic of my next exam.

One of the most interesting things I have learned from this book is how useless eyewitness testimony is. Our memories as bystanders who witness events are so easily manipulated and biased. With the subtlest suggestions, those incidents can be morphed into something completely different based on what our minds expect to see rather than what we actually saw. Take, for instance, someone witnessing a mugging. The whole event lasts maybe ten or twenty seconds. Later, that bystander is asked to give evidence, and the interviewer asks them if they saw "the weapon", even though the attacker was unarmed. Some bystanders will take this extra information and incorporate it into their memory and become convinced, beyond any doubt, that there was a weapon involved.

I forgot to mention that sitting in the library always gets me worked up. Nothing beats library sex, but around exam time there is no such thing as a quiet corner. I find that the shelves dedicated to such fascinating topics as Mathematics and Computer Science aren't the most popular, so they are my preferred destination for a sneaky study break to quickly whack one out and regain my ability to concentrate. I also figure that most guys studying Mathematics or Computer

Science are probably gay or curious, so if I do get caught, they probably won't go running to security.

If you push any guy to be totally honest with you, he'll eventually admit that around exam time he pays a visit to Mrs. Palmer around five or six times a day to break up the tedium and get his focus back. I wonder if girls do something similar. Perhaps they naturally have better concentration spans.

There's a hot stud sitting a few desks away from me who I can't stop staring at. It must be his girlfriend sitting beside him, 'cause she keeps putting her hands all over him and showing him whatever she's been looking at on her iPhone. She won't stop giggling, but he doesn't seem all that impressed. I hope he doesn't look up from his books, because I'm cracking the biggest woody just watching him.

Shit! He peers up and catches me undressing him with my eyes. My gaze drops to the psychology textbook sitting in front of me, and I don't dare look up again. Maybe he'll think I was just staring into space. I read the same sentence ten times over and realize my efforts are proving pointless. I'd better find myself somewhere private, or I'm going to make a damp spot in my pants.

I open the door to the men's room on the top floor of the library. There's usually minimal foot traffic up here, so I'm less likely to be disturbed. But first, I need to pee. The concept of a urinal is kind of hot—a row of guys all standing intimately close to one another, holding their dicks and enjoying the blessed relief that comes with emptying your bladder. Somehow, I always get shy and stand there for what feels like an inordinate amount of time, trying to relax. So whenever I'm alone in a public restroom, I like to use the urinals for practice.

Just my luck. As I unzip and pull out my dick, someone walks in and stands right beside me at the trough. I keep my eyes locked on my own penis and keep repeating the mantra, "Relax ... relax ... relax." I sneak a peak of the guy's dick standing beside me. It's a fine specimen. The guy catches me checking him out, and then I realize who it is—the hot guy I was staring at while studying.

"Almost lost you back there," he says in a hushed tone.

I step back from the urinal and pack away my junk, but the guy catches me with one hand.

"Wait," he says. "Where are you going?"

"Bro, what are you talking about?" I answer in my most masculine voice, leaving the guy hanging.

I would never cheat on Kyle. We discussed this very scenario early on in our relationship. It's okay to ogle other guys, but no touching, and that's what works for us. The only problem is that now the hot guy is occupying my private masturbation theatre. I lurk nearby the restrooms, pretending to look for a book, but really I'm waiting for the hot guy to leave. A few seconds later, he casually strolls out and back to the stairwell. I sneak into the restroom and lock myself in a stall. For the next ten minutes, I fantasize about everything I would have liked to do with the hot guy, which includes Kyle walking in and joining us. My fifth load of the day. I swear, my balls are half their normal size.

I return to my books, feeling renewed enthusiasm for

forensic psychology, and get stuck into my study. The hot guy is still there with his girlfriend. Only now he doesn't seem as hot as he did before I knew he was into guys. She looks like a sweet, albeit vacuous Barbie doll who doesn't deserve to have her boyfriend cheating on her. Although there is another possibility that I entertain—perhaps she knows about his taste for boys, and it's something that they like to incorporate into their sex life occasionally. Or perhaps she lets him have his fun on a "doesn't need to know" basis. The possibilities are endless when it comes to human sexuality. Perhaps that's what I should do as a career; become a sexologist? I'm midway through a sentence when Barbie slides a folded piece of paper in front of me.

"If you change your mind." She winks at me as she walks out with the hot guy in tow.

I open the piece of paper and blush like a twelve year-old boy whose mom just asked him if he's got pubic hairs yet —*"You're cute. I want to watch you fuck my boyfriend sometime."* There's a phone number scrawled below. I let the fantasy swirl around my dirty mind for a minute or two, then toss the note into a nearby trashcan. Now I need to pay another visit to the masturbatorium. Number six for the day.

I have to do a double-take at the clock when I check what time it is. I can't believe it's already gone past 11 PM. I text Kyle a good night message. He doesn't reply, which means he's either already gone to bed or he's still pissed at me for canceling dinner. We have one more week of study before exams are all over. He'll get over it. I know he's just stressed. I would be, too, if I had economics, accounting, finance and statistics exams to study for. I'll make it up to him and surprise him tomorrow with a morning blowjob. That should put a smile on his dial for the day. My phone vibrates loudly on the desk beside me, much to the annoyance of all those studying hard in the vicinity. I check the message. It's from Kyle—*"Night night, babe. Don't study too hard xo."*

Why do I overthink things all the time? I'll probably still swing by Kyle's place in the morning, though.

The damn librarian has been pacing backwards and forwards from her desk for the past fifteen minutes. I get that she probably wants to lock up and go home, but the library technically only closes at midnight—it's half past eleven—and I don't appreciate her disrupting my precious study time. When she starts tapping her fingers on the edge of her desk, that's the last straw. It's like Chinese water torture to my ears. I gather my things in my bag, and march out of there, glaring at the pent-up bitch as I walk past her desk.

She gives me a smarmy smile. "Good night."

I'm not falling for her pseudo sweetness. "Whatever," I say like a petulant child, flinging the exit doors open like a total prima donna.

An icy blast of wind hits me, and I realize that I forgot my coat. Dammit!

I backtrack to the library and tap my access card on the keypad at the door. It flashes red and reads—*"Access Denied"*. The librarian stares vacantly at me from her desk. I knock on the door and wave to get her attention. She acknowledges me with a tilt of her head. I point at the desk where I was sitting, my coat still hanging over the back of the chair.

"I forgot my coat!" I shout through the glass.

Her eyes follow the general direction of where I'm gesticulating madly. She scoots around the side of her desk.

"Thank you!" I'm just about freezing my tits off out here with nothing but a t-shirt on.

She strolls up to my coat and picks it up with a pincer grip like it's a filthy rag. She turns and walks towards me, carrying the coat at arm's-length.

I press the palms of my hands together like I'm saying a prayer. "Thank you!"

The librarian stops just short of the door and holds my coat over a large basket labeled "*Lost and Found*". Don't you dare! She squints at me like Clint Eastwood in his old cowboy movies just before a quick-draw duel … and drops the coat.

I stare at her, stunned and shivering. She smiles, turns on her heels, and walks back to her desk.

"Come on!" I shout and bang on the door, but she completely ignores me. "Bitch," I mutter under my breath.

I sling my bag over my back and slip my arms inside my t-shirt to keep warm. The dorm rooms are on the opposite side of campus, so it's at least a twenty-minute walk home. Every shiver makes me reflect on what just happened. If I hadn't been so rude and immature, she would have probably helped me out. I'll acknowledge that I'm partly to blame for what just happened, but I still think she was out of line.

I hear a voice behind me yell out, "Hey, Todd. Wait up."

It's my old friend, Samuel the Mormon. He's not in his door-knocking uniform. Guess he had the night off from trying to sell his religion to innocent strangers. He jogs up beside me and gives me a friendly smile.

"Hey," he says.

"Hey."

"I saw you studying at the library."

"Oh? Were you just there too? I didn't see you."

"Yeah, I was upstairs. I also saw what happened with the librarian. That wasn't very nice of her. I thought you might need this." He opens his backpack and pulls out my coat. Just the sight of it warms my bones.

"Oh my God," I say, forgetting that he probably finds blasphemy offensive. "Thank you so much."

Samuel offers to hold my bag while I stop to put my coat on.

"It's all good. Why were we placed on God's great Earth, if not to do good to others?" He smiles, but the biblical overtones make me grimace in response.

"Well, thank you, Samuel," I say, "I've got to head back to my room. It was nice bumping into you again. And thank you for the kind gesture."

"Can I walk with you?" he asks.

"Uh ... sure."

I can't help but think that he has an ulterior motive. This seems strange and out of the blue. We follow a concrete path that leads through the gardens to the student housing. I don't like walking through here at night. There's not much lighting along these paths, and I'd usually take the longer, illuminated route through the main campus, but it's faster this way and I've got Samuel with me.

"About the other morning," he says.

It takes me a few moments to figure out what he's talking about.

"When you came by Kyle's apartment?"

"Yeah," he says, staring at his feet. "You're gay, right?"

"If by 'gay', you mean that I am sexually attracted to other males ... then yes. I am gay."

Samuel looks at me funny.

"Did you always know you were gay?" he asks.

I wasn't expecting to get into this conversation on the way home tonight. He'd better not start with any of that "homosexuality is a sin" shit. He may have rescued my coat, but I'm not in the mood.

"I don't know. Since I was eleven ... twelve, maybe? What about you?"

He shoots me a horrified expression.

"I'm not gay," he says.

"Oh, I didn't mean that. I meant how old were you when you first had sexual feelings."

His gaze trails along the ground. "I'm not sure."

I peer at him curiously out the corner of my eye.

He continues with the same line of enquiry. "What's it like? Being with another guy?"

This is ridiculous. I step in front of Samuel, put a hand to his chest, and stop him.

"What is this about? Is there something you're trying to tell me?" I ask.

Samuel grasps my coat with both hands and wrenches me towards him for a kiss. His embrace takes me by surprise and

I feel his tongue slip inside my mouth before I have a chance to react. I try to pull away but he's holding on tightly. I give him a firm shove and he stumbles back, falling over his own feet. Samuel is the last person I ever expected to do that to me.

"What the heck was that?" I yell at him.

He stands up, lip trembling and shamefaced. "I'm sorry," is all he says before running away into the darkness.

I'm unsure what to do. Do I tell Kyle about what just happened? I really don't want to have to deal with him getting angry, or worse, insecure about Samuel. He knows I used to have a mad crush on the guy. But I don't have any feelings for Samuel, not any longer. Kyle doesn't need to know. Oh man, he'll kick Samuel's butt from here to next week if I tell him. Last thing I need in my life is a dead Mormon's blood on my hands and a boyfriend in prison.

At least I got my coat back.

Chapter Twelve

My psychology classmates are the most antisocial group of people I've ever met. The vast majority of students who sign up for Psych 101 only ever show up for the final exam, so I'm talking about the dedicated bunch of nerds who would never skip class. I'm guessing they'll be huddled in the library, doing a post-mortem of every exam question, and dissecting their essay feedback.

I, on the other hand, have tagged along with my boy to an end-of-exams celebration party for the accounting students. It seemed like a good idea at the time, but now I understand why Kyle never talks about what he's studying. *Why did the accountant cross the road? To bore the people on the other side.* I chuckle, and every head in the vicinity swivels in my direction.

"Did I say something funny?" says the guy who spent the last twenty minutes discussing the absolute benefits of investing in hedge funds over managed accounts.

I panic and blurt out, "I have Tourette's."

Their heads all swing back to the dull orator. It baffles me how they could be hanging on every bland word that he says. The topic of conversation shifts to accounting-client privilege. That's the last straw. I'm going to need more alcohol to get through tonight, so I go in search of a full keg.

What does an accountant use for birth control? His personality.

My intoxicated state causes me to pause and reflect on the last few months. Life has felt like it's on fast-forward since I met Kyle. Every day, the thing I look forward to the most is coming home and seeing his handsome face.

Somehow ... don't ask me, because I think I just had an en-bloc memory blackout ... I survive the next four hours listening to the most inane conversation I've ever had to endure in my adult life. It's almost 1 AM. I'm ridiculously drunk, and feeling crazy horny. I put this down to classical conditioning. Before I met Kyle, alcohol just made me drunk. Now, whenever I over-imbibe, I need his fat dick in my butt. I'm always brutally honest when I've had a few too many.

I go in search of my boy and find him right where I left him. He's still talking conspiracy theories about the fall of Enron. I give Kyle a squeeze.

"Babe, I think it's home time."

He knows what I'm hinting at, and can't put his drink down or say his goodbyes fast enough.

He whips out his phone, and five minutes later we're in a taxi on the way to our favorite hookup spot at the moment—*Manhandle*, the gay bar with the back room reserved just for sex.

Our modus operandi is simple. We split up as soon as we

walk through the door and separately approach the bar to order a drink. We make eye contact across the room and play it cool. When Kyle has finished his drink, he makes his way to the tiny dance floor. The older gentlemen in the bar leer at my hot boyfriend, and we pretend to be total strangers meeting for the first time. He acts like he only has eyes for me and gives me a wink. With a subtle flick of his head, I know it's time to follow him into the back room. It makes me feel like a hunter stalking my prey, and when I finally track him down, trap him, and have my way with him, the thrill is indescribable. I like to call this game hide-and-go-fuck. The rules are self-explanatory. Seeing as I'm drunk tonight, we switch roles and I go ahead of Kyle to hide.

The back room is so dimly lit that it takes a few minutes for my eyes to adjust. In that time, I've already been molested by a couple of unrecognizable, dirty old men walking past, but I couldn't care less. I start to wind my way through the maze of small corridors and rooms. The excitement sets my heart racing and my dick throbbing for release.

But something doesn't feel right. The whole illusion is shattered when I become aware of someone whimpering through a glory hole in a nearby wall. I peer through the hole and see the outline of a man walking away while another slumps onto the floor. The slumped man starts to sob. Something isn't right with this situation.

I scamper around the corner, but there's no entrance to that part of the maze. I backtrack and try another route. This time I'm more successful, and I find the young man who was crying curled up on the floor.

"Hey, buddy, are you okay?" I fall to my knees beside him.

"Doooon tush meee!" he pulls away.

The guy is wasted, which is saying something, because I'm pretty drunk myself.

Just then Kyle appears behind me.

"Jesus, Todd, what's wrong with him?"

"I don't know. I just found him like this, crying."

"Let's get him up." Kyle helps me to lift the drunk guy to his feet and carry him out. The men lurking in the shadows and lined up against the bar eye us with suspicion as we carry the young man to the door. I realize that they're staring at his bare backside, so I pull his pants up as best I can with one hand.

We get to the street. The guy fights free of our supporting arms.

"I cin lukaffa m … self!" he protests, unable to even string a sentence together he's so wasted. He brushes his messed up hair away from his face, and we both recognize him.

"Samuel, are you okay?" I catch him before he falls. I pull open his eyelids. His pupils are blown, and his skin is hot and clammy.

"Samuel, have you taken anything tonight? Any drugs?"

He shakes his head and manages to answer, "Jsssst beer."

Kyle freaks out. "He's been fucking date raped, Todd."

"We don't know that," I say, although I'm inclined to agree.

"You found him face-down, with his pants off, in a fucking back room. What do you think happened to him?"

"Washn't raped," insists Samuel. "I wanted it."

"Maybe we should take him to a hospital," I say.

"No hopsital," Samuel slurs.

"He needs to go to hospital," says Kyle.

Samuel lashes out and tries to run. "I said no!" He falls flat on his face and lies on the ground, whimpering.

"Let's take him home. I'll stay up and watch him. If he gets worse, I'll call an ambulance right away. He can make a decision in the morning when whatever he's taken has worn off."

Kyle begrudgingly agrees and we make our way home, hauling the Mormon boy along with us. I begin to have a crisis of conscience. I feel like I should tell Kyle about what happened with Samuel on the way back from the library. But this isn't the right time, and I doubt that Samuel will mention it. I was totally unambiguous that I wasn't interested in him.

"I don't see why I have to sleep on the couch," whines Kyle.

"Babe, he's in a bad way. Just let the guy have a good night's rest."

Kyle grabs the duvet off our bed and makes himself a nest on the couch.

Kyle gives me a peck on the lips and mutters, "Good night."

"Night, babe."

Samuel lies on our bed, sound asleep. I sink onto the floor in the corner of the room and watch him. It makes much more sense now why he acted so strangely after he found out I was gay. He believes that he's trapped in a world where he has to live a lie, and I pity him for it.

I open my eyes, and it's morning. So much for staying up to make sure Samuel is all right. Kyle is still dead to the world on the couch. Samuel's eyes flutter open, and a look of terror washes over his face. He panics and jumps out of bed.

"Why am I here?" he screams at me. "And where are my pants? Who took off my clothes?"

"Whoa, man!" I stand and put my hands up in the air. "We found you out in town in a rather bad state."

"So you brought me back here, and you and your faggot boyfriend—"

"We found you wasted in a gay club and brought you home because we were worried about you."

Kyle appears in the doorway. "Yeah, man. We thought that something bad had happened to you."

"I don't need your help! If anybody found out that you two had lured me back here—"

"We never lured you anywhere!" says Kyle.

"I'll be excommunicated from the church. Do you understand? This is my life you're messing with!" Samuel sits down on the bed and puts his head in his hands.

Kyle leaves the room and calls out from the kitchen, "Anybody want coffee?"

"Look, Samuel. I understand that you're dealing with some big issues at the moment—"

"You have no idea what I'm going through!"

"Well, we're not going to say anything about this, all right? Do you understand me?" I stare him dead in the eyes. He submits and nods his head.

"Now, be honest with me. Did something happen to you last night?"

Samuel doesn't say a word.

"Do you need to go to a doctor ... or the police?" I ask.

"I'm fine," he utters through his teeth.

I've never seen a guy put his pants and shoes back on so fast. I don't know what to say, and he clearly doesn't want to talk about it. Even if he wasn't raped, whatever happened in the back room left the guy in a teary mess.

"I need to go." He makes a beeline for the front door and slams it closed behind him.

"You're welcome!" snarls Kyle with two fresh cups of coffee in his hands. "I hope we never have to put up with his drama ever again."

I plop down on the couch beside Kyle and rest my head on his shoulder. This whole incident with Samuel has made me depressed. I could do with a cuddle.

"Do you want to talk about it?" says Kyle.

"I'm okay, babe. His reaction took me by surprise, that's all."

"Never underestimate just how fucked up people in this world can be, and you'll never be upset when they disappoint you."

"That is so cynical ... and wise. Come here you sexy, wise old man." I give Kyle a smacking kiss on the lips and we spend the rest of the day on the couch blobbing, watching movies. I love him so much.

Chapter Thirteen

Booking an extra ticket to Denver at the last minute for Kyle was going to be prohibitively expensive, but Felix came to the rescue and let us borrow his car. We left Los Angeles at 4 AM and we've been on the road driving almost non-stop to get to my parents' house in time for a late Christmas Eve dinner. I can't describe how excited I am about coming home, and how desperate for the bathroom I've been since we reached the Denver city limits. My mom comes running out the house to the car with her arms flung open to greet us. I've hardly set foot outside the car before she's wrapped her arms around me in the tightest squeeze, and gives me a big, smothering kiss on the lips. I'm just as quickly discarded when she sees Kyle and repeats the same affectionate welcome. My legs are jelly from being cooped up for hours. Dad appears on the porch with a glass of red wine in his hand and a merry smile on his face.

"There's my boys!" he yells out. I love seeing my dad a tad tipsy.

"Hey, Dad," I call back.

"Hey, Mr. Chambers," says Kyle.

We grab our bags and head into the warmth of the house. Dad gives us both a big bear hug and takes our coats.

"Damn, it's cold here," I say shivering.

"Already forgetting what it's like at home?" My older sister Sarah walks into the hallway with a grin on her face. I drop my bag and jump on the spot in excitement, making the gayest squeal before pouncing on my beloved Sarah.

"Like my new figure?" she says, showing off her pregnant belly.

"You really let yourself go, sis," I snicker.

Someone smacks me on the back of the head. "Don't you talk to your sister like that!" says a stern male voice, but I know it's in jest.

I turn around to see my brother-in-law Olsen standing there. "Give me a hug, you big fairy."

"Sarah ... Ols ... I'd like you both to meet Kyle."

I put an arm around my boy. He's so nervous about meeting my crazy family. I've never seen him this tense.

"Nice to meet you," says Kyle.

He offers to shake hands with Olsen, who looks at him strangely. "Bro, we hug in this family. Come here!"

Olsen gives Kyle a big squeeze. I watch Kyle relax now that the scary introductions are over.

"Come on, you lot. Dinner was ready over an hour ago," says Mom. "What took you boys so long?"

"The traffic was terrible!" says Kyle.

I can't believe he could lie without hesitation to my mother, and with such a straight face. The truth is that we got bored and horny during the trip, and pulled over at a service station to have some fun in the restrooms. We were brave and did it against the hand basins, out in the open. Almost got caught by a trucker at one point. What a rush! I shoot Kyle a knowing smile and his face flushes pink.

"Traffic is always terrible this time of year," says Mom in agreement. "Okay, hurry up and sit down."

We move through into the dining room, where we take our seats. My mom and sister bring out plates of delicious Christmas food.

It feels good to be home again.

After dinner, I help Mom and Sarah clear away the dishes, and leave Kyle and my dad to bond over accounting talk. Olsen works in television, so the second he realized that we were abandoning him with the finance nerds, he excused himself and headed up to bed. Before I even have the dishes set down on the kitchen counter, Sarah bounds over and hugs me from behind.

"Nice work, girlfriend!" says Sarah.

Mom shoots her the evil eye.

"Could you not?" says Mom. "I hate when you refer to your brother as a girl."

"It's okay, Mom. She's just messing around," I say.

"I agree, though, he is very easy on the eye," says Mom with a lecherous sparkle in her eyes.

"Gross, Mom!" says Sarah. She picks up a cloth and starts wiping the stove clean.

I laugh at Mom's comment. I must have inherited her

taste in men.

"Mom won't admit it, but she's relieved that you didn't end up bringing home a big hairy bear twice your age."

Mom throws a dirty rag at Sarah, but she misses.

"Honey, I would be supportive of anyone you chose to be with," says Mom.

I laugh. There's definitely some truth to what Sarah just said. "I know that."

"Where did you say the two of you met?" asks Mom as she passes me a pile of dishes to stack in the dishwasher.

"At a party."

"A gay party?" My mom is clueless.

"No, at this big house party on campus."

"Have you met his parents?" she says. She's so transparent. She always wants to be top mom, and I know that she would have been devastated if we'd met Kyle's parents first.

"They don't speak much."

"Oh? That's unfortunate. He seems like a lovely boy … young man, sorry."

"Are you gonna marry him?" asks Sarah. She never beats around the bush.

I can feel both of their eyes burning holes in the back of me.

"Maybe one day. Right now I've only got one ring to offer him, and it won't look pretty if he walks around with it on his finger all day."

It takes them a few seconds to catch my joke.

"That's disgusting!" says Sarah.

She punches me on the shoulder. I chuckle, and Mom chooses to ignore what I said.

"Do you think he likes us?" asks Sarah.

Mom stops what she's doing and steps closer to me.

"Yeah, he likes you guys."

As the words leave my mouth, it brings the biggest smiles to their faces.

"We want you to be happy, my darling," says Mom. "It's the most important thing to your father and me."

Olsen walks into the room with his usual boisterous exuberance.

"Who do we want to be happy?" says Olsen.

"Mind your own business, Big Ears!" says Mom. She winks at me.

"I've come to take my little lady to bed," he says, tugging on Sarah's shirt.

"I'll be up in a minute. You go ahead." She shoos him off.

"I see you've got your Viking well trained," I say.

Sarah pokes her tongue out at me. Kyle and Dad join us in the kitchen. Kyle is grinning from ear to ear.

"Babe, guess what?" says Kyle excitedly. "Your dad just offered me a summer job working at his accounting firm."

I can't believe my ears. I've dreaded the thought of being apart from Kyle for a whole three months over our summer vacation. "That's awesome!"

"This means we won't have to spend the whole vacation apart."

My dad is smiling in the background. I run over and give him another hug.

"Thank you so much, Dad."

He pats me on the back. "I had a word with the partners at our last meeting, and they all thought it was a great idea."

"Thank you, Mr. Chambers. This is unexpected ... and so generous of you to help me out," says Kyle.

I throw my arms around my boy and give him a squeeze.

"Think nothing of it, Kyle," says Dad. "You're family now."

"Go on, you lot," Mom says to us, and gives me a gentle nudge. "I'll finish tidying up the kitchen with your father."

Sarah hightails it out of the kitchen. "Night."

"You sure?" I ask.

Mom squinches up her face and smiles.

I take Kyle's hand and lead him away. I glance back over my shoulder and see my dad walking up to my mom. He spins Mom around and presses his body up against hers, then gives her a tender kiss. My parents still have the magic.

My old bedroom got fitted out a few months ago as a new sewing room. It's nothing like how I remember it. It's eerie to think that I slept here for almost my entire youth. Now every trace of me ever being here has been wiped clean. As if I never existed. There is one improvement, though; the brand new queen-size bed that they had to buy because there was nowhere for us to sleep. Mom must have had the heating and electric blankets switched on. It's nice and toasty, maybe even a bit too warm in here.

We lie in bed together. I've got my arms folded behind my head, staring up at the ceiling. Kyle lies on his side, drawing imaginary shapes on my chest.

"Your parents are really cute," says Kyle.

"They're a bit nauseating sometimes," I say dismissively.

Kyle playfully swats my face. "Did you just say what I think you said?"

"No, really. There's something creepy about couples who travel the world together and renew their vows in exotic locations every year."

"Well I think it's romantic," says Kyle. He lays his head on my chest and sighs. When I first met Kyle I wouldn't have picked him as the Mills and Boon hopeless romantic type.

"Is it wrong that I'm envious of my sister?" I ask.

"Envious of what?"

"That her and Olsen can have babies."

Kyle shoots me a serious look.

"We can have babies too," he replies matter-of-factly.

"Yeah but they won't be both of ours."

He props himself up on his elbows.

"Babe, just because we can't mix our DNA to make a child does not mean that any kid we have with a donor egg will be any less yours or mine."

"You're right. I guess my point is that straight couples have it easy."

"In a few years' time we're going to be a power couple— doctor and accountant. We'll be able to make ourselves as many babies as we want."

"Got a number in mind?" I say.

"At least two. Minimum. Boy and girl."

"I don't think you get to choose."

"It would be great if it worked out that way, because I want both."

Kyle kisses each of my nipples.

"Do you have any names in mind?" I ask.

"If it's a boy ... Logan ... girl ... Ivy."

He covers my chest in delicate kisses.

"I like those. Where did you get the name Ivy from?"

"My gran's name," says Kyle.

"Who is going to be the stay-at-home dad?"

"We'll draw straws."

"Or take turns?" I suggest.

"Or that."

He spreads his kisses down my abdomen, following the happy trail towards my underwear.

"Babe?" I say.

"Yeah?"

He starts to run his mouth along the outline of my hard-on.

"My parents are in the next room."

He looks up at me with one eye. "Seriously?"

"I can't do it."

"Pussy!" he mumbles, then smacks me on the dick.

I bite my lip to stop from yelping.

He is right. We could try to be quiet, but unlike sex in public places, where it's a thrill almost getting caught by a stranger, I would rather die than have my mom or dad walk in and catch us in flagrante delicto. He'll just have to go without tonight.

I nuzzle into Kyle's neck and play big spoon. I know he

likes it when we fall asleep like this.

Chapter Fourteen

On New Year's Eve, Kyle and I borrow my parent's four-wheel drive and we head up into the mountains where our family has a small log cabin. It's rustic but luxurious. Real country folk would cringe at how us city slickers have corrupted their way of living. My dad has never gone without his creature comforts, so it's fitted out with all the rural mod cons, including a generator, running water and solar heating. It's freezing when we arrive. I don't think anybody has been here since last winter, and the air inside the cabin is stale.

"This is awesome!" says Kyle. "We need to come here more often."

We set about unpacking our belongings, and I get the fire going in the hearth. As the evening begins to fall, we illuminate the cabin with more candles than you'd find in a cathedral. It's overkill, considering we could start the generator and put the lights on, but this is more fun. The chores take a few hours to complete before the place is livable once again. We had planned ahead and brought along a ready-made macaroni cheese and bacon meal for tonight. A few minutes heating up in the fire, and its delicious smell teases our nostrils. We devour our meal, having worked up an appetite today.

When dinner is done, Kyle snuggles up close behind me.

"No parents next door listening. Now it's just you and me," he says.

His soft lips press against mine, and I drift away in his tender embrace. He slides a hand behind my ear and runs his fingers through my hair. I love it when he does that. I feel so safe in his strong arms. We undress and sit in front of each other on a rug by the fire. In the candlelight, his skin is golden. I can see the flames from the fire reflecting in his eyes with an almost supernatural glow. We touch each other's bodies like only lovers do, overflowing with lust and desire. Our lips lock again and our bodies entangle. Our hands and tongues explore one another.

"I want you inside me," says Kyle seductively.

He rolls onto his side, facing away from me.

I run my hands down his muscled back and caress his perfect butt. He tilts his hips back towards me, his cheeks brushing against my erection. I spit in my hand and lubricate myself with saliva. Kyle grinds back onto my pole and swallows the length of it, inch by tumescent inch. I reach my arms around him and we lie there, holding each other so tightly. I pull his face towards mine and we kiss over his shoulder, making gentle love.

"I love you," he says.

"I will always love you," I reply.

I reach around his waist and jerk him off with the same

slow pace. Kyle whimpers in delight with every stroke. Right here, right now is about making him feel good. His legs begin to tremble, his eyes close, and he loses himself in the ecstasy of the moment. His dick becomes engorged in my hand. He pulls my hips, trying to get more of me inside him. We French kiss, even more deeply and passionately than before. He looks at me briefly before his eyes roll back and his eyelids flutter shut. I feel the rhythmic contractions as Kyle shoots his load across the floor in front of him. I hold him close to my chest and can feel the pounding of his heart. I lie there, still erect inside him, close my eyes, and drift off.

The next morning, I wake up to the delightful aromas of fresh coffee, bacon and eggs wafting on the air. Kyle walks in wearing nothing but a chef's apron, carrying a tray of breakfast delights.

"Good morning, my handsome man," he says, grinning like a Cheshire cat.

"Morning, babe. How did you sleep?"

"Like a bear in winter. And speaking of bears," he runs a finger along the three-day stubble growing on my face, "you look so sexy with facial hair."

"You think?" I say in surprise. Since I hit puberty, I've never gone more than a few days without shaving. I didn't think it suited me.

"Hell yeah! I wouldn't be able to keep my hands off you if you grew a beard."

"I thought you found me irresistible anyway?"

"I do." He gives me a big, sloppy kiss. "You hungry? I'm

starving!"

"So what would you like to do today?"

"After breakfast, you're going to fuck me in the woods." He takes a bite from a piece of toast and I choke on my coffee. I watch him run back into the kitchen and admire the sight of his naked, furry butt. We'll definitely come back to the cabin again soon.

In the afternoon, Kyle receives an unexpected phone call. He reads the name on the screen, and I see the color drain from his face—"*Mom*". I put my arm around him and we sit on the couch together.

He takes a deep breath and answers the phone.

"Hello."

He starts to hyperventilate and his face crumples.

"Oh my God, no. When?"

His expression changes from sadness to confusion.

"A week ago? When is the funeral?" The sadness turns to anger.

His face turns beetroot and I can see a vein pulsating in his neck. "WHAT? How could you?" he screams into the phone. "We're supposed to be a family, don't you know that?"

He throws the phone on the couch and paces in front of me.

"Babe, what did she say?"

He holds his face in his hands. He's furious. I can see that he wants to hit something, there's so much anger boiling up inside him.

"Kyle?"

"My brother died in a fucking car crash and they didn't even invite me to the funeral."

"Jesus! I'm so sorry."

I'm at a loss for words.

"My father said that it was enough of a tragedy, having the only son he was proud of die so young. He didn't want his faggot son coming home to add shame to the occasion. I fucking hate him!"

I try to comfort Kyle, but he brushes me aside and storms out the cabin. I know it's best to give him some space. I'll wait a short while before I go after him. Nothing I can say will change the hurt. I just need to be here for him.

It takes over an hour for me to find Kyle out in the woods. I sit on a rock beside him and sling my arm around his waist. He rests his face on my shoulder and cries.

I lie on the bed next to Kyle. His face and pillow are stained with tears. He looks up at me and I think I see a fleeting smile. I can't begin to imagine what it's like for him, being so isolated from his family at a time like this.

"Do you want to talk about it?" I ask.

His response is a shallow sigh.

"I didn't know you had a brother," I continue. "I'm so sorry."

"He was my best friend," says Kyle, his voice breaking, "… until the day my father threw me out. He couldn't even look me in the eyes. I guess he saw it as his opportunity to finally be the golden boy and make Dad proud. The fucked up thing about it is … I still love him. He was my baby brother. And now he's gone."

I squeeze Kyle tightly in my arms.

"We'll go back home tomorrow."

"No," Kyle says firmly. "Let's stay here a bit longer. It's peaceful."

"We can stay as long as you like."

Kyle turns his head to look at me. "I don't know what I'd do without you in my life, Todd."

"You don't have to. We're going to spend the rest of our lives together."

If I could choose a moment in my life to push pause and stay there forever, I'd choose now, with my arms wrapped around the man I love, comforting and holding him, knowing that because we have each other, everything is going to be all right.

Chapter Fifteen

I show up at Kyle's apartment with flowers, chocolates, and everything I can think of to lift his spirits. Things between us haven't really been the same since his brother died. He's distant and depressed. I knock on the door to his apartment. There's no reply, so I turn the handle and let myself in. I see Kyle sitting at his desk with his headphones on. That explains why he couldn't hear me knocking. I think I'll sneak up and surprise him.

A few steps away from Kyle, I almost shit myself when he shouts at his computer screen. I hadn't noticed that he was chatting to someone online.

"Just put him on the phone!" he growls.

I stand there, frozen. It's probably not the best time to surprise someone when they're in the middle of an argument. Now what? I slink back to the front door.

"Dad, is that you?" says Kyle. His voice is calm and steady, but his hands are trembling against the desk in front of him. "I will probably never get the opportunity to say this to your face, but I hope that one day you'll be able to forgive yourself for the way you treated me … your son. I never chose to be this way, but I'm proud of the man I've become. I wish you could see that." Kyle starts sobbing and pulls the headphones off his head.

I knock loudly on the front door and act as if I just walked in.

"Babe, you okay?" I whisper.

"He put the phone down on me," says Kyle.

I hug him from behind and pretend not to know who he was talking to.

"Who put the phone down on you?"

"My dad. I told him how I feel, and he never said a single word back to me."

"You've got me. We've got each other," I try to reassure him. "We don't need anyone else."

Kyle says nothing, but I see in him a sadness that reaches deep into his soul.

"I believe in you, babe. We're here for each other." I kiss the crown of his head and hug him again.

I don't think that I'll ever fully comprehend what Kyle has had to go through with his family. They sound like a bunch of rednecks refusing to catch up with the times. When Kyle came out to his parents, they threw every homophobic line of scripture at him, which is beyond hypocritical coming from a couple who never got married and haven't set foot in a church in decades. Regardless, they're Kyle's parents. I daren't tell him my honest opinion of them. As far as I'm concerned, he has a new family now, and we love him just the way he is.

Chapter Sixteen

It's a Wednesday night, which alternates between wrestling practice and date night each week. But tonight, I'm going to be the one groping Kyle's crotch, not his teammates. We're going on a double date with Felix and Georgina to some fancy restaurant near the beach. I would be satisfied with fish and chips on the sand, but the others want an excuse to dress up smartly for a change. That means full suit and tie to get through the front door.

As usual, Georgina is running late. I'm not sure why she takes so long to get ready. All she does is put on a little mascara and pull her hair up in a ponytail. She's naturally drop dead gorgeous—I always tell Felix he's punching well above his weight—and yet somehow manages to take over an hour to shower, shampoo, shit, and shave before a big night out. It's painful. Felix isn't much better. He takes at least fifteen minutes to get his hair "just right" in front of the mirror at the gym. They really are made for each other.

Kyle doesn't seem to be interested in hearing my thoughts

on Felix and Georgina's bathroom logistics. He's already started playing a game on his phone. I tease him for being an iWhore, but the truth is I'd trade my own grandmother for a smart phone if I could find a sucker who would take the deal.

Speaking of my gran, she's started a budding romance with one of the men in the rest home where she lives. It's sweet in theory, but also kind of gross because it turns out that the women outnumber the men like eight to one, and she only gets to be this old bastard's girlfriend once a week. So she's sharing him with six other women, assuming he doesn't need a night off to recover here and there. I think she has Tuesdays, which means straight after bingo, it's back to her room to freshen up for her gentleman caller. Still, she doesn't seem to care. One day a week of affection seems to keep her happy. I try not to think about them going further than first base, though.

Suddenly all I can think of is saggy tits hanging down to knees, old couples having toothless, gummy kisses, and shriveled sausages squishing into sloppy tacos. Yuck ... that's going to be me one day, well, not exactly. I really hope that Kyle and I both make it to old age, because the statistics are lined up squarely against us, being male ... and gay.

Come to think of it—I'm sure I read something about gay rest homes in the newspaper the other day. Could be an interesting prospect. Gross. Now all I can think about is old men having sex, or falling in love with and marrying the young male nurses. I blame Kyle for not listening to me and setting my monkey brain down this track.

The back doors swing open. Felix and Georgina jump

into the car, rescuing me from my own twisted imagination, and not a moment too soon. Felix cleans up pretty well for a straight boy. I envy his v-shaped torso, which makes everything he wears look like it came straight off a catwalk.

"Sorry, we're running so late," says Felix.

"We've both been chasing our tails all afternoon," adds Georgina.

I look at Kyle and we both see through their lame excuse. They were totally having sex and lost track of time.

"We know whose tail was being chased all afternoon," I say.

Kyle and I both laugh. Felix turns a shade of ketchup, while Georgina pretends not to understand. She's such a lady.

We arrive at the restaurant and the maître d' eyes us out like we've come to the wrong place. He's correct in assuming that this isn't the type of venue a group of students would ordinarily frequent, but Georgina has expensive taste, and her parents also happen to know the owners. When it comes time to pay the bill, we're hoping for a "friendly" discount.

We're led to a table in the far corner of the restaurant, where the maître d' is satisfied we'll be hidden away from view. Most likely for the benefit of the snobby patrons, so they don't feel as if they're dining among members of the underclass. What a dick! One day I'll be earning fantastic money working as a doctor, and he'll still be a pretentious, glorified restaurant server. Jobs like his should be a stepping-stone to better things, not the pinnacle of your career.

I realize that my future self sounds like a stuck up a-hole, so scratch that last comment. It takes all kinds of people to make the world turn around, and what this guy epitomizes is that some of them are not very nice. We hang our suit jackets over the back of our chairs and take our seats. At least the view of the ocean from our cramped little table is spectacular tonight.

When it comes to ordering, I'm stumped.

"Do you serve steak?" I ask the rather handsome young waiter, which provokes rolled eyes and muttered expletives from my companions.

I'm a creature of habit, and fish freaks me out ... the smell, the texture ... the eyeballs. They knew this before they decided we should come here. I don't see why it comes as that big a surprise to them.

"No, sir, I'm sorry. This is a seafood restaurant," says the waiter in some variation of a sexy South American accent. Explains the dark and handsome looks.

"A plate of fries please," I say with a smile, handing the menu back to him.

"Again, I'm sorry, sir, but we only serve steamed vegetables," the waiter says most apologetically.

Kyle kicks me under the table and glares daggers at me.

"Order something!"

"Do you do surf 'n turf?" I say.

Before the waiter can respond, Kyle interjects. "Can we please have a mixed platter for two?" This brings a smile to the waiter's face.

"Todd, you frustrate the fuck out of me sometimes," grumbles Kyle.

"You don't even know me," I say in mock defense.

"You two should totes get married," chuckles Georgina.

I savor every scrumptious mouthful of dinner—prawns, crab, lobster, and fresh-baked fish. I'm in culinary Heaven. If Kyle hadn't forced me to eat this delicious array of seafood or starve, I might never have tried it on my own. If you're inflexible and you know it, clap your hands. *Clap. Clap.* I do draw the line at oysters, though. Those things are fucking disgusting. They look like someone jizzed on a shell, which appeals to my kinky side, but they taste more like salty, congealed snot. Fu–cking dis–gus–ting.

Felix and Georgina can't keep their hands to themselves right the way through dinner. They barely finish their last mouthfuls before making their excuses and disappearing to find the nearest accessible toilet.

We pay for our half of the exorbitantly overpriced meal — the restaurant charged us full price — and head outside to wait for the gruesome twosome to finish their business.

Kyle offers his hand to me. "Care to join me for a stroll on the beach?"

He leads me out onto the deck and down the wooden stairs to the beach. We leave our shoes and socks at the foot of the stairs and step onto the soft, cool sand. Starry skies, warm breeze and the sound of waves crashing against the shore: a beautiful night. We walk along the smooth patch of sand between where it's dry and where the water breaks. The last remnants of waves that have made it up the shore lick at our feet before being pulled back into the ocean.

It's dark, but our eyes soon adjust to the moonlight. We almost never go for walks holding hands. A part of me feels so vulnerable and insecure about doing that, even in today's more accepting world. I have an irrational fear that any public display of gay affection is going to bring menacing stares from passers-by. It's probably all in my head, and I feel ashamed about that. Why should I care what someone else thinks, and why do I let it stand in the way of showing my darling man how much I love him?

Out of nowhere, Kyle pulls me in for a kiss. The tender warmth of his sweet lips and his body pressed against mine makes the whole world around us disappear. We stop to stare into each other's loving gaze.

"I saved some room for dessert," he says.

Kyle draws me even closer still for another kiss. He takes his time opening the buttons on my crisp white shirt without our lips ever breaking apart. I do the same to his. I feel his hands fumble with my belt, and my pants come undone. They fall to my ankles, and I stand skin to skin with the man I love. He unbuckles his belt and drops his pants and underwear to the ground.

His lips pull away from mine. "Skinny dip?" Kyle gives me that sexy smile of his that raises my flag to full mast. He's off running through the waves before my mind has processed what he said. On instinct, I run after him into the cold water. Kyle charges through the waves, letting them break against his beautiful body. He turns around and splashes me.

"I'm going to get you for that!" I cry out.

He laughs and runs back onto the sand, knowing full well

that I have no hope in hell of catching him. He's way fitter than me.

"Is the water a weeny bit cold?" He taunts me and holds his thumb and index finger a fraction apart.

I look down to see my pride and joy has shriveled up to the point where I can't even see it beneath my pubes. Kyle is killing himself laughing on the beach.

From somewhere deep inside me, I channel my inner football tackle and charge him on the shore. I lift Kyle into the air and bring him down onto the soft sand with a thump. I land on top of him. It doesn't completely knock the wind out of his sails, but it does shut him up. I kiss him again, and my cold body starts to warm against his. My hand inches down his athletic frame and I make circles with my fingers along the edge of his abs. I almost reach his pubes when Kyle begins to twitch and jerk beneath me. He yells out and pushes me away.

"There's something on me!"

He screams like a girl and swats at his back, butt, and legs. Now it's my turn to laugh at him.

"Jesus, Todd, don't just laugh! There's something crawling on me."

I inspect him from behind, and apart from a bit of sand stuck to his fuzzy butt, there's nothing else there.

"Probably just crabs," I say, which horrifies Kyle.

He squeals and starts swatting at his back again. I giggle and walk up to him, wrap my arms around him, and hug him tight.

"I told you. There's nothing there, you big wimp."

I give him a peck on the lips.

"Let's go home. There's a comfy bed waiting with our names on it," I say.

We gather our clothes, and I hold his hand tightly in mine as we walk back to the restaurant.

"I'm going to tell my mom that you got crabs," I say, trying to be witty.

He punches me hard on the shoulder.

"Okay, I deserved that."

Chapter Seventeen

Lee finished his exams a week ago and already moved back home, so I've had the whole room to myself for a change. I won't miss his snoring. And I definitely won't miss the awkward knocks on the door from random bratty, fugly chicks trying to find out why he hasn't called them back. I swear I'm not a misogynist, Lee just has really bad taste.

School policy is that from the last official day of exams, we have precisely four days to vacate the premises. Georgina has an awesome townhouse that her parents bought for her when she started college. She offered to let me stay in her spare bedroom for a few weeks until Kyle and I head home for the long summer break. We'll have to commandeer Sarah's old room downstairs so that our sex life doesn't suffer. I just can't bring myself to do it when I know Mom and Dad are on the other side of paper-thin walls.

Kyle's been away for the weekend at a wrestling tournament. It's the last one for the year, and I've never seen him as excited as he was before he left my place on Thursday night.

The team's ranking has skyrocketed, and he's almost guaranteed a spot again next year based on his performance this season. I'm expecting him home in time for dinner this evening.

Georgina thought it might be nice for Kyle and me to have the house to ourselves this evening, so she and Felix have been hard at work, tidying the place from top to bottom. Kyle is also in for a special surprise this evening when the clothes come off. I've done my research, and now consider myself to be an expert on the fine art of manscaping. Once I've gathered the necessary supplies for tonight, I shall attempt to put said theory into practice.

Felix and I head out to collect the first items on our list from the cheap Asian store around the corner. We find a variety of red candles in different shapes and sizes and an assortment of glass containers. We tick the next few items off our list at the grocery store. Felix watches me scanning the rows of personal care products in the feminine hygiene aisle.

"Hey, Todd," says Felix. There's a strange hesitation in his voice. "I don't mean to be awkward ... but why are you looking for sanitary pads?" His voice becomes hushed as the sentence trails off.

I laugh at him. "No, you tool. I'm looking for hair remover."

He exhales and looks relieved. "Use a razor."

"Speaking from experience?"

"Bud, girls won't go down there unless it's shaved, groomed and freshly washed ... with soap."

"You're kidding, right?" I ask him in all seriousness. "I thought girls liked their men to be MEN."

"Nah. That was like back in the day. I figure it's their way of getting revenge for decades of men forcing them to pull, pluck, and rip everything out. Which makes me curious … are you being mussy-whipped into doing this?"

Mussy? Oh wait, I get it.

"I'll come clean with you—" I stop to allow a woman pushing a trolley to walk past and out of earshot. "I want to shave my ass for Kyle."

"Well, bud, sing out if you need a hand," says Felix.

"You're a fucking weirdo, you know that?"

"You'll be wishing you took me up on the offer when Kyle gets random tufts stuck in his teeth."

"You reckon I should just go with a razor?"

Felix nods his head. Razor it is.

Our final destination is a store tucked away downtown that I read about online. We walk around the block twice before plucking up the courage to go inside the neon-lit store. The window display is full of naked mannequins clothed in lingerie and strap-ons, some simulating sex in reverse cowgirl and doggy-style. The young lady working at the counter peers up from packing sex toys into boxes and smiles at us.

"No stealing my shit, boys, or I'll shove that," she points to a twelve-inch black dildo shaped like a fist, "right up your assholes."

I laugh, but Felix stands there, shell-shocked.

"If there's anything I can do to help or assist you with,

just let me know, okay?" She returns to her packing.

Felix and I wander around the store in absolute awe. I had no idea that any of this stuff even existed, not in my wildest dreams—studs, clips, ties, cages, ropes, and much more. We arrive at the wall of dildos. Felix takes one look and throws his hands in the air in surrender.

"I can't do it. How do I compete with that?" he exclaims.

He picks up a ten-inch dildo in a box that claims it was molded from some famous porn star in the nineties.

I decide to feed his insecurity. "Isn't that average?"

"Shut up," he says, walking off to browse through 3D lesbian porn Blu-Rays on sale.

I pull my phone out and send a text to Kyle—*"You'll never guess where I am. Everywhere I look reminds me of you. xo"*

While Felix is distracted, I sneak two cock rings off the shelf and a gay sex card game that looks like fun. I can't wait!

My heart races as I pay. The girl behind the counter eyes me suspiciously. She has bizarre piercings in weird places all over her face. I can't take my eyes off the inch-long metal bar that she has sticking through the skin on her forehead. I can understand why some people might want to get a ring put through their penis, nipple or taint, but I can't fathom what purpose that ugly chunk of metal would serve.

She raises an eyebrow, looks at Felix, who is hypnotized by the abundance of boobs in the lesbian section and not even trying to hide the bulge in his pants, then back at me.

"I take it you guys are just friends?" she says.

"Who? Me and Felix? Yeah, just friends."

She glances at the card game. "You need any amyl?" she

asks as she puts my purchases into a black plastic bag.

"What's that?" I must sound like such a newb.

She looks at me, somewhat puzzled. "Never mind. It's a bad habit."

"Yeah but what is it?" Now I'm intrigued.

"You sniff the fumes from the bottle. Makes your whole body relax, especially your asshole. Your heart races, and this wave of pleasure passes over you. Only lasts a minute, but it's long enough to help get it all up in ya."

"That sounds amazing. Is it bad for you?"

"Kid, I'm not a doctor. I sell sex stuff. Ask Google if you got questions like that."

"Okay." I think about it for a split second. "Can I get a bottle to try?"

"Sure."

She smiles at me sweetly.

I have to drag Felix from the adult store. It's like trying to pull a kid away from playing with his favorite toys. Thank God he didn't cry. There is no way Georgina would ever consider having another girl guest-star in her bedroom, so Felix will need to come to terms with his favorite fantasy forever remaining exactly that.

It's almost 5 PM, and there's a ton of stuff to still get organized, so we have to rush back to the house. Georgina has already set the dinner table and put out all the ingredients for me to cook Kyle's dinner tonight. She and Felix head upstairs to get ready for their big date-night, and I start to precisely lay out the candles around the room. I double-check that I have everything I need for dinner, pour a bowl full of warm water, and sneak into my bedroom.

Free-standing mirror pushed up against the wall? *Check*!

Bowl of water? *Check*!

Shaving foam? *Check*!

New razor? *Check*!

I lie down naked on my back in front of the mirror and pull my knees up to my chest. There is my butthole, in all its glory, winking back at me in the reflection. I've never felt so stupid in my entire life, but I have a purpose—to boldly shave where I've never shaved before. I lather up the foam and spread it liberally.

There's a sudden knock on the door and Felix calls out, "Todd!"

I almost jump out of my skin, hit my head on the floor, and knock the mirror over. Thankfully, it doesn't break.

"You okay in there?" Felix shouts through the door.

"Um, yeah, just give me a moment," I say, scrambling to my feet.

"Are you shaving your asshole in there? No, Georgina, he's all good ... he's just shaving his asshole!" he shouts at the top of his voice.

I die just a little bit on the inside. This was such a dumb idea. I wrap a towel around my waist and open the bedroom door.

"Is the shower free?" I say.

Felix tries to poke his head inside the bedroom to see what I was up to, but I close the door quickly behind me.

"Sure is, bud."

In spite of how long he takes, Felix's idea of dressing up smartly is a pair of jeans, clean sneakers, and a polo shirt. Georgina will undoubtedly descend from her bedroom dressed like a princess. If it weren't for the fact that her dad was friends with half the restaurant owners in town, I doubt he'd make it past the bouncers dressed like that. But what he lacks in style, he makes up for in total loving devotion towards her. They're the cutest couple.

Once I've got myself showered and dressed, the two lovebirds help me light the candles and spread them all around the house. With the lights dimmed, the flickering candles cast the most romantic, shimmering light. I say goodnight to Felix and Georgina and chase them out the door. My boy is going to be here in about fifteen minutes, and I'd better get started making dinner.

On the menu for tonight are chicken breasts wrapped in bacon and stuffed with wholegrain honey-mustard, pesto and cream cheese, served with a side of salad and a garlic roll. For dessert, I have a chocolate mousse in the refrigerator that I prepared earlier. It grossed me out that the recipe required raw eggs, but once everything was whipped up to a light froth, the flavor was divine and I completely lost my squeamishness.

I become engrossed in what I'm doing, and hardly notice that an hour has passed. I put dinner in the warmer and check my phone. No messages from Kyle. I'd bet real money that he forgot to charge his phone. How the heck did he manage to look after himself before he met me?

Even though I know he's probably not going to read it

because he's obviously running late, I bash out another text to Kyle—"*I'm feeling needy and I miss you. Hurry up.*"

I head back into the living room and put on some Michael Bublé. With the album playing softly in the background, I slump on the couch. It's been a long day, and I'm exhausted from all the excitement. I'll just give my eyes a short rest until Kyle arrives, because I'm going to need my energy for the fun night ahead.

Chapter Eighteen

"Hey, sleepy head," slurs Georgina.

She jiggles my leg, waking me from a deep sleep. I must have drifted off on the couch. It takes a minute to orient myself in the room. The candles, which I had so carefully placed throughout the house, are now either dead or giving off their last flicker of light before the wick runs out.

"What time is it?" I mutter, wiping sleep from my eyes.

"Uh ... like 2 AM," Felix replies, swaying on his feet. "Where's Kyle?"

Felix hiccups, and the two of them giggle. They're both drunk as skunks, and by the looks of things, had a great night out.

Suddenly it sinks in just how late it really is. Holy shit! Where is Kyle?

"I don't know," I reply.

I start to feel desperate. I fumble around in my pockets, trying to find my phone. No, wait, there it is, on the coffee table. No missed calls. No messages. I call Kyle, but it rings through to his voicemail. "Hi, you've reached Kyle. I'm not here, but if you'd like to leave a message ..."

"He's not answering."

I dial again.

"When did you hear from him last?" asks Felix.

I stop and try to remember, but a million things are racing through my mind. What if something happened to him? What if he's been in an accident?

"I'm not sure," I say. "When he left my place on Thursday."

I dial again.

"Could his flight have been delayed?" suggests Felix.

"He'd have called by now ... surely?" says Georgina.

"And he was definitely coming home today?" asks Felix.

"Yes. He should have been home by now. Why isn't he answering his phone?" I say, feeling increasingly uneasy.

"We should go round to his place. See if he's home," says Georgina.

Felix looks at me and nods in agreement. "We'll take my car."

I snatch the keys from Felix. I'm the only one of us sober enough to drive a car.

The short drive to Kyle's apartment takes forever. Every traffic light conspires against us, and there must be a bad driver convention on in town because they're out in full force tonight. As we leave Georgina's upmarket leafy suburb and enter the shady downtown area that Kyle lives in, I feel nothing but dread. I have such a bad feeling about this. Kyle would never just not show up.

We arrive outside Kyle's apartment and I pull into a free parking space. I slam on the brakes and bring the car to an abrupt standstill, mounting the sidewalk with the front tires. I throw open the door and race to the entrance. An old white station wagon parked outside the building pulls out and almost knocks me off my feet. Fucking drivers need to pay fucking attention to pedestrians. I hit the hood of the car with my fist. The station wagon tears off down the street.

I sprint into the lobby and push the button beside the elevator doors. I push it again ... and again. Finally the light comes on. It's sitting on the twelfth floor. His apartment is only three floors up. I can get there faster if I run, so I take the stairs.

I knock frantically on Kyle's door and reach into my pocket for the key, but I don't need it. The handle turns freely in my hand and the door swings open. It's eerily quiet inside, and the lights are out.

"Kyle," I call out. "You here, babe?"

There's a *ding* as the elevator doors open. Felix and Georgina rush into the hallway to find me.

"Is he there?" asks Felix.

I switch the main light on and we step into the apartment. Nothing looks out of place or disturbed.

Georgina walks into the bedroom and calls out, "Shit!"

"What is it?" I race behind her.

The bedroom is stripped bare. All that remains is furniture. Every cupboard and drawer is empty.

Felix walks out of the bathroom. "Same in the bathroom.

Everything of his is gone."

Georgina looks at me with a downturned mouth and sad eyes, like I'm some kind of hurt puppy.

"Oh sweetie," she hugs me. "I'm so sorry."

I stand there, frozen.

"You okay, bud?" Felix places the palm of his hand on my shoulder.

I pull away from both of them. "I don't understand what's going on. Where is he?" I say. I fall back onto the couch and hold my head, which feels like it's going to explode.

Felix and Georgina stand there watching me, like sympathy is a spectator sport. I wish they would say something reassuring, anything at all, but they don't.

"Could there be a logical explanation for why all his stuff is gone?" says Georgina. "What if he was robbed? He could be at the police station." She almost gets excited about the prospect. "We should call."

Felix puts his hand on my shoulder again. This time, I don't pull away. "Bud, do you want me to call the police?"

I nod and say, "Please."

Felix walks out of the apartment and into the hallway. I can hear his muffled voice through the paper-thin walls.

Georgina crouches and holds my hands. "Things were good with you guys, right?"

From nowhere, tears well in my eyes and stream down my face.

"Sweetie, don't cry." She sits beside me and puts her arms around me. "We'll find your Kyle."

Felix storms back into the room, furious. "Fucking assholes won't do anything until he's been gone for forty-eight hours."

I dial Kyle's number again, this time with my phone on speaker. It goes straight through to voicemail. I burst into tears. Georgina takes the phone from me and leaves a stern message. "Kyle, honey ... this is Georgina. You didn't show up tonight and you're not at your apartment." Her calm voice starts to crack. "We're really fucking worried about you, so would you call back ... please?"

She hands the phone back to me and looks at Felix. "What now?"

What now, indeed. If Kyle has decided to leave then we'll never find him. If something has happened to him, where would we even begin to start looking? All we can do is wait.

Georgina turns to Felix and whispers, but I can hear every word she says. "They might need to sweep this place for evidence. We should get out of here."

She's right. My mind starts racing through all the terrible possibilities of what might have happened tonight. What if we already removed any traces of whoever did this? Kyle would never just leave.

Stop overthinking things, Todd. It's going to be all right.

The waiting is unbearable. I haven't slept in almost two days. I've left a hundred messages on Kyle's voicemail, and sent twice as many texts. All I've done the last half hour is sit in the corner of Georgina's living room and stare at the screen on my phone, hoping that I'll receive something, any kind of sign, that will let me know he's all right.

"Can I get you anything?" asks Georgina.

A gush of raw emotion hits me again and I splutter out tears.

Georgina slumps on the floor beside me and rests her head on my shoulder.

"It's going to be okay, Toddy," she says. "We'll figure this out."

Forty-eight hours later, the three of us are sitting in front of a police officer down at the station. He's such a cliché. There's a pile of files sitting on his desk, and his bin is overflowing with empty soda cans and take-away boxes. He shows all the outward signs of metabolic syndrome—the skinny arms and rotund belly. I bet he'd have a heart attack if he had to run half a mile.

Kyle never materialized, never answered his messages. I called his landlord, and the asshole laid into me because Kyle left without giving notice.

The police officer reclines in his chair and stretches out, yawning without covering his mouth. I secretly hope the strained screws holding his chair together will snap and he'll slam onto the floor.

"I've seen this kind of thing a lot with you people," the police officer blurts out.

None of us fully understand what he's saying.

"What do you mean?" I ask him for clarification.

"You gays," he pauses for effect. "You're always getting in these fights, and then one or the other ends up running away. Happens all the time." He slaps his hands down hard on the table. "Every time there's a breakup—another restraining order. Especially the lesbians. God, they're a nightmare." He shifts his gaze to Georgina. She makes a face like "Why the fuck is he looking at me?"

"We didn't have a fight. Kyle came home from a wrestling tournament over the weekend and he's vanished into thin air."

The policeman chortles.

"Look kid, I spoke to the coach already. There was no wrestling tournament. Your boy ... friend lied to you," he sneers at me.

This comes as news to the three of us. Georgina and Felix stare at me, hoping I'll have some kind of defense.

"Spoke to the parents too," the officer continues. "They said he's done this before."

I interject. "Yes but the situation with his parents—"

"I wasn't finished speaking," he interrupts. "This young man has a history of packing up and shipping out when he doesn't like the way things are turning out."

"We were happy."

The officer glares at me.

"Was there any sign of a struggle at his house?" he asks.
"No."

"Did anyone ever threaten to harm him?"
"No."

"Do you see where I'm coming from?" His voice drips with condescension. "Based on what the parents have told us ... and they say they're not interested in opening up a missing persons case ... this boy was troubled ... he's done this before. There's a very real possibility that Kyle has simply decided to move on with his life … and not include you in it."

I want to reach over the desk and stab him through the eye with a pen, and smash his fat head with a paperweight.

"What if you're wrong? What if he is missing?" says Georgina coldly.

The police officer sighs.

"There's no evidence of any struggle. He left the apartment spotless. His personal items packed up and gone. I'd say it's reasonably compelling evidence that he's lied to you and moved out without telling anybody."

I let out a frustrated groan. "This is fucking bullshit!"

The officer crosses his arms and glares at me.

"What are we supposed to do now?" says Felix.

"I'd like to help, but there isn't enough here for me to justify the manpower looking for someone, who for all intents and purposes, might not want to be found," says the officer with a pitiful expression. "You have to trust me, I've seen this before."

I start to sob uncontrollably. Felix and Georgina escort me from the building, shielding me from the inquisitive eyes of onlookers. We drive back to Georgina's place. On the way I get a call from my mom. I put her on speaker. Her voice is calm, soothing and safe. My composure disintegrates as soon as I hear her speak.

"Mom, I want to come home," I cry into the phone.

"Darling, we've changed your flights. Can Felix and Georgina get you to the airport this afternoon?"

"Yes, Mrs. Chambers. That won't be a problem at all," says Felix.

"Is that Felix? Thank you for helping my boy," she says.

"That's what best friends are for, right?"

"Toddy, be strong. We'll see you soon. I love you," says my mom. We both hang up.

We sit in silence for the rest of the car ride home, and I stare blankly out the window. Every time Kyle's face springs into my mind, another tear wells in my eyes and runs down my cheek. I feel completely abandoned, even in the presence of my best friend and his girlfriend.

It's like having your soul torn apart or your heart ripped out through your throat. Raw, bleeding and dying. I can't breathe. I can't scream. I can't move. I'm numb … detached … hollow. I miss him so much, and I would do anything and everything to get him back. Just to feel him next to me one last time.

Just like that, the man I love, my first everything, the one I want to be with forever, has vanished without a trace.

Chapter Nineteen

I haven't left my bedroom in days. For the past three hours I've been staring blankly at the same fluffy yellow toy sitting across the room on the bookshelf. Even blinking seems like too much of an effort. My body is sapped of all its energy and will to live.

Mom opens the door and walks in with a tray of food. She lays it down on the bedside table and sits on the bed. She rubs my back and runs her hands through my hair.

"Honey, you have to eat something," she says.

"I can't."

Mom crouches on the floor and puts her face an inch in front of mine.

"Todd Chambers, I know you're sad, but I am not leaving this room until you have eaten every morsel of food on this plate."

I glance over at the tray. She's made my favorite—bacon carbonara. The smell suddenly hits my nostrils and my stomach gurgles.

I sit up, which brings a smile to my mom's face. She passes the tray to me.

"Can I get you something to drink?" asks Mom.

"I'd love a glass of water, please," I reply.

"Coming right up," she says, walking towards the door.

"Mom?" I say, about to take my first mouthful. "Thank you."

She smiles again and leaves.

I devour the pasta, not realizing how starving I was. My mom returns with a glass of water and sits beside me.

"Your father disagrees with me, but I think we need to come up with a plan for how to deal with this." I chew on my food and listen to what she has to say. "I'm worried that what's happened with Kyle is going to derail your plans for the future. You've always been problem focused when dealing with stress, and I think we should play to your strengths."

"I don't understand," I say.

"We don't know what has happened to Kyle, whether he's coming back, or why he left ..." Her words make me get a little choked up, and it's hard to swallow my mouthful of food. "... So I need you to focus on you for now. Focus on getting those grades you need for medical school. And focus on the positive things going on in your life. Control the things you have the power to control."

"What did Dad say?" I ask.

Mom sighs. "He thought we should give you as much time as you need to ..."

"To move on?" I say.

Mom evidently doesn't like my choice of words, but she

was clearly struggling to find a diplomatic way of saying it.

"I can't move on. I don't want to. I love Kyle."

"He's gone, Todd," she says, firm but caring.

I glare at her, angry that she would try to force me to see things from such a logical perspective when I'm still hurting so badly inside.

"I'm sorry," she says. "I didn't mean it like that. I hate to see you hurting like this. And I'm angry with Kyle for what he's done to you." She wipes a tear from her eye. "You didn't deserve any of this."

I give my mom a hug. I'd been so wrapped up in my own self-pity that I never considered how this might have affected anyone else.

I say softly, "Do you think this would have happened if I'd been in a straight relationship?"

My mom sits bolt upright. She's never looked so serious in her entire life. "Why would you even think that? Don't torture yourself, Todd. You can't change who you are, and don't you dare venerate heterosexual relationships. They're not perfect."

I nod, but even though I know she's right, I can't help feeling it's somehow my fault. What that police officer said about things like this happening to gay couples all the time has been preying on my mind ever since.

"Were you disappointed when I told you and Dad that I was gay?"

Mom smiles and rubs her hand up and down my arm.

"Honey, we always knew." She stops and rethinks her words. "Well, not that you were gay, but somehow your father and I never expected you to one day come home with a girlfriend. It's hard to explain."

I manage a chuckle. "I know what you mean, Mom."

She walks over to the windows and opens up the curtains. The sun streams through and momentarily blinds me.

"It's a beautiful day outside," says Mom. "Let's go do something special. Just the two of us."

I sit out on the porch with my phone, deleting Kyle's messages one by one. I'd saved everything we ever sent to each other, and going through them is like repeating every special moment of our time together. With every message I discard a little piece of me dies, and the fire that burned so brightly in my heart for Kyle is slowly snuffed out till all that remains is ash.

I stop when I come to the last text he ever sent me. My finger hovers over the trashcan icon, but I can't do it. I can't say goodbye for good.

Fifteen Years Later

Chapter Twenty

As I read through my list of scheduled appointments, I think to myself, "It's going to be a long day today". First up is one of my least favorite patients, a twenty-one-year old named Chad who has Obsessive-Compulsive Disorder. When I met him six months ago, I knew after the first session that he was using this behavior to disguise an inability to come to terms with his sexual orientation. He still lives at home with his controlling mother, and she'll no doubt have come along with him today, like she does every week. She's such a nosy bitch. Can't bear the sight of her. The kid doesn't stand a chance of exploring and figuring out what he wants in life and love.

I make a quick trip to the restroom before Chad arrives. Our new receptionist, Vicki, waves me down on the way back.

"Dr. Chambers, your first patient arrived early. He's waiting in your office."

"Thank you, Vicki."

Chad's mother is sitting on one of the sofas in the waiting area, flicking through a magazine. Thankfully, she doesn't notice me, otherwise I'd be obliged to engage in conversation with her. She has an irritating habit of trying to extract information about my sessions with her son, which pisses me off. I sneak into my office and see the top of Chad's head poking up above the back of the leather psychiatrist couch.

"Good morning, Chad," I say as I walk into the room. "How are you this morning?"

He pays no attention to me and carries on staring vacantly at the ceiling. I pick up my tablet and flick to his file before taking my seat.

"Last time I saw you, we were discussing how college was going. You're almost at the end of your computer science degree, right?"

I swipe through a few more screens of notes.

"Are you gay?" Chad blurts out, taking me by surprise.

He makes eye contact and holds it without blinking.

"Tell me why it's important for you to know about my sexuality."

This puts Chad on the back foot. "I heard you were gay, is all."

"Would it make any difference, Chad?"

He squirms in his seat and picks at his fingernails.

"Haven't really thought about it."

The kid has an IQ in the genius range. He's smarter than me. Of course he's thought about it. He's also a complete narcissist, so it won't be hard to deflect the conversation back to him. If I pause long enough, he'll want to fill in the silence, so I wait.

"It feels weird," he says.

"Why is that?"

"Just does."

"When we spoke about it before, you said that you were unsure of your own sexuality. Is that still valid?"

He peers around the room, everywhere except at me.

"Could I get a coffee or something? I'm real thirsty," he says.

Coffee doesn't sound like a bad idea. Give him a few minutes to digest his thoughts.

"Sure, Chad. I'll be right back," I say.

I step out of my office. Chad's mother is right where I saw her last, still sitting on the couch. Maybe if I stand extremely still, she won't see me.

"Dr. Chambers! How lovely to see you," she says.

Fuck.

"Good morning, Mrs. Harris. How are you today?" I say with my sweetest fake smile.

"Just wonderful, thank you."

If only she would continue reading her magazine and stop looking at me, expecting the conversation to go on.

"If you'll excuse me, I need to collect something."

I turn on my heels before she has a chance to reply, and scoot into the kitchenette behind the reception area to make two cups of coffee.

When Mrs. Harris is looking down and the opportunity presents itself, I scurry back to my office.

I can hear Chad breathing heavily on the couch, but I can't see him. What grabs my attention is the pile of clothes sitting neatly folded on the floor. I close my eyes and pray that God will grant me the strength not to murder this little shit today. I can't say anything more or I'll spontaneously combust with fury.

I finish typing up my notes on Chad's visit just as Vicki opens the door to allow my next patient, Cassie, into the room. Cassie traipses into my office bundled in a warm coat and wearing a woolly knitted cap on her head. We both went to the same high school, but we had different circles of friends and didn't talk much in those days. That all changed six months ago when she started coming to see me.

"Morning, Todd," she says, wincing in pain.

"Good morning, Cassie." I quickly run to her aid and let her hold onto my arm for support. She's frail, like a little old lady, when she should be in her prime. I sit beside her and hold her hand.

She's wearing no makeup. Her face is pale and tired. She collapses back onto the couch. Cassie shuts her eyes while she waits for the pain to subside and regain her strength after the exhaustion that comes with moving.

"Thank you, Todd."

"Cassie, you know I can come visit you at home."

She shakes her head. "No. It's good to get out of the house."

"It looks like the bone pain is worse. Have you called your oncologist?" The cancer has spread to her spine and sternum, and she's been in constant pain for months now. When I see someone with metastatic cancer struggling to walk, alarm bells start ringing.

Cassie mouths the numbers as she silently counts backwards from "ten". She reaches the number "one", takes a deep breath, and sits up tall on the couch, smiling bravely.

"I had an MRI yesterday. The cancer is choking my spinal cord. I have zero sensation below my knees, and it's getting hard to walk. But I'm still alive."

Her words confirm my worst fears: she has spinal cord compression. She sits there, stoic and strong in the face of terminal illness.

"I've got an appointment with the radiation oncologist tomorrow. She's going to zap away the pain. The medical oncologist gave me a pill to take in the meantime. It's meant to make me feel like the Hulk, but I think he's full of shit." I've never heard her swear before and the profanity grates on my ears.

"Have you had any luck with the insurance company?" I ask.

Cassie looks at me like I'm stupid. That answers my question. Her medical insurers refused to pay a cent towards her treatment because she failed to disclose a family history of breast cancer. How they discovered that her aunt had died of breast cancer is a mystery to me, because she died long before Cassie was even born. Cassie never even knew her aunt's name. I fucking hate insurance companies.

"I sold my house," she says.

"Jesus, Cassie. I'm so sorry."

"It's not your fault. I got a good price. It should be just enough to cover the mountainous debt of medical expenses that I've racked up. They don't need to know that I can't afford to pay for any more treatment. I'll be dead, anyway. What are they going to do about it then?"

"Nothing. There's nothing they can do about it," I say, and she smiles at me. Her lip begins to quiver, but she manages to hold it together.

"Enough about me. How are you doing?" Cassie asks, trying to act sprightly.

"Good. Can't complain."

"You're so full of shit, Todd." Cassie laughs. "You're just as lonely as me."

"You know how it goes. Peaks and troughs."

She raises one eyebrow and titters.

"I don't want to take the pills you gave me anymore," she says suddenly. "They aren't working."

"You don't have to do anything that you don't want to."

Her face wrinkles up and her head hangs limply on her neck. She slumps against me, resting on my shoulder.

"I don't want to die." A solitary tear runs down her cheek.

I feel myself choking up. Keep it together, Todd. She needs you to be strong.

I ask Vicki to please apologize to my next patients, and tell them that I'm running a bit behind schedule. I need a few minutes by myself to process my appointment with Cassie.

My next session is with a married couple, Julio and Rita. They've been seeing me for a few weeks now about intimacy issues in their relationship. I can't imagine it's easy being in a relationship with the same person for almost twenty years, and I applaud them for that achievement.

"How did you both get on with the homework I gave you last week?"

The body language tells me everything I need to know. Julio and Rita lean against opposite ends of the couch, not touching and gazing off in different directions.

"If you're not going to tell him, I will!" Rita snaps at Julio.

"No, honey—" he tries to stop her.

"He wants an open relationship." Rita gives Julio a cold stare.

He rolls his eyes. "Dammit, Rita! Would you get over it? I never used those words!"

"Julio, where did this come from? Until now, Rita has been the one taking responsibility for the lack of intimacy—" I say.

Rita interrupts me. "I just don't feel sexy since I went through the menopause. It's not easy for me to be intimate. Now he wants to sleep with other women!"

Julio shakes his head and sighs. Rita glares at him. "He wants to try swinging," she says.

"I take it you're opposed to the idea?"

"Yes! I'm insecure enough as it is."

Julio opens his mouth to speak, and Rita blocks it with the palm of her hand.

"Shh. I wasn't finished talking. I want to feel sexy again. And you going off with some stranger at a sex party is not going to help my insecurities."

"Rita! Stop it!" says Julio, growing brusque and impatient. "You're missing the point. I'm not palming you off onto someone else or running away from you. We've tried every-thing, and no offense to you, Doc, but these homework exercises are not working. Maybe I can't light your fire like I used to? Maybe that spark between us has burned out? I just thought that if we added some excitement, it could ignite what we had before."

They sit in silence, but after a couple of minutes I see something change in the way Rita looks at him. His words seem to resonate with her, and she shows him tenderness for the first time today by placing her hand on his knee.

"Do you really think we need that kind of help?" she says to him.

They both look to me for an answer.

"The statistics will tell you that it's not … uncommon. But this is a decision that you two have to make together, and consider all the possible benefits and consequences. If you do this, it can't be undone if you don't like the outcome."

"I told you it was a bad idea," says Rita.

"And I told you not to say anything!"

Julio and Rita cross their arms and assume the same posi-tion as before, staring into the distance at opposite sides of the room.

"So how's your bag of mixed nuts today?" jokes Felix, sinking his teeth into a juicy chunk of medium-rare fillet steak.

We're both creatures of habit and always eat lunch at the same French restaurant just around the corner from our practice office.

"The usual. Remind me again why we love this job?"

"The money." He laughs.

"Well, speak for yourself." I pick at my chicken salad.

"You doing your charity work this afternoon?" asks Felix in a condescending tone.

"Yes, Felix. There's only so much I can take of private patients' first-world problems and woe-is-me relationship struggles."

"I bet they literally pay you with peanuts there, right?"

Felix can be such a dick sometimes.

"Like a well-trained monkey."

I got into medicine because I wanted to help people, not to get rich. The patients I see at the hospital are the ones who need my help the most. This is one of those contentious topics that Felix and I are never going to agree upon.

Time to change the subject. "Did I tell you I'm going on a date tonight?"

Felix drops his knife and fork and looks at me in surprise. "No fucking way! With who?"

"This guy I met the other day," I say with a coy smile.

"Uh huh?" he says, prodding for more information.

"I'll tell you more if it goes well."

Felix looks a bit dejected at my lack of sharing. He chews on another piece of steak, and I can see the cogs turning in his twisted brain. "There's something I've been wondering for a while now," he asks.

"Here we go," I exclaim.

"Do all gay guys douche before they go on a date?"

"Fucking hell, Felix! Where do you get this shit from?"

"What? It's a valid question."

I shake my head in despair. For someone so intelligent, Felix sure does ask the dumbest questions sometimes.

Going on a date will be a welcome change. It's been almost a year since my last official date, and even longer since I had a proper relationship. For as long as I can remember, I've gone from one disastrous coupling to the next. A true serial monogamist. Nowadays I spend most of my nights at home alone whacking off to porn. Not that I don't enjoy it, but there's comfort in a relationship: knowing that you always have someone to turn to when you're having those down moments, and it's way more fun celebrating big occasions with someone special.

This isn't healthy, and Felix is right when he says that it's time I put myself out there and make an effort to find someone. You can't win the lottery if you don't buy a ticket, likewise you can't expect to find yourself a partner if you don't go out on dates.

"Yourself? Anything interesting?" I ask.

"Oh you know. The usual. Insecure business executives having midlife crises and chronic fatigue fakers."

I snort. "You can't say that. It's a diagnosable medical condition."

"More specifically, a diagnosis of exclusion. All it means is we haven't been able to find a legitimate medical reason to explain their 'symptoms'. I'm not saying it doesn't exist, but I'd bet real money that not a single one of my patients actually has it. And If I don't give them a condition to label themselves with, then someone else will."

This kind of head-shrink stuff is private practice gold,

and I despise how my profession has medicalized completely normal behaviors like apathy and self-pity.

"Why can't perfectly healthy people celebrate the fact that life is good instead of inventing problems for themselves?" says Felix.

"Finished ranting?" I ask.

"Mmm hmm."

"There was an incident this morning with Chad," I say as I finish off the last of my meal.

Felix takes a sip of water and raises an eyebrow. "What happened?"

"I walked in and he was …" I hush my voice and lean over the table closer to Felix. "He was jerking off on my couch."

Felix spits his mouthful of water out all over the table. Tears of laughter begin to stream down his face, and the other patrons in the restaurant turn and stare at the commotion he's creating.

"This isn't funny," I say in all seriousness.

Felix calms himself down enough to speak.

"You need to refer him on to someone else, bud."

"You know what? I feel violated by the whole thing. I'm there trying to help this confused kid figure his shit out, and then he goes and pulls a stunt like this. What the fuck was he thinking?"

"You want my take on things?"

I sit back and listen.

"Chad is dangerous. You want to know why?" Felix pauses, but the question is rhetorical. "Because he's an over-indulged brat with mommy issues. I don't think he's confused about his sexuality. He's probably been jerking off to hard-core gay porn since before he had his first wet dream. He needs a hard slap in the face with a big dick, and his mother needs lessons on how to parent properly. Isn't he twenty-one years old? Guy needs to grow the fuck up."

It's then that I notice the elderly couple sitting at the table beside us have gone silent and are staring blankly at Felix. He smiles at them briefly and flicks his eyes between them and the meals in front of them. They get the idea. Felix locks eyes with me again and reiterates the point. "Refer him on to someone else."

After lunch, Felix and I both go our separate ways. I'm running a bit late for a patient assessment at the psychiatric hospital where I work part-time. When I arrive, the head of department, Linda Fierstein, is not in the finest of moods.

"You're late!" she scolds me from the end of the hallway.

"Is the patient ready for me?" I ask, ignoring her snappy comment.

One of the first lessons I ever learned in medicine is to never apologize for anything, even if it is entirely your fault. It's not so much about avoiding liability, although that is important from a legal perspective, but rather acknowledging that human error is a fact of life, and there's really no point spending our lives saying "sorry".

Linda and I were in the same graduating year at med school, but we hardly spoke in all those years together. I had no idea when I accepted this job that she'd been fighting with the board for months to employ someone else. Instead, they chose me. I later discovered that the "preferred candidate" was actually her partner at the time, and the candidate was counting on the position to get a visa to stay in the country. I think she blames me for forcing her to have an international relationship that was doomed to fail. Needless to say, our working relationship has been strained from the very beginning.

"He's in consulting room four," she says.

"Restrained?"

"Heavily. He broke a prison guard's neck yesterday and the lawyers are demanding a psych eval. We have the pleasure of playing host to Mr. Jenner for the next ninety days."

"Why couldn't this be done in the prison?"

Linda gives me a look that tells the entire story without words. We stop outside the consulting room, which looks more like an interrogation chamber. A lonely table and two chairs in the center of an otherwise empty room.

The prisoner's face starts setting off alarm bells in my head. "What was he in for?"

"You remember those murders a few years ago where the guy was approaching random people in the street and snapping their necks with his bare hands?" says Linda.

The story is vaguely familiar. If I remember correctly, the guy got away with it for months until he got unlucky and was hit by a car as he fled the scene of his last attack.

"Defense pled insanity, didn't they?" I look at her for confirmation.

"The car that hit him broke his back and left him with a

major contusion on his brain in the frontal lobe," says Linda. "He walks all right, but he has no conscience ... no emotion ... I won't say much more. He was dangerous before the accident, but now he's a monster. Have fun." She gives me an insincere smile and pushes a wad of paperwork into my arms. I read the name on the top of the patient notes, "Peter Jenner", greet the two armed guards standing outside the consulting room with a nod, and step inside the room with all the confidence I can muster.

The assessment of the patient lasts well over an hour. He communicates with me in a series of monosyllabic answers, but my gut tells me that he's not as brain damaged as he wants us to believe. I make a recommendation for solitary confinement, where we can keep him on lockdown for the protection of our other patients and staff. I've crossed paths with more murderers on a professional basis than I care to remember, but this sort of brute is volatile and ruthless. Is it wrong to say that I "prefer" murderers whose crimes are premeditated? They're so much more predictable and less prone to violent outbursts. This Peter guy scares the living shit out of me.

Chapter Twenty-One

My detour past the psychiatric hospital took longer than expected. Now I'm stuck in rush-hour traffic, and I'll be lucky if I make it to my appointment on time. Better call ahead to let them know. The phone rings through the car audio system.

A girly voice answers, "Manscapers. You're speaking with Jess."

"Hi, Jess," I say, unsure where to direct my voice. I've had this car for over a year, and still can't figure out where the microphone is hidden. "It's Dr. Chambers."

"Oh hi, Dr. Chambers. How are you today?" Her voice is so saccharine sweet. I bet she's faking a smile while she talks too. When did I get this cynical?

"I'm fine thanks, Jess. I just called to let you know that I'm running late today."

"Dr. Chambers, you know we can only hold appointments for fifteen minutes."

I bite my tongue. "That's fine. Will you let Melody know that I'll be fifteen minutes late?" Melody is the young lady who usually does my grooming. I've been to see her every six weeks for the past five years and I don't trust anyone else with my junk.

"Um … your appointment is scheduled with Sally today."

"There must be a mistake." Now I'm starting to get irritated.

"Let me check." Her voice drifts away, and I can hear the muffled sounds of her speaking to someone in the background. "No, it says here that you specifically requested Sally."

I change lanes, because this one is going nowhere. The guy in the car behind me flips me the bird.

"She's very good," says Jess. Her insistence pisses me off even more.

I consider whether I should enter into a heated debate with Jess, but it's just not worth the effort, and I'll never get another appointment anywhere else in town at this late notice.

"See you in ten."

I hang up the call before she can reply. I'm not going to let this spoil my evening.

When I arrive at the Manscapers reception, I'm greeted by a blonde bimbo with big boobs and fake blue eyes. This must be Jess. Why couldn't they use young, vapid, muscly studs like the other places in town? I feel guilty for being here and for buying into the culture of outward appearance being so important. When did I become this vain? And why is my anxiety about this date tonight turning me into a complete bitch? Take it easy. Just relax.

"Todd Chambers, here for an appointment with Mel … uh … Sally."

Jess looks up the appointment on the computer. "Oh yes. Dr. Chambers. You're a few minutes late. Has it been a busy day?" Does she not recall speaking to me on the phone a few minutes earlier?

"It has," I say.

Jess gives me an understanding nod and says, "Please take a seat and Sally will be through shortly."

I go to sit down, but my conscience gets the better of me and forces me to turn around. "Jess?"

"Yes, Dr. Chambers."

"I'm sorry for being so curt and rude to you."

"That's okay, Dr. Chambers, you should see me when I'm about to have a Brazilian. This bitch be feisty." She flips her hair over her shoulder like she grew up in a ghetto and carries on typing at her computer. That lightens my mood and brings a smile to my face.

A dainty Asian lady walks in and claps her hands together. "Todd Chambers?"

I'm the only person in the room. She has a 100% chance of guessing who Todd Chambers is. "That's me!"

"Come with me please, sir. Have you had a good day?"

"Not particularly."

"Well, Sally is going to make it all better now."

We enter one of the therapy suites, which always remind me of an operating theatre: full of strange equipment and that horrible sterile odor.

"Put your clothes on the stool and make yourself comfortable on the bed. I'll be back."

She pulls the curtain and disappears out the door again. I

disrobe and lie back on the torture table. I miss Melody already. Sally returns after a few minutes with a handful of towels.

"Todd?"

"Yes, Sally."

"Jess at reception tells me there was a mix-up. You thought you booked with Melody?"

"That is correct." I just want her to get on with it already.

"Well, I'm going to throw in a free massage to make up for the inconvenience. That sound good?"

My ears prick up at the word "massage". "Yeah, that sounds great."

"Good. Maybe we do that first before I rip the hair out your balls?" Oh God, this is going to be an interesting experience.

Sally gets me to turn over onto my stomach and starts massaging my back and shoulders. She works my back with consummate skill. My body unwinds and sinks deeper into a state of relaxation. Just as I start to doze off, she breaks the silence. "Okay, time for the back-crack-and-sack wax. Roll over."

I do as instructed. So far she's been a complete sweetheart, and it's taken all that awkwardness of out getting an intimate wax from a total stranger.

She spreads a layer of warm wax down my groin, which feels rather pleasant. Sally places a strip of fabric over the wax and brushes the fabric with her fingers so that it clings like cement to the wax.

"Okay, on the count of one … two …"

Rip.

Scream.

On the way out, I give Jess at reception a big smile. I might be walking bowlegged for the next couple of hours, but the nervous anticipation has melted away, and I'm starting to get excited about my big date tonight.

I swing by my apartment to have a quick shower and get changed into something more appropriate for my date. No time for dawdling. I need to hurry up and get my ass into gear or I'll be late.

These days, most of my personal prep time is dedicated to manicuring my beard. I keep it sculpted and cropped close to my face, which I think adds a certain level of distinction to my appearance. I've been told before that it makes me look like a total DILF. I wish that Kyle could see me now, but I quickly push the thought from my mind.

Still have an hour before I'm meeting my date at the yacht club. I'm not a member, but he is. There's no way in hell I would willingly hand over close to ten thousand a year just to have the privilege of dining from an overly priced menu surrounded by a bunch of snobs.

My clothes for the evening are neatly laid out on the bed where I left them this morning. I have a last-minute change of heart and decide to go for a more casual style instead of the blazer and smart pants that I had chosen earlier. The last thing I do before leaving the apartment is grab a condom from my bedside drawer and slip it into my back pocket. To be honest, sex with a stranger hasn't happened in a very long time, but it's better to be prepared than remorseful later on. It's not like back when Kyle and I were dating monogamously. I haven't barebacked with anyone since him, and it just doesn't feel the same with that layer of latex. It spoils the intimacy, but I would never be stupid enough to go without one.

One of the great tragedies of modern dating, especially gay internet and phone app dating, is the over-sharing of information. If I ask anyone from my parents' generation what characteristics they look for in a partner, the answer is usually some variation of tall, dark and handsome with a good sense of humor and stable job. Nowadays, you can filter down your potential matches based on an almost infinite list of inconsequential features, ranging from preferred sexual positions to dietary choices.

I only have two things that would rule out a potential partner—female or vegan. So when I meet a new guy, I would rather know nothing about him sexually and let things in that department evolve on their own. In a perfect world, every date would be like a Christmas present that I get to unwrap. Ninety-nine percent of the dates I've gone on in the past fifteen years have started with an instant message on a dating site or phone app, so needless to say, I've had very few surprises.

I've been looking forward to tonight's date for just that reason. It was a spontaneous invitation, made offline—in the real world—and from a guy whose wrapping I have fantasized about opening more than once.

"I must admit, I was amazed when you approached me at the gym," I say to the man sitting opposite me at the dinner table.

Did I really just let those words escape my lips? What a stupid thing to say to someone on the first date. He'll sense my insecurity a mile away.

Johnny laughs and I relax a little. This guy is gorgeous. No, that doesn't give him enough credit … he's fucking sexy, with a jawline that would make a superhero jealous.

Johnny Owen was one of the first football stars to prove that gay and sports can mix successfully. His sporting career may have ended early, no thanks to a severe shoulder injury, but that didn't stop him from becoming a television personality. Now he's sitting across the table from me, sipping a glass of pinot noir and waiting for our dessert to arrive.

"You didn't see me staring at you in the sauna?" says Johnny.

I choke on my wine. He was cruising me in the sauna?

"Forgive me, that came out wrong," he starts to explain. "I mean that I had noticed you earlier when we were in the sauna and kept trying to catch your eye."

"I'm shy in saunas."

"Not sure why," he says with a sexy smile. I flush with embarrassment at his shameful flirting. This is how the entire night has been so far, and I'm loving every minute of it.

I lean further onto the table and put on my serious face. "Can I ask you a question?"

"Of course. I'm an open book." He leans back in his

chair, folding his arms across his chest.

I'm distracted by his muscled biceps and forget what I was about to say.

"What's your workout program?" That is not the question that I had in mind. I instantly hate myself. There are so many things I want to know that I'm too terrified to ask, in case I come across desperate, needy, or insecure. The last thing I want to know about is his gym routine.

For the next ten minutes, he regales me with intricate details about every set, rep, bench day, leg day, rest day, and supplement, but all I can think about is what he will look like naked. I start to panic. It's always at this part of the date that the anxiety kicks in, when the perfect date is drawing to a close and we'll inevitably reach that awkward point where one of us bravely asks the other if we'd like to go back to his or my place. Or worse—we say nothing and go our separate ways, full of regret, and most likely never to see one another again.

"Hey, what do you say? Shall we get out of here?" he says.

His words bring a sense of relief and I grin back at him.

"Back to your place?" I ask.

"Well, mine ... yours ... it doesn't matter."

I hesitate just a moment too long in responding.

The desserts arrive at the table, and I thank the waiter. "I guess we might as well have dessert after all," I say, knowing that I just ruined the moment. "Would you mind if we took a rain-check? I have an early morning meeting that I have to do prep work for this evening."

"Oh?" he says, surprised by my response. He probably

never gets turned down. "Yes, of course."

Maybe it's better that I don't sleep with him on our first date anyway. I'd prefer to make a good impression than come across as too easy.

"You, I would definitely like to see again," he insists with a wink and a smile that makes the dessert taste even more delicious.

I walk into my apartment and straight to my bedroom. Everything is immaculate, the way I left it, just in case Johnny had ended up coming home with me. I let out a small sigh as I slowly undress. At just the right angle and with a bit of a crunch I can see my abs, but I'm no Adonis. I'm thirty-five years old, so I have to work hard to keep fit and my body looking good, but I don't live at the gym like most other gay men in this town. It disturbs me how hard they push themselves, obsessed with achieving the perfect physique. To what end? They're objectifying the wrong role models and striving for a goal that is unachievable unless you're a professional sportsman, on the juice, or some kind of hormonal freak of nature.

I climb into bed, pick up my laptop and a bottle of lube from the bedside drawer. I'm fully aware that what I'm about to do makes me a total hypocrite. Because right now, I'm going to lie back and masturbate to videos of hot guys, who epitomise everything I despise about the quest for physical perfection, watching them engaged in lurid acts of man-on-man sexual intercourse. Good night.

Chapter Twenty-Two

Sunday has to be my least favorite day of the week. I know that I should be celebrating the fact that it's a day off work and I have no commitments, but I just can't seem to shake the feeling of Monday looming over me and having to start with the same old bullshit all over again. Felix and Georgina have invited me over for dinner tonight, so that is at least something to look forward to. I enjoy hanging out with them and their two kids over a Sunday roast or barbecue. The girls like to call me "Uncle Todd", which always puts a smile on my face.

On the way to Felix and Georgina's place in the late afternoon, my mind switches to autopilot and I take a surprise detour to the zoo. I haven't been here in years, and yet it looks exactly the same. But it isn't like the romantic strolls that Kyle and I used to take. This is a perilous journey, with children running amok and parents pushing baby strollers the size of small cars that clog up the walkways between enclosures. I find my way to the center of the zoo and the grass lawn where Kyle and I spent our first night together, staring up at the stars. I lie back on the soft grass and squint into the bright blue sky above me. A little girl runs over and peers down at me, puzzled.

"You okay, mister?" she says.

"I'm doing great. Thanks for asking," I reply with a friendly smile.

She smiles back at me and runs off to play a game with her friends. I put my hands behind my head and soak up the sunshine. If only Kyle was here with me now. I just hope that wherever he is in the world, he's happy and healthy. It's been fifteen years and I still haven't got used to him not being around. Maybe I never will.

Felix and his brood live in a beautiful suburban home with a landscaped garden, two dogs, a pool, and everything you would come to expect in the Stepford dream home. I don't think I could ever live out here. The forty-five minute commute into the city every day would drive me insane, but maybe that's just the bitterness talking. I'm sure that one day when a handsome, successful and loving guy comes into my life and sweeps me off my feet, we'll be adopting babies quicker than Angelina and Brad, and settling into a life of pleasant domesticity.

Georgina's meal doesn't disappoint. She cooked the most delicious lamb roast with "heart attack" potatoes—the kind where you let the potatoes bake in the same tray as the roast and they soak up all the mouth-watering flavor … and fat. So succulent and tender, they literally melt in my mouth.

"Wife cook meat good," says Felix, channeling his inner caveman. It earns him a kick under the table from Georgina.

"Wife make husband do all dishes and clean up." Georgina shoots him a wink.

"Mommy, I've had enough," says their youngest girl, Becks, who is three years old.

Their five-year old, Rowena, echoes her baby sister. "I'm full, Mommy."

"If you two don't want any more, then I think it's time for bed," says Georgina.

The girls both pout and sulk.

"Shotgun putting the kids to bed. Come on, my angels." Felix scoops his two girls up under his arms. "Time to go visit Mr. Sandman."

They giggle and scream as he tickles them in his arms and carries them away.

I help Georgina with the cleaning while Felix does his daddy duties. We carry everything through to the kitchen and stack the dishwasher.

"Todd, I feel bad doing this, but I need to talk to you about something," says Georgina.

"What is it?"

"Has Felix spoken with you about us trying to get pregnant again?"

My face lights up at this unexpected news. "He hasn't. That's so exciting."

Georgina shakes her head and groans. "No it's not."

My smile dissipates rather quickly.

"You know how we tried for over a year before I finally

got pregnant with Becks?"

I do remember. To say it was a rough patch in their relationship would be an understatement; they almost got divorced.

Georgina covers her mouth and tries to hold back the tears.

"We've been trying again. It's not happening. I went to see my gynecologist and it's not me that's the problem. She said these days it's the guy fifty percent of the time."

"Have you spoken to Felix?"

"You try telling a guy that his little soldiers don't march like they should." She sobs.

"Hey, don't get yourself all worked up. There are options," I say in my calm doctor voice.

"You're gonna say 'IVF', aren't you?"

I nod enthusiastically.

"Already crossed it off the list. We can't afford it," she says. "We don't have the disposable income since we bought the house."

"What about going back to work?" I ask.

"Who is gonna employ someone who's trying to get pregnant? And it won't leave us any better off. I'd have to put the kids in daycare, and you know how expensive that is."

"I had no idea things were so tight for you guys. Felix has never mentioned it to me."

"He's too proud," she says.

I give her a hug and kiss on the forehead. Georgina wipes the tears that are welling in her eyes.

"Talk to Felix. If you guys need help paying for treatment,

let me know. My dreams of growing mini-mes aren't getting any closer to fruition."

"I'm so embarrassed," says Georgina. "I wasn't asking for a handout, Todd."

"It's not like that at all. I love you guys and I want to help in any way I can."

"Are you sure?"

"I'm not gonna change my mind."

Georgina smiles. She stands taller than before, like a heavy weight has been lifted off her shoulders.

"You're too good to us, Todd."

"That's what friends are for."

The girls go down without much fuss, and Felix joins Georgina and me in the living room for some grown-up time. We sink onto the sofa and put up our feet, which is blissful. Georgina is fading fast and can hardly keep her eyes open.

"Why don't you go upstairs and get ready for bed, babe?" says Felix, giving her a quick cuddle. She gives me a wave and staggers off.

Felix gets a glint in his eyes and says, "I just remembered. You went on a date last night and you haven't said a word about it."

The date had completely slipped my mind.

"It wasn't too bad," I say.

"Okay, we can work with that."

"I'm not sure. I've thought about it a lot today, and re-playing the conversations we had at the dinner table in my mind, I realize that the attraction is all physical. He didn't stimulate me intellectually."

Felix screws up his face. "All right. Tell me again how you two met each other."

"The old-fashioned way."

"On the internet?"

"Fuck off!" We both laugh. "It was at the gym, actually."

"Classy," says Felix. "I hear that's where all the slutty guys hang out."

"You want to talk about classy? Like you and Georgina on the night you met?" I shoot him the evil eye and continue, "If I recall correctly, you two spent your first night together playing pool in a dirty Irish bar downtown. If she hadn't projectile vomited all over you—"

"Okay ... okay ... that's enough," he shushes me and makes a timeout gesture with his hands. "Such sweet memories." He puts on a serious expression. "Promise me you won't ever tell my kids how Mommy and Daddy met."

"Secret is safe with me, pal," I assure him.

We both take another sip of wine. There's a moment of silence.

"Did you fuck him?" Felix asks inquisitively.

"No, we did not have sex."

"Seriously?" He sounds extremely disappointed by this news. "Come on, bro! When are you going to start sharing hot stories about getting loads of man-puss? Aren't you gay guys supposed to be total sluts? Georgina works with a guy who's such a manwhore he's never slept with the same dude twice. She always gets to hear about his dirty antics."

"I don't know. I think I'm at a stage in life now where

seeking no-strings fun doesn't hold the same kind of appeal that it used to. I need more than that."

"How many dates have you been on lately? Two? Three?" he says.

"Last night would be the first."

"This month?" he asks.

"Year," I say.

"Oh man, I don't care how the date went; you need to sext him this minute and get those pipes cleaned out. Show me his profile pic."

"We didn't meet online. Are you even paying attention?"

Georgina slinks up behind Felix in her nightgown and wraps her arms around him.

"I'm sorry, Toddy, but I'm going to have to steal my husband away from you. It's time for bed," she says.

I glance at the clock on the wall. It's close to 11 PM, and time for me to head home. I thank them both for the delicious meal and their splendid company.

"Text him," shouts Felix as I pull out of their driveway. I watch them both disappear into the house together and a pang of envy stabs me in the gut. I pull over before I reach the end of the street and sit there, staring blankly at my phone. Why is it so hard for me to do this? I've decided that I have no intentions of ever dating the jock, so what is stopping me from fulfilling the base, primal urge that I so desperately need satisfied?

Nothing. Stop being such a pussy.

I'm usually the sort of person who labors over every word I write, spending far longer than is necessary, even when texting, but tonight all I can be bothered sending is—*"What are you doing?"*

About a minute later, as I'm about to give up my half-hearted efforts and drive home again, my phone vibrates —*"Hey sexy. Was wondering when you'd text. Wanna come over for a nightcap?"*

What a surprise! It must be a sign, right? I say that sarcastically because to be honest, Felix wasn't too far off the mark with his insinuation that most gay men are sluts.

Fifteen minutes later I pull up outside the gate to Johnny's grotesquely modern mansion. The electric gates swing open before I even wind down my window to push the intercom. He must be waiting for my imminent arrival, which I shall take as a compliment.

I park my car beside his Lamborghini. My Audi, which isn't exactly an inexpensive car, looks emasculated and inadequate beside such a masterpiece of machinery. The front door is slightly ajar and I assume this is an invitation to come in. The house is an interior designer's wet dream come true, but I try not to dawdle and get distracted by the opulence.

"Good evening," booms Johnny's deep voice from another room.

The sound echoes through the house. He saunters into the entrance hall in nothing but a tiny pair of silk boxers, carrying two glasses of champagne. I want to spend all night staring at his smooth, muscular physique.

"Just keeps getting better," I say without any subtlety.

He passes the champagne to me and we clink glasses.

There's something a little strange about his behavior, but I just can't put my finger on it. He takes my hand and leads me to the back of the house. A warm mist rises from the bubbling spa beside an infinity pool that overlooks a jaw-dropping view of the city. Not only is it breathtaking, but the neighbors' houses are also completely obscured by trees, making the space feel intimate and private.

Johnny drops his underwear and walks naked to the spa pool. He turns around and gestures for me to follow him. He hasn't a tuft of body hair anywhere on his ripped torso, and it amplifies the massive length and girth of the weapon of ass destruction swinging like a pendulum between his legs. One more thing for me to feel inadequate about. No wonder this guy has such a huge ego. I turn around to preserve my modesty while I undress, fold my clothes, and place them on a deck chair.

"Stop teasing me and turn around," demands Johnny.

There's a towel lying across the end of the deck chair, which I scoop up and wrap around my waist.

"You turn me on so fucking much, you know that?" he says, licking his lips. I feel like a piece of meat.

Johnny reaches for a small brown bottle that's sitting beside the spa.

"You want some?" he says. He blocks one nostril and takes a giant sniff from the bottle. His face flushes red and he drops back into the water, totally content.

"No, thank you. Amyl gives me a headache," I reply.

I amble over to the spa and sit on the edge, dangling my feet in the warm, soothing water. Johnny swims up and rests his arms either side of my legs. He takes his time unwrapping the towel from around my waist. My semi bounces free against my leg. Johnny hardly says a word. He's like an animal examining the prey it's just caught, looking for the perfect angle and opportunity to attack. He cups and tugs at my balls while staring down my cock.

I tilt my head back, stare up at the stars and wait for his warm, wet mouth to envelop my manhood … but nothing happens. Johnny yanks me into the spa and rams his tongue down my throat without any warning. I choke and try to pull away to breathe, but he won't let go. He releases the death grip he has on my head and I take a gulp of air.

"Fuck, you're a good kisser. Can't wait to see what that mouth does to my cock," he says.

He slides back onto a step, and his monstrosity rises to the surface like a periscope.

I'm normally not submissive; actually, totally the opposite. For some reason—let's call it lust and stupidity—I allow things to continue. He takes my head in his hands and spears my face in his crotch. I gag and choke. My teeth scrape the sensitive skin of his shaft, and he loosens his grip.

"Whoa there! Careful with the teeth," he says.

He slips up against me and attacks my face with his tongue. He swirls it around in my mouth like some kind of alien probe. That isn't the only probing going on. He forces a finger deep inside my ass, and I nearly hit the roof.

Johnny stops everything he's doing. He stares deep into my eyes and runs his hand along my jawline. This almost feels romantic. Perhaps the worst has passed.

"You should shave. You'd look much sexier without the beard," he says.

I'm absolutely flabbergasted. Did he really just insult my facial hair while he's trying to woo me to have sex with him? "You definitely clean, as in, HIV negative? 'Cause I prefer bareback," he says, leaving me in stunned silence.

That's it. I think I've had enough of this moron. First, he treats my penis as if it's a decoration that doesn't deserve any of his attention. Second, he tries to dominate me, when clearly I'm not into that. Third, he just wants to fuck me senseless, without any attempt at foreplay. And last but not least, he wants me to have unsafe, receptive anal sex with him after the first date. He's got to be fucking dreaming.

Without another moment's hesitation, I extricate myself from the spa, collect my clothes from the deck chair, and head for the front door.

"Babe, where are you going? You all right?" he calls after me in a soft and compassionate tone. How many guys has this predator molested … or worse? What a creep!

I slam the door closed behind me, ignoring the torrents of abuse that begin to stream from Johnny's mouth as he realizes that I'm not coming back. I'm still as naked as the day I was born and dripping wet when I climb into my car and start the engine. Suddenly, the fancy sports car parked beside me takes on a whole new meaning of desperation and egomania. There's absolutely nothing aphrodisiacal about it any longer.

I put my foot flat on the gas and speed down the driveway. Once I'm out the gates, I drive as fast as the speed limit allows. I want to be as far away as I can from what just happened. When I get home I'm going to take a long, hot shower to wash away the feeling of disgust that keeps sending shivers up my spine every time I think of Johnny.

Chapter Twenty-Three

Getting out of town for a few days for a conference—or as doctors like to call it, going on "confroliday"—is one of my favorite things in the entire world, and something I look forward to every year. They're opportunities to discover the latest research, catch up with old classmates and colleagues who I haven't seen in years, and have a break from other responsibilities for a few days.

When I found out that this year's big psychiatry conference was going to be held in Las Vegas, I didn't hesitate to confirm my attendance and make arrangements with my travel agent for flights and accommodation. Naturally, Felix made up his mind about coming only days before the event. He's flying with some budget airline and won't be staying at the same hotel where the conference is being held. Part of me would like to offer to let him share my room, but then I remind myself that it would make me an enabler, and he really does need to learn how to organize his own life better.

I check into my hotel and head up to my room. This trip,

I decided to spoil myself to a spa suite, which includes a bathroom with spa, steam room, and massive shower. It's big enough that I could invite an entire sports team over and still have room for spectators. I unpack my suitcase and take a quick shower before changing into a nice pair of jeans with a polo shirt and blazer. I go down to the lobby to meet up with Felix. At least that's the plan.

Felix is nowhere to be seen, so I stroll into the snazzy bar, which is buzzing with patrons. Most of them, I assume, will also be here for the conference. I recognize a few faces from previous psychiatry events. My disastrous date with Johnny has me thinking that I need to get back in the saddle again and hone my dating skills. I've been single for far too long. I spot five guys within the first two minutes who are exactly my type—tall, broad-shouldered, strong facial features, and a killer smile. One of them is dressed like a cowboy. Yeehaw!

Statistically, around one in ten men enjoys sex with men, which means approximately ten of the men in this room. But when you factor in preferences, be that appearance or sexual proclivities, the number of potential mates plummets. So, if my math is correct, I have about half a chance of getting lucky tonight. At least I can rely on my good old buddy Felix to supply me with interesting conversation and a few hearty laughs.

I can already see the bottom of my first drink by the time Felix's text arrives—*"Flight only just arrived. Gonna head to the hotel and call it a night. Sorry."*

There go my plans for a fun night out.

I reply—*"That's okay. We'll catch up tomorrow morning."*

Now I'm left to entertain myself for the night. I don't really feel like going exploring on my own, so after I finish this drink, I'll probably make my way back to my room.

I play with my phone for a few minutes and then polish off the rest of my drink. As I start to slide off my seat, a handsome stranger leans up against the bar beside me. I glance across at him and he smiles back at me.

"Hey," I say.

"Hi," he replies.

He tries to get the bartender's attention, but the bartender is too busy flirting with a couple of rich older women. The handsome stranger rolls his eyes and sighs. I chuckle and he looks in my direction again.

There's something about this guy that captures my interest. The way his hair is neatly styled, the crispness of his ironed shirt, the shine on his smart black shoes. He sits down on a barstool and slouches over the counter.

"I should have just gone straight to the gay bar," he mutters to himself.

He turns and smiles at me again. His eyes drop to my drink.

"The cocktails here any good?" he asks.

"Pretty good," I reply, bobbing my head.

"Well with that glowing recommendation I shall have to try one."

The bartender finally saunters over.

"What can I get you gentlemen," he asks.

The handsome man says to me, "Can I buy you a drink?"

I stare at him in surprise. "Oh? Uh ... yes, thank you."

"Two more …" he looks at me to fill in the gap.

"Mojito," I say.

"Two more mojitos please." He gestures to the bartender with two fingers and gives me a wink.

"Careful, I'm a cheap drunk," I say without thinking.

He laughs, but I cringe at myself for making the comment.

"I'm Simon," he says.

"Todd. Pleasure to meet you."

"So did your best friend also stand you up tonight?" I ask.

"No. I came here with some of my co-workers for drinks. I'll be straight up with you … I was intending to head home, but then I saw this handsome man sitting up at the bar … and I just had to come over and say hi."

I blush at his blatant flirting and charming personality. I feel like I need to pinch myself, because this couldn't possibly be happening for real.

"Were you planning on heading out this evening?" he says.

"Would you like to be my tour guide?" I ask half-jokingly.

"We're role-playing already!"

I like his sense of humor—naughty but nice.

The bartender slides two freshly made cocktails in front of us.

"After this drink, I'll show you the town," Simon says, grinning cheerfully.

"What are we waiting for?" I throw caution to the wind and down my cocktail in seconds. Simon follows my lead and drains his glass with only a couple of gulps. The bartender

shakes his head in disgust at our flagrant abuse of his cre-
ations. There is something special about this guy. I pay the
bartender and we go outside to hail a taxi to take us to our
next destination. I can sense an adventure is about to happen.

Reflections from the bright city lights dance across the windows of the taxi. We sit together in the back seat, Simon's
hand curled over my thigh. It might just be the alcohol, but it
feels good to be with him.

"Driver, could you please stop over there," says Simon,
pointing at the drop off zone outside a nearby casino. I'm not
much of a gambler, and Simon must sense my hesitance
because he adds, "They make the best cocktails in town."

That's all the reason I need, and we both shuffle out onto
the sidewalk.

"This is our first stop. You get to choose our next destination."

We dash up to the host standing outside the cocktail bar,
who gives us both the once-over. He looks unfriendly to me,
and I don't think we've got much of a chance of getting in.

Simon whispers in my ear, "He's family, we'll get in."

"How can you tell?"

Simon slides his hand in my back pocket and pulls me
close. The host smiles lasciviously and I know he's undressing
us both with his eyes.

"You boys are in luck tonight," says the host. From the
way he talks, he's definitely gay. "We just had a table become
available. Follow me."

The host sashays into the bar and directs us to a table for

two in a private corner of the bar. A waitress flits across to our table and takes our order for two paradiso cocktails.

"I want to play a game with you," says Simon.

"What kind of game?"

"Truth or dare."

"Okay."

"But you have to do it without thinking. First thing that comes into your head. Bam!"

The waitress returns with two ice-cold cocktails. The twist of lemon sends a shiver down my spine before the sweet aftertaste hits and soothes the flight of butterflies in my stomach.

"Okay … truth," I say.

He grins and makes a big show of trying to come up with something witty to ask me, but I'm ninety-nine percent sure he's already planned the next ten questions that he wants to ask me.

"I've got one," he says. "Tell me something about yourself that you've never told another living soul."

"Ooh, that's a hard one."

He sits back in his chair and waits for my confession. "No thinking about it!" he says, reminding me of the rules.

I lean across the table and speak in a hushed voice. "I've always wanted to be in a home-made porno. One of those hot videos that makes its way onto an amateur site and goes viral."

Simon chuckles. "I don't see it happening. You're too much of a prude."

"I am not! Anyway, you have to tell me a truth now too," I

say.

"I've got a fake nut."

"You've what?"

"I had a scare a few years ago with cancer and they had to take out one of my boys. I got a prosthetic one in its place."

"And you didn't tell anyone? Not even your family?"

"I didn't want to frighten them before we knew that it was cancer for sure. It wasn't, so I kept it to myself."

"You all good now?"

"Oh yeah. I bet you couldn't tell which of them is fake."

I laugh at his shameless invitation.

"This time it's a dare," he says. "I want you to take the piece of ice from your drink and put it in your underwear."

I try to read his face to see if he's pulling my leg—he's not.

"Seriously?"

He's unflinching. I scoop a piece of ice out of my cocktail and hold it between my thumb and forefinger. Simon smiles. I scan the room in case anyone is watching, and slip the ice down my pants.

The cold. The pain. The icy discomfort. I writhe in my seat and try to think happy thoughts while Simon pisses himself laughing.

"I didn't think you'd actually do it," he guffaws.

"It's your turn next, remember," I say through gritted teeth.

"Nope. It's time we moved on to our next destination."

"Hey, that's not fair."

"It'll give you more time to dream up a suitable revenge

for me."

"Evil bastard!"

We settle the tab up at the bar and walk outside to find a taxi. Last time I was in the city, I was on a tour group that went up to the top of the Stratosphere Hotel, the tallest building in Las Vegas. Turns out it's right around the corner, so the taxi driver gives us walking directions instead.

We walk into the Stratosphere and jump into the first available elevator. It takes us to the observation deck, one thousand feet up in the air. The elevator rises so quickly that I have to pop my ears several times, and it makes me feel queasy. I slip my hand around Simon's and give him a squeeze. He turns to me and smiles.

We reach the top and lurch out onto the solid ground of the indoor observation deck. There are loads of tourists indoors, but only a handful standing outside. I lead Simon to the outdoor observation deck. We find a quiet spot where we can look out at the view of the city undisturbed. Simon holds my hand, and we gaze out at the city lights in complete silence.

"Your turn," he says to me. "What's my dare?"

For the first time in an extraordinarily long time I don't hesitate with my answer. "Would you like to come back to my hotel room?"

He doesn't answer. He just keeps staring out at the city below. Why is he taking so long to respond? The tension is killing me. But then a smile creeps across his face and I know he feels the same way.

I fall face down on the bed and sink into the soft mattress. I reach for my phone on the bedside table and switch it to "silent". It's unlikely that anyone will try to contact me at 3 AM, but tonight, I don't want anything to disturb us. It's been a lifetime since someone last excited me the way that Simon does. I sense his presence looming over me, but I don't look back. His skin glides over mine as he climbs onto the bed behind me. His soft hands knead my cheeks and pull them apart.

His tongue flicks across my skin and right into my hole, sending sparks of pleasure racing through me. I wasn't expecting that, and it makes my heart pound in my chest. I raise my hips to offer his tongue easier access and bury my face in the pillow to muffle my moans. Simon plants what feels like hundreds of tiny kisses in the small of my back and up my spine.

The weight of his body rests on top of me and he nibbles on my earlobe. His warm breath passes over my skin, and it makes me feel alive. I roll onto my back and our bodies entwine.

No one has kissed me with this kind of red-hot passion and looked at me with such sensual, loving eyes since I was with Kyle. The memories of my time with Kyle come flooding back. The feelings overwhelm me. There's nothing I can do to stop the tears from welling up in my eyes and spilling onto my cheeks. Simon lifts himself up and looks at me with such sincere concern.

"Are you all right?" he asks.

"I'm sorry," I say, trying to pull myself together. "You

remind me so much of someone I once knew."

He lowers his body down beside me and lays his arm across my chest.

"Tell me about him," he says, wiping a tear from my cheek.

It's so abundantly clear now that I never came to terms with what happened to Kyle. It's a stumbling block in the way of finding happiness with someone else.

"I should have moved on by now. It's been almost fifteen years since he went away."

"He must have meant a lot to you," says Simon.

"He did. He was my first everything."

"You never get over your first," says Simon with a sigh.

It's impossible to move on when you suppress the emotions and try to examine everything for a purely intellectual perspective like I did. It's all coming out, and I don't want to hold back any more. I want to be free of the past and move forward with my life.

"What happened with you guys?" asks Simon.

"He vanished off the face of the earth," I say.

"No goodbye?"

I shake my head.

"Fuck! That's rough," says Simon. "And I thought my first breakup was bad. I cried for weeks when he left me for a girl."

Simon's confession snaps me out of my solemn mood.

"A girl?" I ask, not sure if I heard him right.

"I should have seen it coming. He told me from the beginning that he was straight." He hides his face under the pillow in shame.

"He couldn't have been all that straight?" I say.

"It hurt all the same," says Simon. "To be someone's dirty secret. I confronted him about it a few years later. He told me I was an experiment in college … and his biggest mistake."

"His only mistake was letting you go," I say. I realize how cheesy it sounds, but I don't care.

Simon lies there in silence, staring at me with soft, caring eyes. There is neither an ounce of judgment in his body language nor disappointment that our evening of fun has come to this. I hardly know the man, yet he shows me such kindness.

He kisses me. It's just a brief peck on the lips, as if to make sure that it's okay to continue showing me affection. His lips draw close to mine again, and we stare into each other's eyes. Time seems to stop while we hover a breath apart. Then we kiss and our whole world shrinks down to just him and me in this precious moment. I need to feel him, to touch him, and have to be inside him.

I'm lying on top of Simon, kissing and caressing him. He reaches for the condoms siting on the bedside table. He deftly tears the packet open with one hand and slides the condom over my erection. We stay in this position, his legs wrapped around my hips, holding each other, as I slowly enter him. He lets out a gasp when I'm completely inside. I throb and he groans. Our tongues meet once again.

We make love for hours, repeatedly holding back before the point of climax. It's intense and tantric. When we simultaneously cross the point of no return, we hold each other tightly as each rhythmic contraction pulses through our bodies. We don't let go. We don't want this moment to end.

I wake up to the sound of rustling clothes. Through sleepy eyes I see Simon getting dressed back into his clothes from last night.

"Good morning," I say with a smile.

"Morning, sexy man."

He comes over to the bed to give me a big kiss on the lips.

"You have to leave so soon?" I ask him. The clock reads 7 AM, and I remember he has to catch a flight out this morning.

"I wish I could stay." From the tone of his voice, he means it.

"Will I see you again?" I ask.

Simon lets out a sigh and perches timidly on the end of the bed. "I have a confession to make."

A feeling of dread comes over me.

"This isn't something I usually do, you know, sleep with a guy I've just met." He pauses. "And I have a kid, so I'm a package deal, and most guys aren't interested in that type of relationship."

"I like kids."

He turns and looks at me, pleasantly surprised.

"How did you end up a dad?" I ask.

"I love my baby girl, but feel ashamed about the circumstances. It was back in college. Not long after I was dumped by the straight guy, I met a girl who was so stunningly beautiful that I fell in love the instant that I set eyes on her ... well, the idea of her ... I was spellbound."

"Are you bisexual?"

"Hell no! Definitely gay. That first night though, we got drunk and slept together. We carried on dating, but never had that spark again. It was like the two of us were best friends hanging out. I realized that I wasn't sexually attracted to her, even though she captivated me. When we closed our eyes and kissed, all I could think about was my hunky roommate, but I was too much of a coward to end things. Then she heard via the grapevine that she was dating a gay guy, and our 'relationship' ended in a rather heated screaming match. Two months later, I get a call to say that I'm going to be a dad. She still hates me for, and I quote, 'stealing' her virginity."

"Ouch. But honestly, how did you think it was gonna work?"

"Like I said, I was in love with the idea of her. It was my naivety showing, thinking that maybe I was also into girls. I've grown up since then. But anyway ... I'm going to be in your neck of the woods in a month's time—"

I cut him off. "It's a date!"

"It's a date," he repeats with a smile. "I better get going, or I'll be late."

I scoot out of bed and press my naked body up against him.

"Thank you for the most incredible night." I kiss his neck, then his lips, while my hands trace the outline of his strong frame.

He closes his eyes and inhales deeply. "Stop ... or I'll miss my flight."

He giggles and pushes my hands away. We share a final kiss, and he disappears through the door.

I stand there in disbelief. What just happened? I'm alive again. Never did I expect that I would meet another man who could make me feel the way that Kyle used to. I want to give life a high five and dance for joy. If I could find a way to bottle this happiness I'd be the richest psychiatrist on the planet.

I see Felix pacing outside the conference venue. I wave hello and smile as I walk towards him.

"You look like shit," he says.

"Good morning to you too, asshole."

He looks at me, perplexed. "But you're still smiling. Did you get some mangina last night?"

I admit nothing that could incriminate myself, but I've got a lousy poker face and he's a pro at reading my facial expressions.

"You stud! Thank God I wasn't there cock-blocking you. How was it?" he says at the top of his voice, attracting the attention of our colleagues waiting for the next presentation to begin.

"Can we talk about this later?" I ask in a hushed voice.

It dawns on him that we're in public. "I want all the gruesome details," he says in a whisper.

For someone who jokes that he's only gay enough to "let another man compliment his dick in a public restroom and no more", he sure does seem to live vicariously through me sometimes.

"You going to see him again?" Felix asks. "And please tell me you're done with that douchebag football player."

"He lives here in Las Vegas, but we might just have a second date lined up. And yes ... the douchebag has been kicked to the curb."

Felix beams from ear to ear.

"That's my boy!" he says, slapping me on the back like we're two macho straight guys.

Like two naughty students, we take our seats at the back of the auditorium. Felix and I have a bad habit of giving a running commentary through talks to keep ourselves awake, so we try to sit as far away as possible from the rest of the crowd. But the attendees keep arriving, and soon every seat is taken.

"The first speaker must be popular," I whisper to Felix.

"Big time! Rosie Keller," he says, like I should instantly recognize the name, "from the Lindeman Foundation."

I shake my head. The name doesn't ring any bells.

"There was an article about her work in *Time* last month," says Felix.

A geeky lady walks out on stage and up to the podium.

"This her?" I ask.

Felix shakes his head.

The geeky lady leans towards the microphone. "Good morning, ladies and gentleman."

A hush descends on the crowd as the audience listens intently.

She reads her speech, taking tremendous care with each word, speaking in a rehearsed tone. "Alfred Lindeman made no secret of his personal war against Alzheimer's disease. The eccentric billionaire was our Nation's largest private donor, and through his philanthropic support, the Lindeman Foundation was established. Unfortunately, Alfred was taken from us by the same disease that robbed him of his mother, and grandmother before her. He died mere months before his team of scientists revealed the spectacular results of their novel Alzheimer's wonder-drug Loidase. But his memory lives on in the research and discoveries taking place every day at the Lindeman Foundation. This morning's first speaker, Dr. Rosie Keller, was a key player in the team that genetically engineered Loidase. Since then, her research has taken her to the bleeding edge of medical technology. Now, if you'll allow me to introduce Dr. Rosie Keller, who will be speaking about her incredible new discovery, the machine named "Moneta" after the Roman goddess of memory. Ladies and gentlemen, I present to you … Dr. Rosie Keller."

She claps her hands and the crowd joins in. A stunning woman, dressed in a navy business suit, and high heels, walks up to the podium. You can tell just by looking at her that she votes Republican.

My phone starts to ring. It wasn't on silent, and a string of heads turn and glare at me.

"I'll be right back," I say to Felix, and run outside to answer the call.

I don't recognize the number on the phone.

"Hello, Todd speaking," I say.

"Hey, it's Simon," says the voice on the other end of the line.

"Shouldn't you be halfway across the country by now?"

"I'm at the airport still. Flight was delayed. Is this a bad time?"

I spin around and look at the closed auditorium doors.

"No. Not at all," I reply.

"I couldn't wait until I got home to call you," he says, which brings a smile to my dial. "I wanted to hear your sexy voice again one last time before I got on the plane, so I can let it echo in my head."

"You realize that I spend most of my day trying to stop people from hearing voices in their heads."

He giggles at my joke. "I know."

"What am I going to do with myself until I see you again?"

"I'm sending my top bodyguard to fight off any other guy who flirts with you."

I sit down in one of the seats in the lobby.

"Are you always this territorial?" I ask, biting my lip.

"I know what I want when I see it."

He's not even talking dirty, and our conversation is turning me on.

"Shit, they're calling my name. I'm sorry. I gotta go."

"Talk to you later," I say.

I hear him kiss the mouthpiece and the call ends.

I sit there with a silly smile on my face, staring at my phone.

As quietly as I can, I sneak into the auditorium, and back to my seat.

"Who was that?" asks Felix.

"Simon," I reply.

"Who's Simon?" he asks, and then the penny drops. "Oh, he's the guy?"

The man sitting directly in front of me turns around and tells me to shush. Guilty as charged.

"I'll tell you later," I whisper to Felix.

I try my hardest to concentrate on Rosie Keller's talk and her impressive PowerPoint presentation, but my mind keeps wandering back to Simon and last night. If I close my eyes, I can envision his handsome face and beautiful body lying next to me. I can imagine kissing his soft lips, and running my hands across his muscled back down to his perfect ass.

I jump in my seat as the entire audience rises to their feet and gives a huge round of applause. Dr. Keller takes a bow at the podium and walks off stage.

I glance over at Felix, who narrows his eyes at me and shakes his head in disgust.

"You were having sex with him again in your head, weren't you?" he says.

"Shut up," I reply.

"I knew it," he says. "You missed out on a great talk, by the way. It was like something out of a science fiction movie."

"Oh yeah?" I say, trying to act interested, but I'm too distracted with thoughts of Simon to actually listen.

"It's going to blow … your … mind," says Felix while miming shooting his head off with a handgun. "This chick has found a way to literally unlock memories from brain tissue, capture them and play them back to you. It's insanely cool."

"Wow." I say vacuously.

"You're thinking about your man candy again?" Felix punches me on the shoulder. "Slut!"

Chapter Twenty-Four

I've hardly been awake for ten minutes, still stumbling around my apartment like a naked zombie, when my phone rings.

"Can you come in this morning?" Linda croaks in my ear. She has the voice of a woman who gets too little sleep, drinks too much coffee, and smokes like a chimney.

"I have a rather full morning," I say, struggling to decide which shirt to wear. Thank God for walk-in wardrobes and abundant hanging space.

"I wouldn't ask unless I was desperate," she says.

"Is this your version of begging?"

"Yes. I'm on my knees." I can hear her inhale deeply from her cigarette. "It's an amnesiac case. You might find it interesting. He's being transferred this morning," she says.

"Let me see if I can reschedule some of my appointments."

"You're a champion. See you shortly." She hangs up.

I don't mind helping Linda out occasionally. She runs a good department on an almost non-existent budget. Psych is always the first department to have its funding cut and finding new avenues of revenue is a hopeless cause. Philanthropists want to put their names above surgical hospital wings and child cancer wards. They couldn't care less about what happens to the nut jobs. So on the odd occasion when the grumpy bitch finds herself in a tight position with staff shortages, I find myself unable to say "no" to her.

I pass Linda in the corridor as I arrive on at the hospital. She greets me with the smallest of nods, barely raising her eyes from her phone. I can tell she's in a rush, so I don't bother to stop and make idle chit chat with her. I walk up to the nurses' station, where I see a patient file at least six inches thick. Shit! This is not going to be a quick patient assessment. A shiver of hatred crawls across my skin and I curse Linda under my breath. The name on the file doesn't make me feel any more optimistic—"*John Doe*".

Linda reappears behind me, clutching a steaming cup of coffee with both hands. She flips open the file and starts talking.

"This one is an interesting case. Mixed-type post-traumatic amnesia. Has almost no recollection of his past, and new memory formation is intermittent. Been in the system a while now. They keep flicking him from one hospital to the next when he's too much to handle."

"What's with the name?"

"What else do you call someone who can't remember his own name?"

"Why couldn't they identify him?" Now, this is starting to

get intriguing.

"Bit of a sad story actually. He was found unconscious, lying in a urinal at a public restroom, somewhere along a state highway in the middle of nowhere. Major head trauma. The neurosurgery notes say it's a miracle he survived the assault. But he still ended up in a coma for almost a year."

"Who footed the bill for that one?"

"The hospital posted security outside his bedroom door. You know, just in case he woke up." Linda stops and gulps down the rest of her coffee. "Fuck, that got cold quickly."

"I assume he did wake up?"

"And within minutes got into an altercation with the security guard."

"An altercation?" I know she's downplaying the events.

"It doesn't say much in the file, but apparently the guard tried to stop him from leaving, and ended up with a cracked skull and a broken wrist. Want to see the photographs?"

I run a finger across the bloody image of the back of the security guard's head and an x-ray of the compound fracture of his wrist.

"Since then he's bounced between facilities from one side of the country to the next, having one violent outburst after another."

"How did we end up drawing the short straw?" I turn through pages of the file, skimming the notes.

"I owed someone a favor," she says. "And you owe me."

Linda walks away and shuts herself in her office.

I pick up the file and take a glimpse at the white board in the nurses' station to find out which consulting room John

Doe is waiting in.

As is customary, I knock a couple of times on the consulting room door before I walk in.

I see a hollow shell of a man, sitting with his shoulders rounded and head drooped forward over his chest.

"Good morning, I'm Dr. Chambers. How are you this morning?" I ask cheerfully.

The man doesn't respond or even acknowledge my presence. I sit down on the chair opposite him.

"This is a little awkward for me because I'm unsure what to call you," I say, trying to make eye contact with my new patient. "If it's okay with you, I might just call you John for now."

The man nods.

"Well, John, I'm one of the doctors here at the hospital. I am responsible for helping people like you, who are struggling or not coping very well in life. Do you think that would apply to you?"

He nods again.

"I believe that you are suffering from amnesia? Do you remember anything from your past?"

"Some things," he replies in a staccato voice.

"Let's start with something easy, then. What's your favorite color, John?"

"Don't know."

"Do you have a favorite food?"

"Steak ... I think," he says sheepishly.

"No need to be embarrassed about that one. Sometimes I think that vegetarianism deserves an entry in the DSM, between obsessive compulsive and pain-in-the-ass disorder."

The man chuckles at my joke and looks up at me.

My stomach churns and I come within an inch of vomiting as I recognize his face. Is this Kyle? This gaunt figure sitting in front of me? Not the same Kyle I loved, but a ghostly pale, emaciated, weathered version. I want to leap over the table and wrap my arms around him, but he doesn't recognize me, not in the slightest. Could I be imagining this? I watch for the most subtle change in his expression, but it's painfully clear that I'm as much of a stranger to him as any random person off the street. All this time, he's been alive. What happened? Where was he?

The guilt overwhelms me. How could I have stopped searching for him? If only I had tried harder, I might have been able to find him and rescue him from the hell he's lived in all these years. All this time I was enjoying my comfortable existence, while he rotted away like some forgotten prisoner trapped in a castle dungeon. Will I ever be able to forgive myself?

"Kyle?" I say his name hesitatantly, but loud enough for him to hear. He looks up at me, and fleetingly I think I see recognition in his eyes, but I'm mistaken.

"Why am I here? Are you a doctor?" he asks, strangely unaware of his surroundings.

"You're in the hospital, Kyle."

Confusion crosses his face. He looks down at his body and tries to raise his arms to find whatever physical ailment is the cause for his admission. That's when I first notice the handcuffs. With a loud *clang*, he pulls on the metal restraints.

He looks at them and up at me in horror.

"What are you doing to me? You can't lock people up like this. Let me go!" He struggles with the restraints and writhes in his seat.

An orderly and nurse burst through the door. The orderly restrains Kyle, and the nurse withdraws a large syringe.

"Half that dose! I don't want him comatose," I say to the nurse.

The nurse scowls and injects Kyle with the sedative. Kyle looks at me with his beautiful brown eyes, so full of confusion and sadness. His expression begs me to help him, but I sit here, frozen. His eyes glaze over as the drugs kick in.

"Could you please remove the restraints?" I say to the orderly.

He's a massive man who I assume was on his high school football team, and had dreams of one day playing among the greats. I imagine he'd have a great story to tell about how he ended up as a lowly orderly in a place like this. The orderly doesn't question my instructions, but shakes his head ever so slightly. I question my own decision, but it pains me to see Kyle treated like a criminal. I thank both of them, and they leave the room.

Kyle reclines in his seat, relaxing in the numbness of the sedative.

"Kyle?" I say his name again, but to no avail. His own name means nothing to him. "It's me, Todd. Do you remember me?"

Kyle's eyes drift closed. It'll be a few minutes before he's alert again.

"Goddammit!" I curse.

I stand up and walk to the corner of the room and become conscious of my heart beating uncontrollably. The feeling is overwhelming. My stomach rises up into my throat again and I feel like I'm about to throw up. The whole world starts to spin. I'm having a panic attack. I can't let him see me like this. I need to get out of here now.

I turn around to look at Kyle, and he's staring up at me with that same stupid grin that made me fall in love with him all those years ago.

"You look like shit, man. You okay?" he says, looking a little intoxicated himself.

"Kyle?" I ask, even more hopeful.

"Who's Kyle?" he replies, and my heart sinks.

"That's your name, isn't it?" I sit down again at the table opposite him.

"I'm not sure." Kyle's eyes dart around the room as he tries to make sense of his surroundings. "Where am I? Why do I feel so woozy?"

"You're in the hospital. You had an injury to your head. It's left you with severe amnesia."

Kyle stares at me blankly, then bursts out laughing. "You're funny. Do I know you?"

I swallow hard to try get rid of the lump in my throat.

"Can you tell me one of your early childhood memories. Something significant," I say, my hands trembling under the table.

Kyle speaks in a meek voice. "Going to church with my parents. I was maybe ten years old. I was so excited that day.

Even insisted on wearing the new suit and tie that my mom had bought me for a wedding that we went to a few weeks before. I remember sitting down and waiting for the sermon to begin. The first words out of the priest's mouth left me cold." He stops and sits in silence.

"What did he say?"

"There is a special place in hell reserved for rapists ... murderers ... pedophiles ... and homosexuals. I never heard another word after that. I thought every adult in that church was going to instinctively know that he was talking about me. That everyone there knew that I was going to hell. That my beautiful mother sitting beside me, dressed in her Sunday finest, would glare at me with disgust because I belonged with the sinners and filth who are condemned to an eternity in hell when they die." His voice trails off.

"Do you remember anything about what happened to you? How you got the injuries to your head?"

Kyle glances at me sideways like I'm crazy. "My head feels fine."

"It happened a few years ago."

Kyle gets lost in thought. His lip starts to tremble. This wasn't the reaction that I was anticipating. Tears run down his cheeks. I want to give him a hug so badly. I feel the tears welling in my own eyes and reach out to comfort him.

Kyle draws his hand away and abruptly crawls up in the fetal position on his chair. "Don't touch me," he says firmly.

We sit in silence for a minute or two before I rise from my chair and leave the room. As the door shuts behind me, I lean back against the cold wall and try to steady my thoughts and emotions.

"What was that all about?" says Linda as she walks out of the adjacent observation room. I had forgotten that someone could have been watching through the one-way mirror.

"His name is Kyle Hansen."

"How do you know this?" she cuts me off, somewhat taken aback by my statement.

I want to tell her that it's complicated and none of her business. Is this wound ever going to heal now that it's been ripped wide open again?

"He disappeared … about fifteen years ago when we were still at college. I thought he'd gone … moved away someplace else to start a new life. At least, that's what they convinced me to think."

"What? Who convinced you? I don't understand," she snaps at me.

"The police. They were right. He must have run away," I say.

"Oh my God, were you two … together?" she says almost compassionately.

My mind drifts back to all the precious memories I have of time spent with Kyle. The word "together" sounds so casual.

"Fuck! Todd, I don't have any spare resources to cover this case. Do you think you can still handle it? Given the circumstances?"

"Can I have an hour to think about it?" I say.

"Of course. We'll reconvene in my office in an hour?" She places a reassuring hand on my elbow. In med school we are taught ways of conveying sympathy through touching that can't be misconstrued as anything but a comforting gesture. It feels good to have that human contact, but a hand on the elbow is just so cold and clinical. What I could really use right now is a hug and a shoulder to cry on. For someone to say, "Honey, I'm so sorry."

She gives me a sad smile and looks over my shoulder through the small pane of glass in the consulting room door. Kyle is still curled up on his chair.

I sit at my desk and read through Kyle's file in meticulous detail. There is so much information missing that I want to throw something at the wall in frustration. I question the competence of my peers at the countless psychiatric hospitals and institutions that he's been passed around to like a hot potato over the years. They invested no time or effort in rehabilitation. The clinical notes are appalling. They've painted this picture of Kyle as a spontaneously violent and aggressive patient who must be handled with extreme care.

I come across an entry from the last facility where he was held.

The kind of skill that this patient displayed in taking down the guard today, and rendering him unconscious, is in my mind irrefutable evidence that this man has a history of similar behavior. It would be unsurprising to discover that he has a criminal background. Will organize for fresh fingerprints to be taken and sent to local police.

I have to step away from my desk to stop myself from

tearing the pages to shreds. Never in my life have I felt such anger. My blood is boiling.

Chapter Twenty-Five

I spent the better part of today trying to track down the senior psychiatric consultant, Dr. John Perdue, at the facility that last unburdened themselves of Kyle. The man claims to have no knowledge of Kyle as a patient until I use the doctor's own words to describe Kyle.

"The monster with no memory?" I quote over the phone.

There's silence from Dr. Perdue's end, and then he finally seems to put two and two together.

"Ah yes, that one. Glad to be rid of him," he says triumphantly. "Lost two of my best male nurses to that waste of humanity. Monster of a man."

"Mr. Hansen was transferred into our care yesterday—" I begin to say before Dr. Perdue rudely interrupts me.

"Who?" he asks.

"The patient we are currently discussing."

"Oh, you must mean Mr. Doe?" he says patronizingly.

I fill my lungs with a giant gulp of air and hold back from unleashing my growing frustrations on this man.

"Look, Mr.—" he says.

"Doctor," I say, cutting him off.

"Well, Dr. Chambers, I am a very busy man and I do not have the luxury of oodles of time to indulge in lengthy chit-chat over the phone. If you wish to discuss this case further, I would suggest you make an appointment."

"What time would suit you best?" I ask in my calmest tone.

He *ums* and *ahs* a bit before throwing a ridiculously early time tomorrow morning at me.

"Excellent. I will see you first thing tomorrow."

I hang up and want to smash my phone, but the stingy bastard inside of me would rather I break my knuckles than the phone. I hit the wall with my bare fist and instantly regret it.

The following morning I arrive ten minutes before my scheduled meeting time with Dr. Perdue. He's nowhere to be seen. His receptionist looks through his appointment book twice and apologizes profusely for the misunderstanding. Apparently, Dr. Perdue only comes in at ten on a Wednesday. I glance up at the clock on the wall—6:56 AM. There was no misunderstanding; the pretentious prick wanted to make a point. I fucking hate psychiatrists who like to play mind games. After making the hour-long trek out here, I'm left with no choice but to wait for him to arrive.

Completely out of the blue, the receptionist walks over with two cups of coffee and a smile.

"I wouldn't take it personally. He's a cunt." She hands a

cup to me.

I accept the coffee graciously.

"I'll say it unapologetically because his childish behavior makes me look like an incompetent fool sometimes," she says.

I start to fear that this conversation is rapidly descending into some form of free counseling session when, like an angel sent from Heaven above, she says, "Is there anything I could do to help? I probably know more about the patients here than any of the consultants. The number of mistakes I find on a daily basis in their clinic letters! My name is Judy, by the way."

"What do you know about a patient named John Doe?" I say with every finger and toe crossed for good luck.

"Please step inside my office."

She gestures for me to follow her into Dr. Perdue's empty office. She sits back in the doctor's leather desk chair and asks, "What do you want to know?"

"I've read through his file, but I now have more questions than answers. I also didn't get copies of any imaging."

Judy chuckles. "We never received imaging from the hospital that had him before us either. But … one of our junior doctors was stupid enough to order an MRI without first checking that the patient had insurance."

"If I could view the radiologist report …?"

"Let me see whether I can dig them up for you."

It feels like I've hit the jackpot, but I don't want to show too much excitement in case I jinx it. Judy spins around and logs into Dr. Perdue's computer, using his logon details. I know that I should be questioning the ethics of accessing another clinician's files in this manner, but my hunger for answers is stronger.

Judy brings up a series of brain scans and associated radiologist reports.

"You might wanna take a look at this one while I go see if there's anything useful in my filing cabinet," says Judy. "Here, have a seat." She scurries back into her office.

I read the report. It's a rather dismal picture of Kyle's prognosis.

"... evidence of small frontal lobe lesions consistent with blunt force head injury. More worrying are the large bilateral lesions in the hippocampus and surrounding medial temporal lobes. This area of the brain is involved in memory recall and formation. It is my opinion that the damage is permanent, and the patient is unlikely to recover. I see little potential benefit in providing this gentleman with any further therapeutic care. We have missed the window of opportunity ..."

I hear a filing cabinet close with a *crash.*

"Ah ha! Found it," says Judy.

She strolls back into the office with a typed report.

"Here," she says, passing the document to me. "Copy of the full report that we compiled. You most likely wouldn't have received a copy of this either." She glances at her watch. "Dr. Perdouchebag won't be here for another few hours. Take your time reading through everything."

"Thank you, Judy," I say.

"It's no problem at all. Let me know if you need anything else. Can I get you a coffee?"

"I would absolutely love a coffee, please."

Judy smiles and shuts the door behind her. I pick up the document and start to read with extreme trepidation.

I drive back to my practice office with a head full of thoughts. These are the details that I've been able to ascertain so far. After he was found unconscious, Kyle was taken to the nearest emergency department at a small rural hospital. Without any form of identification or proof of insurance, they refused to treat him, and bumped him to a larger hospital two hours away. By the time he arrived, the swelling on his brain was causing respiratory depression, so he couldn't even breathe by himself. Then the convulsions started.

Kyle was rushed into neurosurgery, where they placed him in an induced coma and performed a decompressive craniectomy. They removed a piece of his skull to relieve the pressure on the swollen brain. He was unconscious for eleven months. The longer a person is in a coma, the less their chances of surviving, let alone making a full recovery.

Miraculously, he regained consciousness, albeit with severe limitations. The guard on duty that day got the fright of his life when Kyle came stumbling out of the room. He attempted to guide Kyle back to his bed, but Kyle threw him to the ground. A witness said that Kyle took the guard down "like a trained assassin". One swift move and the guard was nursing a cracked skull.

Kyle was charged with assault, but due to his altered state of mind the trial was swift. He found himself in one of these hellhole psychiatric hospitals where no one has the faintest hope of getting the treatment they need. The same thing happened time and again with other prisoners and guards. Anyone who dared touch him ended up with his head smashed in or broken body parts. They think he's a monster. I know he was simply defending himself. It's the only plausible explanation. But now I'm afraid that he's going to spend the rest of his life medicated behind bars.

What happened to my sweet Kyle, who couldn't bring himself to crush a cockroach when we were together, that could make him so afraid and angry at the world?

It's not something that most psychiatrists will willingly admit to doing, but there is the rare occasion when we might need to seek the assistance of a private investigator. If I have suspicions about a patient and some solid evidence of illegal activities, albeit inadmissible in court, it does help guide me in passing the case over to the police. I know it might seem like overkill, but on a day-to-day basis, I hear a lot of messed up shit, things that would send chills down an ordinary person's spine, coming out of people's mouths. But I can't go handing over every patient who threatens to kill himself and his dickhead boss.

If anyone is able to dig up the truth about what happened to Kyle, it's Douglas McGill, the private investigator I've used for the past ten years. He's discreet, thorough, and very expensive. I pick up the phone and give him a call. He instantly recognizes my voice. Now that's good customer service!

I rack my brain to come up with a novel approach to Kyle's

treatment. Now that the initial horror has sunk in, I'm able to be marginally more objective. I have to admit there were a few doctors along the way who invested a great deal of time and energy into Kyle, but their efforts were for naught. Now I'm scratching my head, trying to figure out if there's anything that could be done differently or some therapy they might not have thought of trying.

There's been a lot of hype lately around transcranial magnetic stimulation for treating neurological disorders. A magnetic field is created around the patient's head and electrical currents are passed through the brain. This theoretically should stimulate brain activity and switch malfunctioning neurons on or off. That's the theory. In reality, the evidence that is actually works is sketchy. Some are even calling it "the acupuncture of neuroscience". But Kyle has nothing to lose and everything to gain if this treatment succeeds in bringing back any part of his memory. I schedule a time with the interventional radiology department for us to perform the treatment later this afternoon.

For the first time in my life, I understand why patients want to grasp hold of any form of quackery that promises a cure. I would do anything to help Kyle. Anything.

When I arrive at Kyle's room to discuss the plan, he's pleased to see me and sits upright in bed.

"Hello, Dr. Chambers." He greets me with that sexy smile of his. Instead of attraction, the sight of him brings only gnawing pain. Is it guilt because I allowed him to become such a distant memory while my life went on without him? Or has he changed so substantially in appearance that I now find him repulsive? Regardless, the fact that he remembers my name does warm my heart, though I know it's probably just a coincidence. Maybe he read it off my name badge.

"Good afternoon, Kyle. How are you feeling?" I sit on the chair beside his bed and notice that one of his arm's is still handcuffed to the bed.

"Not sure what kind of kink goes on in this place, but I'd like to get this off," he says, examining the restraints.

"Well ... if I have your permission ... I'd like to try a form of hypnotherapy on you to see if we can help jog your memory."

Kyle is confused by my request. "Why would you need to do that?"

"Kyle, you have severe amnesia from an injury you sustained to your head a few years back. It's called mixed-type post-traumatic amnesia. Your brain is unable to recall many of your long-term memories, and has difficulty forming new ones." I watch his face as he tries to take in all of this information, as if it's the very first time he's being told. "I'm hoping that we can stimulate your brain and see some return of function. Would you like to give this a go?"

He says nothing, but nods slowly.

"I'm going to put you into a hypnotic state while we place a magnet over the areas of your brain that have been injured. You won't feel any pain or discomfort. It will be as if you're awake in a dream. Does that sound okay?"

"You're the doctor," he says.

Kyle lies in the therapy chair with an electrode cap placed on his head. His nervous eyes dart around the room, watching the nurses and technicians preparing for the procedure. The radiologist places the magnetic coil over the side of Kyle's head and gives me a nod. The staff leave the room, and it's just me and Kyle left alone. I dim the lights and take a seat beside him. The room is silent and I'm ready to begin.

"Close your eyes, Kyle," I say. His eyes drift shut. It's strange to see him lying so serenely. "I'm going to give you a series of instructions that will help you relax. Imagine that you are standing at the top of a small set of stairs. I'm going to count back from 'ten' and you're going to take a single step. With each step, you will feel yourself drifting deeper until I reach the number 'one'. When we reach that final step, your eyes will stay shut and you will feel more relaxed than ever before.

"Ten ... you take that first step and feel a weight lift off your body."

"Nine ... you feel calm and relaxed."

"Eight ... drifting deeper and deeper."

"Seven ... let your body melt away." I watch the EEG machine beside Kyle's chair. The waves of brain activity begin to slow and grow taller and wider. "Six ... deeper and deeper."

"Five ... your mind and your body drifting down."

"Four ... way down."

"Three ... drifting even deeper."

"Two ... you're almost there now."

"One ... you've reached tranquility."

Kyle lies absolutely still, his chest hardly moving with quiet respiration. I'm so transfixed by Kyle that I almost don't notice the radiologist waving madly at me from the control room, trying to get my attention. He gives me a thumbs-up.

"Allow yourself to travel back in time to your most recent happy memory," I say. "You're in a safe place now. You feel content and happy. Can you tell me what you see?"

"Not see … hear … animal sounds … they're everywhere. It's nighttime. I'm alone. Waiting."

Is he talking about the night we met, when he waited for me outside the gates to the zoo?

"You're doing well. What else can you tell me about this memory?"

"My hands are sweating. I'm so nervous. My heart is going to jump out of my chest." Kyle breathes deeply and smiles from ear to ear.

"Good. Now I want you to hold onto this feeling. It's going to protect you and keep you safe. Now you're traveling again through time, but forwards."

Kyle squirms in his seat and the machine begins to beep. He's moving around too much, and it can't lock onto the areas of the brain that it's been programmed to target.

"You can travel through these memories because you're safe, and nothing bad can happen to you now. You can relax."

He relaxes back into the chair. The machinery stops making the incessant and annoying beeping sound.

"What do you see now?" I ask.

Kyle's face scrunches up and his lip trembles. "Nothing," he whimpers. Suddenly, his body jolts upright and he thrashes about. Another jolt follows, and another, as if he's being shocked by an invisible electric source.

"Get him out of the machine!" I yell at the shell-shocked radiologist and technicians behind the control room glass.

"I've never seen this happen before. What did you do to him?" asks the radiologist.

"I don't know." My eyes scan the EEG machine printout. It was a focal seizure that's gone tonic-clonic. Shit! I dose Kyle up with benzodiazepines to control the seizures and take a step back. His whole body becomes limp and he loses consciousness. He looks so peaceful as he drifts off to sleep. We'll have to try again another day.

Just when I thought the day couldn't get any worse, I feel a vibration coming from my phone. I check the screen and see a new message sent through my gay dating app. I feel another pang of guilt over what happened to Kyle. I open the message and almost fall over backwards.

It's from none other than Johnny Owen, gay sports hero and complete asshole of a human being. After the way he behaved the other night, he has some nerve messaging me —"*Hey sexy. Wanted to say sorry about the other night. Will you forgive me? JO*".

I'd rather watch him choke to death on a fish bone. *Delete.*

Chapter Twenty-Six

Kyle lifts his king and places it on the chessboard.

"Checkmate," he says triumphantly.

I sit there trying to figure out how I lost the game so badly. I had the upper hand for the first half, and then out of nowhere, he wiped out most of my pieces in a handful of masterful moves. I scan the board in the hope that he's wrong, that there's still one last chance for me to weasel my way out, but it's hard to concentrate with the noise of the other patients chatting and playing games. A disappointed sigh escapes my lips and I tip my king over.

"You got me," I say.

I look up at Kyle and catch him staring at me.

"Can we play again?" he asks.

"Of course we can. But first I want to try another game." I reach into my pocket and take out a pack of cards. They're not your everyday deck of playing cards; rather, a set of easily recognizable shapes with two of each kind in the pack. "Do you know how to play the card game 'Concentration'?"

Kyle screws his face up. "Doesn't everybody?"

"Okay. So to reiterate the rules in case they're a little rusty in your head. I'm going to lay these cards out on the table, and you're going to flip them over, two at a time, and try to find the matching pairs."

"Do we really need to do this?" asks Kyle, sounding bored.

"Shall I make it more challenging? I'll time you," I say, taking out my phone and turning on the stopwatch.

Kyle looks at me, waiting for permission to start.

"Go," I say.

His hands race across the cards, flipping them face up and back down again. He searches feverishly. I spot the first possible matching pair, but they go unnoticed by Kyle. He continues with his frantic search, until he turns over two of the same kind.

He flexes his arm. "Yes!"

Kyle gets the next three pairs in a row. Is this progress or random chance? He's been at it for three minutes now. The test should take the average person no more than seven minutes to complete. He misses another possible match. I cringe and have to restrain myself from helping him. And yet another set of identical cards is flipped that he should have spotted by now. I shouldn't have got my hopes up. I watch the stopwatch as it ticks past ten minutes and only half the cards have been matched.

"You can stop now, Kyle," I say.

He ignores me and keeps playing. I reach over and place my hand on his. He stops suddenly and looks at my hand, and then my face.

"But I've only found half the cards," he says, confused.

I pat the back of his hand. "You did well."

He leans over the table towards me, his eyes skirting briefly down to our touching hands. "Are you flirting with me, Doc?"

I realize that I probably just overstepped the mark. I quickly fold my hands on the table in front of me.

Kyle winks at me. "It's okay if you were."

A nurse walks over and taps me on the shoulder. "Excuse me, Dr. Chambers. Sorry to disturb you."

"No. Not at all," I say.

"There's a call for you." She gestures to the nurses' station.

"Who is it?" I ask.

"Dr. Fierstein. I told her you were with a patient, but she insisted."

"If you want to keep playing, I'll be back shortly," I say to Kyle.

I follow the nurse. As I walk across the room I can feel Kyle's eyes watching my every step.

I pick up the phone. "Linda?"

"Come to my office … now."

Linda is slumped over her messy desk with her head in her hands.

"Everything all right?" I ask.

She peers up at me and rolls her eyes.

"Close the door. This is a fucking nightmare," she says.

I take a seat and get comfortable in case she's planning on venting to me for the next half hour.

"Wanted to give you a heads up that I'm moving a few more patients to your ward," says Linda.

"You're joking, right? We're at capacity."

"There's always room to squeeze in a couple more beds."

I throw my hands up in the air. "And I have no say in the matter?"

"They're starting repairs on the east wing and I need to find beds for twenty patients."

"East wing? Does that include the patients in solitary?"

Linda's eyes widen and she groans. "They'll have to go in the single rooms that can lock from the outside."

"And you're going to have a guard posted outside every room?"

She stares at me, deadpan.

"Reschedule the repair work and limit our patient intake for a few weeks so that the situation is more manageable."

"I can't do that, Todd," she says firmly. "Anyway, this wasn't a discussion. I've told you how this is going to work."

I stand up. "Fine. But I'm letting you know that I think it's a bad idea."

"Noted. And thank you for being so accommodating."

"Was that everything?"

She gives me a smirk. "Yes."

An alarm in the building begins to blare. Linda and I rush into the corridor and catch a guard running towards the east wing.

"What's happening?" I ask.

"Patient attacked a nurse. He's putting up a fight."

We run down the criss-crossing hallways until we reach solitary confinement, where a crowd of nurses watch in horror as three burly guards wrestle a patient to the ground. A smaller group of nurses tend to one of their crying colleagues, whose nose is broken and her uniform splattered with blood. Another nurse runs past us with a syringe in her hand. She plunges the needle into the fighting patient's neck and almost instantly he slips into a dreamy haze.

"Somebody explain what is going on here!" booms Linda.

"That monster attacked me," cries the wounded nurse.

"How? He was supposed to be handcuffed," Linda snaps at the guards who shrug their shoulders.

"It was my fault. He pretended to handcuff himself to the bed. When I walked into the room he grabbed me."

I take a closer look at the patient's face. It's Peter Jenner, the prisoner we have in the hospital for psychiatric evaluation.

"You're lucky he didn't kill you," I say, which pushes the poor nurse over the edge. She starts bawling her eyes out.

Linda glares at me.

"This is exactly what I'm talking about, Linda. You can't put these patients on the wards with the others. You're asking for trouble."

She raises a hand to my face and shuts down the conversation, lowers her head, and walks away. I sometimes wonder if that woman has a single caring bone in her body.

I race back to the patient lounge on my ward where I'd been working with Kyle. He's still sitting at the table, and from where I'm standing, it looks as though he's finally finished the card game. I wander over with a huge smile on my face.

"You got there in the end," I say, giving him a congratulatory pat on the back.

Kyle gazes up at me. "Who are you?"

He might as well have punched me in the face.

Chapter Twenty-Seven

Hopeless doesn't begin to describe how I feel today. Weeks of intensive therapy with Kyle, and I have nothing to show for it. Yesterday, he broke a guard's arm. The nurses reported the incident as an unprovoked attack, but I saw everything with my own eyes. Kyle was sitting, peacefully staring out the window when the call was made for lights out. One of the guards yelled at him twice, but he didn't move. I watched as the guard strode across the room and grabbed Kyle's shoulder, forcefully spinning him around. It took less than a second for Kyle to pin the guard to the ground and twist his arm so far back that it came out of its socket with a grisly *pop*. I cringe even thinking about it.

Kyle was always an amazing wrestler, and these responses are nothing but reflexes. The common theme in every incident report from his assaults seems to be that someone, be that a guard or another patient, approached Kyle in a manner that he misinterpreted as threatening. How come I'm the only clinician who can see that?

I slouch over my desk with my head in my hands. It's already past nine, and I should be at home by now. I start packing my bag when I get an unexpected phone call from an unfamiliar number. Usually I would let it go to voicemail, but tonight I'm curious, so I answer.

"Dr. T," says the voice on the phone. It's Douglas, my private investigator. "Can you talk?"

"Of course." I sit bolt upright in my seat. "You have my full attention."

"You know I hate talking business, but we should probably get that out of the way first." He hesitates and waits for me to respond.

"Go on," I say.

"Well, I had to call in a few favors this time ... and I'm sorry, but I have to double my usual fee to cover the ... shall we call them, 'expenses' ... that I incurred obtaining this information from various sources."

"You found something?"

"Well, I'm not sure if it's going to help you much, but it does raise a whole load of extra questions."

"What questions? What did you find?" There's more than a hint of desperation in my voice.

"Check your email. I've sent a few files," he says.

I immediately open the mail application on my laptop.

"Well, I got my paws on Kyle's credit card statements from the three months prior to his disappearance, and two items caught my attention."

I wish he'd hurry up and get to the point.

"The first is bus tickets. So I called up the bus company

and they were kind enough to send through a copy of the itinerary, which I have also sent to your inbox."

His email comes through, and I open up a scanned copy of the bus ticket. It's for a round-trip bus ride that was scheduled the weekend Kyle disappeared. I read the "Destination" several times. Why would he be going to Denver? Now I'm confused.

"What was the second thing?" I ask.

"Did I send you the credit card statements too? Look at the last entry on page two."

I click on the email attachment containing the credit card statement and scan down to the bottom of the second page. Kyle spent over two grand at a local jewelry store the day before he disappeared.

"I'm struggling to make sense of this," I say.

"Turns out your boy chose to take out optional insurance on the sale, which listed two gentleman's engagement rings." As the words come out of Douglas's mouth, this new revelation brings me to the brink of tears. What was Kyle planning? Those rings were for us! That's why he bought the bus tickets. He was going to ask my parents for permission to marry me.

"Now," Douglas continues, "I was able to find something that could prove useful from the night he disappeared. One of those attachments should contain the city zoo security access logs. It looks like Kyle swiped himself in sometime around 8 PM and left shortly before 11 PM. I went to the trouble of locating the address of the security guard who was working that night. Should be at the bottom of the email."

I scroll to the bottom of the screen, and sure enough, I

find an address for a Mr. Lyle Bennet.

"I don't know what to say."

"Don't say anything. It's always a pleasure doing business with you."

He hangs up the phone, and I'm left dumbfounded.

The following morning, I drive out to the address that Douglas gave me in the hope of finding the security guard who used to work at the city zoo. It's on the extreme edge of the city limits, in a rather unsavory part of town. These streets were once filled with commuting workers and bustling stores. Since the last economic downturn, the area has been hit hard, with businesses closing down and gangs establishing new territory here. I have to admit that I'm nervous driving these streets.

I pull up to the address, expecting a shabby apartment building, but instead I find myself outside the gates to an old people's home that looks like a prison. I walk into the building, through two sets of security doors, and up to the front desk. The receptionist looks up at me through the bars that separate us.

"Can I help you?" she says in a dismissive manner.

"I'm looking for a resident. His name is Lyle Bennet."

I show her my hospital access card as if it'll lend me additional credibility. She raises an eyebrow and types something into her computer.

"And who are you?"

"His doctor," I lie, knowing it's probably my only hope of getting in to see the man.

"Fine. Come through."

She leans across her desk to press a button on the wall. I hear a buzzing sound, and the security gate to my left swings open.

"Follow me," orders the receptionist. She spins around and heads down an empty corridor into the bowels of the facility.

There's not an ounce of natural light inside this place. I wonder if they wheel the patients out into the courtyard for their daily dose of vitamin D. Is there even a courtyard? The receptionist leads me along one dingy hallway after another. The smell of stale urine makes me want to gag. Such a cruel fate, to end up in a place like this.

"Over there," she says when we reach the communal living room.

She points at a frail old man reclining in a La-Z-Boy chair that's been pushed up against a window. Out the window is a view of nothing but the neighboring building's brick wall.

"Thank you," I say to the receptionist, but she's already left the room.

I'm not unfamiliar with the stench and sense of impending death that shrouds old people's homes, but I don't think I'll ever get used to it. No one would choose to spend their last days in a place as depressing as this, and yet so many elderly folk are abandoned by their families or left with no alternative, due to debilitating medical conditions.

The old man sitting across the room from me might just be the last person who ever saw Kyle before whatever happened to him. Just my luck: he'll have Alzheimer's, and this will have all been a colossal waste of time and emotional energy.

I crouch beside the old man and recognize him instantly. He was the guard who was always snoozing at the desk when Kyle and I snuck into the zoo together.

"Mr. Bennet?" I say. It's then that I notice he's missing both legs. Knowing that his disability is physical, I almost feel relieved.

He wakes with a huge snort. "The one and only," he says with great exuberance.

"My name is Dr. Chambers. I've come to see you in the hope that you could answer a few questions for me."

"My, my … this does sound intriguing. Go on, but grab yourself a chair first. You'll wreck your knees crouched down like that." I can't help myself from staring at his amputated lower limbs before I pull up a nearby chair and sit down. "I don't have that problem any longer," he chuckles.

"How did it happen?" I ask.

"I was hit by a vehicle a few years ago." He shakes his head. "My fault entirely. Tried to cross the road before the lights changed, and a truck came out of nowhere."

"I'm so sorry."

"Oh, don't be. It was an accident. Anyway, you had some questions for me?" he says.

"This may sound like an arbitrary question, but do you remember your days working at the city zoo?"

"All too well. They had to wheel me out of there in the end." He winks at me. "I worked at the zoo for almost forty years. Can you believe it?" he says proudly.

"And do you recall working with a young man named Kyle Hansen?"

Mr. Bennet holds his chin and stares glassy-eyed out the window at his view of the brick wall.

"He worked Saturday nights. Cleanup crew?" I add, hoping it will spark a faded memory.

"Oh yes! K-dog! He used to bring pizza and soda for dinner every Saturday night. Wonderful young man. Although he'd be about your age now. Not so young any more ... but that's all relative." He pauses and smiles. "I wonder how he's getting on."

"What do you mean?"

"Well ... he stopped coming to work very suddenly. This was years ago. But I can recall the last night I saw him. He was so excited."

"Did he tell you why?"

"He told me everything!" He laughs, and I sit back, rather surprised. "I called him 'K-dog' because he was a bit of a man-eater ... until he met that other boy. I can't remember his name now."

"Todd?" I say.

"Yes, Todd. That's it. He sounded like a lovely boy, too. That's why Kyle was so excited. He came in specially to tell me the good news." Mr. Bennet's gaze drifts off and he goes silent.

"Mr. Bennet?" I say and he snaps back to attention. "You said that Kyle came in to share his good news with you?"

"Yes. He was going to get married." An incredible sadness falls over me upon hearing those words. "All he still had to do was ask the other boy's parents for permission. I never did get an invitation to the wedding. Never saw Kyle again after that night either. I heard he left town." He looks at me forlornly. "Why do you want to know about Kyle? Is he in trouble?"

My voice trembles slightly. "No, Mr. Bennet. Not at all. The truth is," I start, knowing that every word that follows is going to be a lie. I clear my throat. "In fact, he wishes he could be here to send his warmest regards himself."

"That's very kind," says Mr. Bennet. "Please send him my regards too."

"I will do." Knowing the truth about Kyle would bring nothing but sadness to this poor old man's heart.

I spend the rest of the afternoon chatting to Mr. Bennet about everything and nothing in particular. He had a special place in Kyle's heart, and I can see now that he was a substitute father figure. This solves the mystery of the engagement rings and the bus tickets. Kyle never made it to my parents' house. I know that because the bus ticket was never validated. Something must have happened to him between leaving the zoo that night and the following morning, when the bus was scheduled to leave.

On the way back to my car after my phone vibrates in my pocket. It's a text from a number I don't recognize.

The message reads—"*Hey you. Hoped you might still be interested in a date. In town for the rest of the week. Simon*".

Simon? I don't know any Simon. I start to text—"*Who is this?*", but change my mind. I'm not really in the mood for playing text tag with a stranger. No doubt they sent a text to the wrong number. I hit *delete*, and both my reply and the original message disappear from the screen.

Fuck! Simon was the guy I met at the conference. I kick my car tire and the alarm blares back at me. My toes start to throb and I instantly regret my juvenile outburst. How could I be so fucking stupid? I breathe a heavy sigh and climb into the car, feeling utterly defeated. I don't know how to deal with these emotions. Kyle coming back into my life has stirred up everything I tried so hard to suppress for so many years. And now I might have just erased my one and only chance of ever seeing Simon again. Maybe I'm cursed.

Chapter Twenty-Eight

It feels like I've stepped back through time. The psychiatric hospital has never looked so good. The yellowed walls have been transformed by a fresh lick of bright white paint. All the dead and flickering light bulbs have been replaced and the intense glow from the ceiling is now blinding. Even the laminate flooring is polished and spotlessly clean, which is unheard of in a place like this where the patients are prone to flinging bodily fluids and creating an awful mess.

A group of fresh-faced nurses walk past and simultaneously smile and say, "Good morning, doctor." This feels very surreal. I arrive at the nurses' station. There's a file waiting for me that has the name *"John Doe"* crossed out and *"Kyle Hansen"* written neatly in its place. I take the file and make my way down several corridors until I reach the patients' rooms. None of the doors is labeled with the name of the patient inside. I peer through each peephole slit and see nothing but empty rooms. I come to the door at the very end of the corridor, and to my relief it has Kyle's name written down as the patient, and mine beneath his as the treating doctor.

I knock three times and walk inside his room.

This isn't how I remember the rooms in the hospital. It's a barren cell covered from ceiling to floor in bright, white padding. At first I don't notice Kyle lying on the soft floor with his arms folded behind his head. Dressed in a white singlet and long white pajama pants, he almost blends into the room. Kyle lifts himself up onto his elbows and gives me that naughty smile that I know so well. He looks good. Great, in fact! They've given him a cropped military style haircut, which instantly makes him look young again. I can't help noticing the definition of his toned shoulders and arms. The door shuts behind me with a soft thud.

"I've been waiting for you," he says.

"Do you remember who I am, Kyle?"

"It's all coming back to me," says Kyle as he springs to his feet. "I remember my name. Whatever you did to me the other day … I can remember things." He circles me slowly. "I can remember some things from my past … people … places I've been … things I've done. Most of it is still a blur." He stops directly in front of me within arm's reach. "And then every now and then, something jumps out at me that I re-member so vividly."

My eyes gravitate to his full lips that are still so kissable, down his neck to his broad shoulders and strong chest. He's standing close enough that I can feel his warm breath on my skin.

"Hello, Todd." He hovers before pulling me in for a kiss.

I forget where I am. It feels so good to be in his embrace.

We hold each other tightly and kiss like we're trying to catch up on a lifetime of lost affection. The hard outline of his erection digs into me through the soft cotton pants he's wearing, and it turns me on just as much as ever before. With my eyes still closed, we move, almost drift, across the room until my back lands against the soft, padded wall. I open my eyes again to look at his handsome face, but he's scowling at me.

"What's wrong?" I ask.

Kyle slams me against the wall. At first I think he's just being dominant, but he pins my hands so hard it hurts. He spits in my face. He's furious. I don't understand what's going on.

He screams at me, "I remember you, Todd. You said you loved me."

He head-butts me in the face and breaks my nose. Blood streams down my chin and I drop to my knees.

"I trusted you! Where were you when I needed you?"

He kicks me in the side, sending me flying across the floor. I curl up in agony, wanting to vomit from the pain and despair I feel.

"You left me lying in a trough full of piss to die!"

He picks me up with inhuman strength and throws me across the room. I smack my head. It's like hitting a brick wall.

"You don't fucking deserve to live, you piece of shit!"

He digs his elbow into my neck and crushes my windpipe. I can't breathe. I claw at his arms and try to throw him off, but he's too heavy and too strong. I'm starting to lose consciousness. I splutter and try to beg, but his grip is so tight that no sounds can escape my throat. I'm going to die.

I wake up gasping for air and drenched in sweat. I clutch at my throat and take several deep breaths to try and calm my racing heart. I switch on the light, half expecting to find myself in some strange location, but I'm exactly where I should be—safe, and completely alone in bed at my apartment. I can't be here by myself right now. I'm going insane with guilt, and I need to talk to somebody.

I arrive on Felix and Georgina's doorstep a little after 1 AM. Felix opens the door, still with one eye closed.

"Bud, you know what time it is?" he says with a huge yawn.

I thought I could hold it together, but I become a blubbering mess.

"Oh shit. You better come in." Felix guides me into the house and sits me down on the couch in the living room.

"What happened?" He wraps a blanket around me and I cry on his shoulder. Georgina appears a few minutes later with two cups of hot chocolate.

"Thanks, babe," he says to Georgina.

"We love you, Toddy," she whispers, giving me a kiss on the head and a hug before going back to bed.

When I finally manage to pull myself together, I explain the whole sad saga to Felix. He sits there in stupefied silence.

Eventually, Felix says, "Todd, you can't keep blaming yourself for what happened. And you can't be his doctor, for God's sake. You … and Linda … should know better than to put yourself in a situation like that. No wonder you're drowning in the deep end."

"I thought I could help him."

"Todd, try to be objective. Kyle has a severe brain injury. He is never going to go back to the way he was before." The words come out more caring than cruel, but it still hurts to hear them.

"I hoped there might be a chance."

"You've done everything and more, but there comes a time when you have to admit defeat. Step away before you dig yourself in too deep."

I pull away from Felix. This isn't how I thought the conversation would go. He's talking to me like a friend and not like a counselor. I want the touchy feely fluff, not cold, hard advice.

"What you're doing is dangerous, more so to yourself than to Kyle. You need to move on," he says, putting his hand on my shoulder.

I sit there with my head in my hands. I really have gotten myself into an awful mess.

"You have no reason to take on all this guilt. If Kyle was able to, he'd be the first to tell you to stop blaming yourself for something that was out of your control."

He pauses, and I nod to let him know that I've heard what he's saying.

"It's time to start looking forward and not back," he says.

I know he's right.

"Let me take the reins from you on this one. I'll take Kyle on as one of my patients. You can be guaranteed he'll be well looked after."

If I was going to let any other person take my place, it would be Felix. I've loved this man like a brother since the day I met him, and I trust him implicitly.

"I would appreciate that," I say. For the first time in our conversation I manage to look Felix in the eyes and form something that resembles a smile.

"Now, you're going to stay the night, and in the morning you're in charge of making breakfast for the kids because Georgina is going to need a sleep in. That's non-negotiable."

"Thank you, Felix."

"Don't mention it," he says. "Now, if you'll excuse me, I have a grumpy pregnant lady to go cuddle back to sleep."

My eyes light up with excitement. "Georgina's pregnant?"

"We haven't told anyone else … yet," Felix says, beaming with pride. "She's around six weeks, so you've got to promise me you'll keep it a secret."

"My lips are sealed tight."

I fling my arms around him and give him the biggest hug. "Congratulations. You guys have been trying for a while now?"

"Nah," he says, too proud to admit the truth. I don't think he knows about the conversation I had with Georgina. "Happened out of the blue."

That's all right. I'm happy for them, regardless.

"Do I get to be a godfather again?" I ask.

"You sure do," says Felix.

I lie in bed for hours, replaying the memories I have of the last few days I spent with Kyle before he disappeared. I keep wishing I had done something different that might have changed the course of events. I spend a large part of my day counseling patients on techniques for total body relaxation and mindfulness. Now, I empathize with how difficult it is to cast aside worries and try to find my own version of inner peace. The worry about worrying and not being able to sleep becomes cyclical. My mind can't take it any longer, and everything goes black.

The house is dead quiet. It's light enough in the room, even with the blinds closed, for me to see everything all around me. I'm feeling rested and calm. I'm guessing it's mid-morning, but I can't bring myself to care. Georgina, bless her soul, must have taken sympathy on me and decided not to let her two little monsters, my adorable godchildren, pounce on me in the early hours of this morning to compete for my undivided attention. It's hard to believe that they're having another baby. It seems like just yesterday we were all hanging out in dorm rooms, or at Georgina's stylish townhouse, and now we're all grown up and having kids. Well ... they're having kids. It's going to cost me the deposit for a nice house to pay for donor eggs and a surrogate to grow my own baby. Straight couples really do have it easy.

Usually, I'd feel unease at the sight of four unheard voice-mail messages on my phone, but today it doesn't even faze me in the slightest. I fall back onto my pillow and play the messages on loudspeaker.

The first one is from Vicki at the office.

"Morning, Dr. Chambers. Wondered if you could please call me back when you have a chance. I'm ringing about your patient, Cassie Wishcroft. She wants to bring her appointment forward a week. Apparently, things aren't going well at the moment, and she really needs to see you."

Poor Cassie. I wonder what's happened now. I don't think I'd have half the amount of courage she has shown through her emotional roller coaster of a cancer diagnosis.

The second message is from Georgina.

"Hey, Todd. Just checking in on you and to let you know that you have the house to yourself for the morning. I've taken the kids to the museum, and we'll be back home lunchtime-ish. See you later."

The third message is from Felix.

"Hey bud, Felix here," he says as if I wouldn't recognize his voice. "I hope you had a good night's sleep. Georgina was a cranky cow this morning, so you owe me big time." The tone of his voice changes from friendly to businesslike. "Look, I had a thought this morning that I wanted to share with you. Do you remember Dr. Rosie Keller from the conference in Las Vegas? ..."

I click my fingers together a few times, trying to visualize which speaker he's talking about. She was the one doing the research on memory retrieval.

Felix's message continues, "... Well, I thought I'd give her a call to see if she'd be interested in Kyle's case ..."

I don't see how she would be much help.

"... Anyway, I think it's worth a shot. I'll let you know what happens." He hangs up.

It feels strange to be so isolated from Kyle's care, but I appreciate Felix keeping me informed.

The last message starts to play and the voice gives me instant goose bumps.

"Well hey, stranger," says Simon. "This feels a bit awkward because I'm not sure if you got my text, but I didn't want to miss out on an opportunity to see you again. I'm here till tomorrow night. Give me a call. Oh, it's Simon by the way. Ciao."

Without hesitation, I save Simon's number to my phone directory.

Chapter Twenty-Nine

It's lunchtime and I've only just snuck through the door at work. I glide past Vicki at reception with the stealth of a trained assassin and slip into my office without anybody noticing that I'm here. I'm yearning for just a few more precious hours of peace and solitude.

Any hope of spending the afternoon catching up on work is dashed when Felix barges his way into the room.

"Oh my God, you're not going to believe this!" says Felix.

He's bubbling with excitement as he sits on my couch and proceeds to make himself comfortable.

"She said yes."

"Who said yes?" I say.

"The memory doctor! Rosie Keller. Only problem is, your name is still on Kyle's medical records as his treating doctor, and she won't talk to me."

My enthusiasm starts to fade as Felix's sentence trails off.

"What does she need to know?" I say, starting to get frustrated.

"She's on the phone now," he says, and stares at me.

"My phone?"

Felix nods enthusiastically.

Before my mind has engaged enough to realize what's going on, I have the phone in my hand. "This is Todd ... Dr. Chambers speaking."

"Hello?" says Rosie. She has a shrill tone to her voice that is like chalk grating on a blackboard. "I've been waiting for over five minutes. I find this very unprofessional!"

"I must apologize, we've been having trouble with the phone lines all week." I'm getting rather good at this whole telling white lies thing.

"I briefly spoke with your colleague, but according to the patient's medical records, you are the treating doctor, is this correct?" she says.

"Yes, that is correct—" I say before she interjects.

"Then I shall speak with you directly. I do not use inter-mediaries. It's like playing broken telephone. Do you under-stand?"

This woman is impossible. Who does she think she is? My mother?

"Yes, Dr. Keller," I say, trying not to let any irritation slip through in my tone.

"Good. That's settled. Well, I only have two important questions that need answering before we progress any further."

I wait for my hopes to be dashed. That's what you're supposed to do, right? Expect the worst and hope for the best?

"Firstly, have you got permission from the next of kin? I know that we don't legally require it, but I would prefer to have permission from the family to perform the procedure. This is experimental and I don't want to be left open to litigation." I try to answer, but she continues speaking. "Secondly, I cannot find anything on the file detailing how this man died."

Felix and I look at one another in befuddlement.

"I'm sorry, did you say died?" I ask.

"Isn't he a 'John Doe'?" says Rosie.

"My colleague," I turn and glare at Felix, "obviously didn't explain the situation very well. 'John Doe' is the name on the file, but it's a mistake. The patient is still alive and he has severe mixed-type post-traumatic amnesia," I state loudly and clearly into the microphone.

The silence from the other end of the line is deafening.

"Shit," she swears over the phone. "How severe?"

"He remembers almost nothing from before the trauma, and new memory formation is patchy at best, from what I can ascertain."

There's more silence that goes on for an uncomfortably long time. "Okay. I can't guarantee it will work. We might be wasting our time."

She's right, though. This may be a pointless exercise.

"We can't know until we try, though," says Dr. Keller.

"Could you send the paperwork today?" I say.

Felix starts fist-pumping the air, but I'm afraid to start celebrating too soon.

"Absolutely. Then once we've received the documents, my office will make all the necessary arrangements. How does that sound?"

"The best news I've heard all day. Thank you." She can't see me smiling down the phone line, but I'm sure she must be able to hear it in my voice.

"My pleasure. I'll be in touch," she says, and the phone line goes dead.

"Felix!" I growl at him.

"Sorry. I forgot to mention that little thing about her research being done on dead people."

This is the part I must have missed when I stepped out to speak with Simon.

I shake my head in despair. "I've just agreed to track down two of the people I hate the most in the world for this woman, and I don't even know what she's planning to do to Kyle. How exactly does she accomplish this modern-day miracle?" I say with skepticism.

"Don't ask me the specifics. I kinda drifted off when she started getting into the nitty-gritty. Neurology isn't my strong suit. We got taught that module at med school when I first met Georgina. I prioritized sex above studying neuroscience. I can't tell an axon from a dendrite ... or are they the same thing?"

I shut my eyes in despair. An academic, he most definitely is not. "You're a shameful excuse for a doctor," I say.

"I'm guessing you don't have next-of-kin contact details?" Felix asks wryly.

"They shouldn't be hard to find."

"Right. Well, I have to get back to my office, bud. Patients to see. I'll catch you at lunch." He skedaddles out the door and I reflect on what just happened. My mind is completely blown.

It takes less than an hour to locate Kyle's parents' new address. I was expecting an address halfway across the country in some hick town, so I'm surprised to find that they're living here in Los Angeles.

My last scheduled appointment of the day is with Julio and Rita, the couple who are seeing me for marriage counseling. When they arrive, the atmosphere turns ice-cold, and I know something is wrong. I ask Rita if she'll wait outside while I speak to Julio separately. I've never seen Julio like this before. He's usually the picture of strength and masculinity. Now he's sitting in front of me, insecure and on edge.

"Julio?"

"Jesus, man. What do you want me to say?"

"When you both arrived here today, I couldn't get a word out of either of you. What happened with you guys?"

"She slept with someone else."

"She did? Wasn't that your idea? To sleep with other people?"

He rolls his eyes, shakes his head and huffs.

"Is this jealousy?" I ask.

"You fucking bet your ass it's jealousy."

"So what happened?"

"We went to a swingers' party that I'd heard about. You know the kind. The husbands put their car keys in a bowl when they arrive, and then later in the evening the ladies randomly pick a set and go off with the owner of the keys? I got landed with this heifer. She was repulsive. I couldn't even get hard."

"And Rita?"

"I don't want to talk about it."

It's Rita's turn in the hot seat. Unlike her husband, she's on top of the world today.

"It was magical. I haven't had someone touch me the way he touched me in a long time."

"You are glowing."

"I think I forgot what it's like to feel special. You know what I mean? He was just my type—a Matthew McConaughey cowboy. Definitely more *Magic Mike* than *Dallas Buyers Club*. You know what I'm talking about? He had such strong, rough hands."

"Have you and Julio talked about this at all?"

"He hasn't said a word since Sunday night when we went to the party."

She casts her eyes to the floor and the excitement vanishes.

"I don't know why he thought it would make a difference. It was his idea. I eventually gave in and went along with it."

"Did you tell him about your reservations?"

"Oh, he knew."

"Shall I get Julio back in for us to have a conversation together?"

"You're welcome to try. You know how stubborn he can be."

I leave Rita in my office while I head into the waiting

room to collect Julio. He looks so nervous, sitting there on his own. Julio glances up and sees me. I gesture for him to come back into my office.

Rita and Julio sit together on the couch. She takes his hand and holds it on her lap.

"Where do I start … it's plain to see that you both love each other deeply, but you have to start communicating better."

Neither of them says a word.

"Well?" I say.

"I'll go first," says Julio. "I made a mistake. Every time I think of Rita being with another man, it makes me physically ill."

She creases her brow and gives his hand an affectionate squeeze.

"Oh honey, I never had sex with him." Her confession takes him by surprise. "I couldn't. I'm just not that kind of girl."

"But I thought—"

"You assume that because it's what you wanted to do. I've never wanted anybody but you."

"So, you didn't make love to him?"

"He wanted to … and I won't lie, I was attracted to him. He gave me a massage and then … he was a gentlemen when I said I didn't want to go any further."

"Will you forgive me?" begs Julio. "I made a mistake. I want my Rita and nobody else."

"My darling, I don't want to be with anybody but you."

She kisses the back of his hand. Julio has the hangdog

look of a guilty man. "You're too good to me, Rita."

He gives her a kiss and they both look in my direction.

"Shall we end things there today?" I say.

It makes me sad to think that a couple like Julio and Rita had to go through an experience like this to realize that they already have everything they need in each other. At least they came to the right conclusion before damaging their relationship irreparably. I never said it before, but I don't hold out much hope for any couple that opens up their sexual relationship as a solution for intimacy issues. There's too much jealousy, envy, uncertainty, and don't get me started on the trust issues it creates. I would choose to either end things and save myself the mounting heartache, or try to make things work by fixing what went wrong with my relationship in the first place. But you can't tell people what to do with their lives. They need to make their own mistakes and learn their own lessons, the same way that I've learned mine.

Julio and Rita leave, walking hand-in-hand. It's sweet to watch, but I'm realistic about the amount of effort those two now need to put into their relationship to make things work again. They've gone down a long road of punishing one another at every opportunity, and old wounds don't heal with a single kiss.

I look at the clock and figure that if I leave immediately, I'll make it to Kyle's parents' house before the traffic gets too busy.

I never met Kyle's parents, not even when we were together. I remember seeing a photograph of his family, but I doubt I'll recognize either of them. Felix agreed to let me go alone to ask Kyle's parents for permission to try out Dr. Keller's Moneta device, on condition that I promise him I'll remain polite and civil, no matter what happens.

I pull up outside their house. It isn't as rundown and shitty as I hoped it would be. At least if they were ignorant rednecks it would be easier to find a reason to forgive them for what they'd done to Kyle. I have to psych myself up with every step I take from the front gate to the porch. The final knock on the door triggers a surge of adrenaline that heightens every sense and makes me feel mildly nauseous.

A plain looking woman wearing no makeup answers the door. I don't see any resemblance to Kyle in her. Could this be the wrong address? Then a middle-aged man with a protuberant belly walks up behind her. He's the spitting image of Kyle, except older and fatter.

"Can we help you, sir?" drawls Kyle's father, whose name I can't remember.

"I wonder if you folks might have a few minutes for me to come in and talk to you about your son," I say with confidence.

"Well, certainly," he answers without hesitation. "Louise, be a sweetheart and make us a cup of coffee. You take milk and sugar?"

"Just milk ... no sugar, thanks," I say.

They invited me in so eagerly to discuss their son? I envisaged a great deal more resistance.

They lead me through to the living room. The house is clean and tidy. They're obviously proud of their little residence. A theme of hummingbirds runs through the decor in the house. I scan the rows of photographs on the walls. There's no trace of Kyle. Not a single photograph. It's as if he never even existed. Then I see a large, framed family photograph up on the wall. It's the same photo that Kyle used to carry around with him in his wallet. Part of the original photo has been cut away to remove their disowned son, so that only the parents and Kyle's brother are left behind. Shit! I forgot that Kyle had a brother. That's why they let me through the door. They think I'm here to talk about their pride and joy, who died in the car accident all those years ago. This is going to be even more awkward than I originally anticipated.

I cut right to the chase.

"We found Kyle," I blurt out, which silences their chitchat. Kyle's mother flops down on the sofa beside her husband.

"What did you say?" says Kyle's father, craning his neck towards me and frowning.

"Your son, Kyle. He has been a ward of the state for the past fifteen years after being violently attacked and left to die by his assailants."

Louise gasps in horror and covers her mouth to shield a whimper. The color drains from her face.

"He's no longer part of this family," says Kyle's father, "and I don't appreciate you distressing my wife like this."

"Is he okay?" she says, trembling all over.

"Not entirely." I don't want her to feel any less guilty about what's happened to Kyle, but I also don't want to devastate the woman. He is her son, after all. "Have you heard of amnesia?"

"The memory thing?" says Louise.

"Kyle can't remember much from his past and can't make any new memories. He's essentially stuck in the present."

"So what do you want from us?" says Kyle's father rather coldly.

"Your permission to use an experimental device to stimulate his brain to try and unlock those memories." I try not to sound too desperate. Kyle's father has already crossed his arms and started to flare his nostrils. I can see where Kyle got his temper from.

"This won't make us liable for any costs?" he asks.

I shake my head. "His care will be covered entirely by us."

I push the piece of paper with the disclaimer across the coffee table towards them. Kyle's father snatches the document and takes his time reading through every single line of legal jargon. After an excessively long silence he grunts and scrawls his signature at the bottom of the page. With another huff, he stands up and walks out the room.

"Is he going to be okay?" Louise asks as she blots her eyes with a tissue.

I open my mouth to respond, but Kyle's father's booming voice drowns mine out. "Please show the gentleman to the door."

"Yes, love," she calls back to him. "This way please," she says, motioning for me to leave.

At the front door, I turn to say my goodbyes, but the door is shut in my face.

There isn't much left in this world that can leave me speechless, but that just floored me. I want to knock on the door again, and when his father opens up, I'd like to land my clenched fist so hard in his face that it breaks his nose so badly he can't breathe properly for the rest of his miserable life. I squeeze my hand into a tight ball until it hurts, then let go and allow the negative energy to pass through me. These people don't matter. I have what I wanted. They can go to hell.

I pull away from the house, leaving a trail of dust hanging in the air and a streak of burnt rubber on the road. I make a quick phone call to Vicki at the office.

"Hi Vicki," I say as soon as she answers the call. "Could you please call Dr. Rosie Keller at the Lindeman Foundation and let her know that we have permission from the family? We can go ahead."

"Sure, Dr. Chambers," she says, as sprightly as ever.

We both hang up and I take a deep breath in and slowly exhale out. It's all happening now.

But before I allow myself to get distracted by anything else I need to call Simon. I pull over to the side of the road and bring up his number on my phone. He answers almost at once.

"Well, if it isn't the elusive Dr. Chambers! How are you doing?"

"What are the chances you're free for coffee this afternoon?" I ask.

"Could do. Dinner might be easier, though …"

I'm aware that inviting someone for coffee is like taking

one giant step back in a relationship, especially after the night we spent together, but the timing is just not right with all the intense emotions surrounding Kyle. I want to give a hundred percent to an amazing catch like Simon, and I can't do that with so much still invested in Kyle. I'm letting go piece by piece, and I hope that he will understand why I have to refuse his invitation.

"I'm sorry, Simon. I want to be completely honest with you because I think you're an amazing guy." There is nothing but silence from his side. "But right now I don't think that I can give you everything you deserve in a relationship. I need to resolve the feelings I have for Kyle first."

Simon laughs. "Let's not get ahead of ourselves, here. I don't even live in the city yet, so let's just think of each other as two people who really like each other, who are getting to know one another better. You take all the time you need to get yourself back into a good headspace."

"When are you back in town next?" I desperately hope that he doesn't brush me off.

"Well that's something I wanted to tell you over dinner," he says, and it sends a wave of guilt through me. "I got the job. Here in the city. I start in three months' time."

I can hear the excitement in his voice, and I wish I didn't have these conflicted feelings. Why didn't I just say "yes" to his invitation? Tonight we could've been enjoying each other's company and celebrating his amazing achievement together. There's no point having regrets. If it's meant to be, it'll be, right?

"That's incredible! Congratulations!" I say.

"I know, right!"

We both let out a nervous giggle, and then there's that awkward moment when neither of us knows what to say next.

"Well ... good luck with the move, and I hope to see you again soon," I say.

"You can count on it." He hangs up the phone.

Chapter Thirty

My hands are dripping with sweat, and no amount of wiping them on my dress pants seems to help. I don't think I've ever been this anxious before. It's times like these that I wish I had a nicotine habit. Smokers always look so calm and collected. All their worries and woes carried away on plumes of smoke.

"Dr. Chambers," says a quiet voice behind me. I turn around to see one of the young female technicians poking her head out of the control room door. "We're ready."

I picture myself dropping the cigarette butt onto the floor and stubbing it out with my shoe, experiencing a sense of total calm. This is it. This is the moment I've been waiting for.

I walk into the control room. Two technicians wearing fitted metallic suits stand in front of several rows of touch-screen glass panels. Everything is transparent and bright, illuminated with LEDs. I see graphs, menu systems and lines of mathematical calculations flashing across the panels. It feels like I've stepped aboard a futuristic spaceship. Felix was right when he said that it sounded like something out of a science fiction movie.

Through the ceiling to floor glass walls in front of us, I see a white room where Kyle is sleeping peacefully on an operating table. There's a transparent cylinder that encircles his head, with two silver balls rotating at a steady pace in opposite directions through the clear tube. I've never seen anything like it before. I was expecting to see electrodes covering his head and monitoring devices surrounding him, but it's just Kyle and this strange device.

My inquisitiveness gets the better of me, and I lean closer to one of the technicians. Her focus stays firmly on the task at hand in front of her.

"Do you mind if I ask what the uniforms are for?" I say.

"They serve multiple purposes," says a high-pitched voice behind me. I turn to greet Dr. Rosie Keller, who is dressed in the same space age outfit as the technicians. "In this instance, they help to block out any electrical currents generated by our bodies that may cause interference. The suit has to be worn when entering the chamber. You can observe from here just as you are," she says in an officious manner. "Spectacular, isn't it? You wouldn't believe how much money has gone into funding this project … but the results …" She throws her hands up in delight. "… Just incredible. I'm going to win a Nobel Prize for this one, Jim."

I wonder if she's still talking to me, and sure enough, she's looking in my direction and waiting for a response.

"Todd … Todd Chambers," I say, correcting her.

She grimaces.

"I'm not sure if we discussed this before, but our work so

far has been with victims of violent assault and traumatic accidents. All deceased. We've helped to solve two murders, which was very exciting." Her voice becomes more somber and serious. "There is a risk of permanent brain injury, though. We have never tried this on a living person, and we still don't know what will happen to Kyle when he wakes up. We'll have him dosed up on anticonvulsants to minimize seizure activity, but there's a very real chance this could kill him."

I realize the risks, but what is the alternative? I can't bear to see Kyle rot away in this state, eternally trapped in the present moment.

"Could you explain to me how the process works?"

"Right," says Dr. Keller. "The simplified version is that Moneta sends millions of tiny electrical currents through areas of the brain associated with memory. We can wirelessly target any region by adjusting the frequency of each impulse. Simultaneously, it captures all cellular and electrical responses happening in the brain. In essence, we create a data dump containing every retrievable memory. Normally, the brain begins to liquefy rather soon after death, so we have a small window period during which we can graft the electrodes and perform the stimulation without turning the brain to soup. But I expect we'll be able to extract a large amount of data from this patient, from Kyle … seeing as he's still alive."

One of the technicians turns to Dr. Keller and says, "We're ready to begin the test sequence, Dr. Keller."

Dr. Keller rubs her hands together and observes Kyle through the glass walls. The silver balls rotating around Kyle's head begin to spin faster and faster. They make a *whooshing* sound that grows increasingly louder. The balls spin at such a tremendous velocity that it looks like Kyle's head is surrounded by a solid silver halo. Then, just as quickly, the silver balls slow down to their original hypnotic momentum.

"Test sequence successful," says the technician. "Steady stream of consciousness recorded."

"Initiate core memory dump," orders Dr. Keller. She turns to me. "This is the exciting part."

I watch as the silver balls accelerate to lighting fast speed. For a second, I see the halo around Kyle's head before the cylinder begins to rotate forwards and backwards, creating the illusion of the balls spinning around his head at different angles, like electrons in a wobbly orbital around an atom. The intense sound of the machine and watching the spinning device gives me a bad case of vertigo, and I'm forced to sit down. Kyle's body begins to twitch.

"Dr. Keller, I'm seeing focal seizure activity in the left temporal lobe," shouts the other technician.

"Are we still receiving data," she demands.

"Yes, we are," replies the technician.

"Then keep going."

Kyle's entire body starts to jerk uncontrollably.

"Seizure activity now generalized," says the technician, louder than before.

Should I be worried? My heart is races, and my whole body breaks out in a sweat.

Dr. Keller swipes through streams of data on the touch screen panels. She smiles and motions to the technicians to stop the machine.

"And we're done!" says Dr. Keller, immense satisfaction in her voice.

Kyle's body relaxes and becomes a floppy heap on the operating table. The device spinning around his head slows to a halt.

Dr. Keller drifts her hand above one of the control panels, and a holographic waveform rises. She pinches and pulls her fingers apart in mid-air to expand the size of the graph and flips her hand to move through the data. She pushes a button. Complex, automated graphical analysis begins to take place. Parts of the waveform swap positions, become compressed, or stretched apart like an accordion.

"Phenomenal," she whispers.

"What is it telling you," I say, unable to comprehend anything that I'm seeing.

"No, no, no." She smacks her hand on the desk in frustration, and the excitement from before is snuffed out. "There's scattered corruption throughout the data. It's a complete mess. I didn't anticipate that the brain was this badly damaged." She sighs.

"What does that mean?" I ask.

Dr. Keller spins her head around and scowls at me. "We're going to need time to crunch the numbers and analyze the data. We'll be in touch." She waves me off dismissively.

"Thank you," I say, but there's no need. Dr. Keller and her team are already immersed in their work.

I make my way to the waiting room where I'm supposed to stay until they're finished with Kyle. I wish I could stop my leg from bouncing. This only happens when I'm on edge.

One of the technicians comes to collect me a few minutes later and says, "Dr. Chambers, he's ready."

I walk into the recovery area and see Kyle lying in bed, studying the LED ceiling lights. I smile at him. He smiles back. Not the empty smiles of the past few weeks, but with the fire in his eyes that I used to know. He recognizes me. I know because he breathes a little faster and the crow's feet around his eyes crinkle even deeper when he sees me. The same way he smiled at me when we were younger. But he doesn't say anything, not a single word.

On our return to the psychiatric hospital, Kyle sits in the back seat of the car staring out the window with the biggest, goofiest grin painted on his face. He has this look of total and utter contentment. I'm afraid to say anything in case it brings him out of this place of serenity that he's in right now. My phone starts to vibrate, and when I see it's the office calling, I get an impending sense of doom.

I answer the call. "Todd speaking."

It's Vicki on the line, and she unleashes a flood of information that I struggle to keep up with.

"Slow down and tell me that again," I say.

"Your patient Cassie … she's dead … committed suicide in the middle of a mall food court. It's all over the news. The police want to speak with you," she says, extremely flustered.

I close my eyes and try to stay calm. My heart starts to pound and there's a ringing in my ears. "Fuck!" is the only thing I manage to verbalize.

"She jumped from the top floor of the atrium and landed in the food court. Thankfully, no one else was hurt. The press has started calling the office. I don't know what to do." She whimpers, and I hear her blow her nose.

"Give me half an hour. I'll come straight to the office," I say, hanging up the phone. I look back over my shoulder at Kyle. He turns his head and smiles at me, then gazes back out the window.

When I arrive at the office, there are two police detectives waiting to speak with me. We move into my office to discuss matters further.

"Your receptionist said that Miss Wishcroft ... Cassie ... had left several messages for you to call her. Were you successful in making contact with her, and what was the content of those messages?" asks one of the detectives, while the other one sits there and nods.

"She left a message a couple of days ago," I say, "but I can't recall ... no, I didn't call her back."

"What did she say?"

"I can't remember. You'll have to ask my receptionist. I'm sorry, but my mind has been on other things lately."

The detectives exchange glances and both simultaneously frown at me.

"Let me remind you, a young woman died. This is no time for brain fade, doctor," he says sternly.

I hesitate. "Could you give me a day or two to go through my notes and put together the appropriate documentation for you? I cannot share our private conversations, but I can give you an assessment of her recent mental state."

The detectives don't seem all that impressed. The one who's been doing the talking grunts at me.

"I don't think there is anything more that could have been done in this instance. When a depressed patient with all of his or her mental faculties still intact chooses death by suicide, it's almost inevitable. I'm sorry that I can't be more help to you gentlemen." I stand and gesture for the men to leave.

"Miss Wishcroft emptied her accounts earlier today and handed out wads of cash to homeless people all over town. She then went on a spending spree, maxed out her credit cards. A witness saw her casually place her handbag and shopping on the ground and run at full speed towards the guard rail. Do you still think she had all her 'mental faculties' intact, doctor?" says the other detective.

They rise to their feet and make their way to the door, disgruntled and leaving none the wiser as to the reasons behind Cassie's dramatic suicide. I think back over my appointments and phone calls with Cassie. Never once did she describe how she might have killed herself. Usually, a person with suicidal ideation will have a well-formulated plan devised to achieve death. Cassie was depressed, but she never expressed a wish to die at her own hand.

"Oh, almost forgot to give you this," says the detective. He passes an envelope to me. "It was addressed to you."

"Thank you," I say. The detectives leave me in peace to open the letter, which I assume is from Cassie.

It's written in neat cursive and signed at the bottom.

"Dear Todd,

You are the only person who I feel the need to apologize to. You have been there from the very beginning of this horrific journey through sickness and depression. If I have betrayed anyone, it is you, always there for me, no matter my hour of need. If it had not been for your ongoing support, I would have ended my life long ago. But I've reached a point now where the pain is ever-present and inescapable, and I choose not to die in an opiate haze. I pray that my actions will not reflect poorly on your professional practice, as you have shown me nothing but under-standing and kindness. Lastly, I want to give you some advice. I see in you a man who has so much capacity for love and greatness in life. Stop wallowing in your own self-pity and seize life. You only get to live once. Don't waste it like I did.

Your friend, Cassie."

"Dr. Chambers," says Vicki, poking her head into my office, "would you mind if I talked to you about something?"

"This isn't a good time, Vicki."

"It's about your patient … Cassie," she says, shamefaced.

"Go on," I urge her.

"I feel like this is all my fault."

"Jesus, Vicki, why would you think something like that?"

"Because I knew she was going to do it. At least I should have."

"Come in and close the door." I sit down and shake my head in disbelief. This can't be happening.

Vicki sits timidly in the chair in front of my desk. Her hands are shaking, and her lip is starting to tremble. I'm getting worried now.

"She told me last week," splutters Vicki. "Well, not me personally, but I overheard her talking on the phone. She was sitting here in the waiting room and the conversation she was having didn't go well ... she ended it by saying that it didn't matter what happened now anyway because she'd 'rather kill herself than die a death like that'. I remember looking up at her and she just smiled back at me. I feel responsible for knowing and doing nothing about it."

Vicki bursts into tears. She's inconsolable, and the only thing I can do is put my arm around her and let her cry it out. It's not her fault, and she'll come to realize that in time. I make Vicki a cup of sweet tea and sit with her for another hour while she lets out all the pain.

Even after all these years of being exposed to every shade of human emotion, it's crying that still gets me in the gut every time. It takes every ounce of fortitude to hold myself together. I'm not a religious man, but I hope that if there is a God, that he shelters poor souls like Cassie, who did nothing to deserve the shitty life they got given, and forgives them whatever sins they may have committed ... even suicide. I cannot see how a benevolent God could further punish someone like Cassie.

I send Vicki home early and direct all incoming phone calls to the office to our voicemail service. The psychiatric nurse is the only person still working studiously in her office. Everyone else has gone home and I think it's time to call it a day. My phone starts ringing and I hang up without looking at the screen to see who called. On second thought, I turn the damn thing off. Whoever it is can wait until tomorrow.

Walking to my car, I notice a slender man loitering in the parking lot with his hands in his pockets. He's wearing a hoodie, so I can't make out his face. I push my car remote and the alarm bleeps, which gives the man a fright. He spins around and looks in my direction.

"Good evening, Chad," I say.

"Hey, Dr. Chambers." He scuffs the gravel with his shoes and looks at the ground, rather contrite.

"You all right, Chad?" I put my briefcase down next to the car and fold my arms across my chest.

"Yeah I'm doing okay." He finally makes eye contact with me and chews the corner of his lip.

I try to adopt a less defensive posture and slip my hands in my pockets, mimicking his stance.

"I need to talk to you about something—"

"I'm not your therapist any longer, Chad."

I open the car door to put my briefcase away. Chad springs forward on his feet and stops only a few feet away from me.

"I wanted to apologize," he says with total sincerity. I stop and give him my full attention. I can sense his relief when I don't outright reject his offer of an olive branch. "I needed to apologize for my behavior. I'm so unbelievably sorry. What I did was unacceptable."

His tone and demeanor seem genuine to me. Perhaps I should give him a chance. We all make mistakes, and there's nothing worse than having a door slammed in your face.

"Apology accepted," I say graciously.

As the silence between us grows, his contemplative expression indicates that he has something more to share.

"Was there something else you wanted to say, Chad?"

His head nods ever so slightly. "I came out to my mom."

"How did she take it?"

"You know ... as well as could be expected. She made it all about her. Had she failed as a parent? What did she do wrong? All that kind of bullshit."

"How are you feeling?"

His face brightens up.

"Good, actually. I finished school end of last month and got a sweet programming gig at a new startup. I couldn't live with my mom any more. Moved in with a bunch of cool geeks. Told them I was gay when I went for the interview for the room and they were super chill with it."

"I'm happy for you."

"Anyway, I'm really sorry for what happened."

"It's water under the bridge now, Chad. Sounds like you're doing something great with your life. Keep it up."

"Thanks, Dr. Chambers. Okay, I better go. See you around."

"Of course," I say.

He gives me a wave and a smile and walks away with his shoulders hunched. There's a slow sadness in his step. I understand the courage it took to approach me and apologize. He'd be feeling vulnerable with such huge changes going on in his life. But he's on the right track, and who knows, maybe great things lie ahead in his future?

Chapter Thirty-One

The proverbial has hit the fan overnight, and there's a string of messages left on my voicemail. They're all from Linda, and as I listen to them, they're getting progressively angrier and more desperate. At first it was just her regular, calm tone of voice asking me to please call her back as soon as possible. That was 11 PM last night. By 7 AM, she's lost the plot, and message after message is just a string of profanity. I try calling back, but all I get on Linda's personal line is a busy signal, and I can't get through to the hospital either. What the fuck is going on? I'm halfway through dressing myself when my phone rings again. It's Linda.

"Jesus, Todd. I've been trying to get hold of you all god-damn night!" she says.

"My phone was off."

"No shit! Look, I don't want to say too much over the phone. You need to come in right now." There's something different about the way she's talking to me; it's more urgent than dictatorial.

"I'll be there in thirty." I hang up. The excitement never ends.

I race down the hallway towards the psychiatric ward, passing a few policemen on the way. Linda is pacing in her office, smoking a cigarette. I walk in and gag on the smoky fumes.

"About time," she snarls at me. "Todd, I need you to sit down. Fuck, I don't know how to do this." She stamps out her cigarette and leans back against her desk. "We had an incident last night." She can't even make eye contact with me as she speaks. "You're familiar with Peter Jenner, the psychopath who we're assessing at the moment?"

"Yes, he was in solitary until you moved everybody out for the repair work," I say.

"Well, someone fucked up." She lights another cancer stick and inhales deeply.

"He didn't hurt anybody else, did he?" I ask with a sinking feeling. "Linda?"

"He killed Kyle." Her voice cracks as she says it.

I hear nothing. I see nothing. This unbearable weight wraps around my heart, and I'm free-falling into an abyss. Linda's lips keep moving, and still she won't make eye contact.

I struggle to form the words. "W … w … what?" I say with a stutter.

She looks me straight in the eyes and says, "He's dead. Kyle's dead."

My whole world stops.

I don't know how I ended up here, but I'm in a curled up

lump in the corner of my bedroom. I've never cried so much. The pain in my head and in my heart is indescribable. I can't cry enough to let out all the grief, and I'm crying so hard that it's impossible to breathe. I need something to numb the pain, anything to take it away. How is it possible that I can feel nothing and yet everything at the same time?

There's a knocking sound. I think it's coming from the front door, but I can't be sure. I open my eyes, but my vision is blurred and my head feels like it's been skewered with a rusty blade that keeps twisting my brain. I hear the knocking again and then silence. My eyes drift shut, and all I see is black.

"Toddy?" says a gentle voice that is so familiar. I can just make out Georgina's smiling face. "We're here for you," she says as she cradles my head in her lap. A strong hand grips mine and I know that Felix is there too. I can't help but cry. I don't know how to explain the hurt inside. I lost him once. By some miracle, I had him return to me … and now he's gone forever.

We stand gathered in the cemetery, watching as Kyle's coffin is lowered into the ground. I wasn't sure if it would be worthwhile placing a notice in the local paper, but now I'm grateful that I did. There are a few familiar faces in the crowd from when we were at college, guys from his wrestling team, and a lot more strangers whose connection to Kyle I'll never know. We stand in somber unison as the priest finishes his prayer. Kyle was never particularly religious, but it just wouldn't feel right saying goodbye to him any other way. The saddest thing about this funeral is the complete lack of crying. Everybody here already said goodbye to Kyle years ago. Today they're just going through the motions of paying their last respects. One by one, the mourners turn and walk away, leaving only me, Felix and Georgina behind.

Georgina squeezes my hand and a rush of emotion passes through me, but there's nowhere for it to go. I have no more tears to cry.

"Let's go home," says Georgina.

It's then that I notice a woman lurking in the distance. She's wearing bug-eye sunglasses and dabbing her tear-stained face with a white handkerchief. There's something familiar about her, but I can't put my finger on it.

"You okay, bud?" asks Felix.

"I'm okay." At least I will be when life regains some semblance of normality.

I look one last time at Kyle's grave before taking that first, brave step away. The sun breaks through the gray clouds and sunlight strikes me in the eyes, blinding me for an instant. As my vision returns I feel a strange catharsis, and some of the pain melts away.

Once again, I wasn't there for Kyle when something bad happened to him. But this time I realize that there's nothing I could have done to change what happened. It could have been me in his position. I wouldn't want him to waste a single minute of his life wondering what might have been or could have happened. I would want him to go on and keep living life to the fullest, and trying to achieve those hopes and dreams we had. I know he would want the same for me.

"Excuse me," says a meek voice from right behind us. It's the woman in the bug-eye sunglasses who was watching us. "Todd, can I speak with you?"

When she says my name, I realize who she is—Kyle's mom.

"Mrs. Hansen." The tone of my voice couldn't be any less welcoming. "Meet you guys at the car?" I say to Felix and Georgina. They walk away, arms linked together in a solemn march.

"I thought I recognized you when you came to the house, but I wasn't sure …" Her voice trails off and she wipes fresh tears from her eyes. "He sent me this photograph." She unclenches her hand, revealing a crumpled self-portrait photograph of me smiling over Kyle's shoulder, tickling him while he's holding the camera.

I remember the day that photo was taken like it happened yesterday. We had walked for hours along the beach, lost in flirtatious conversation. We stumbled upon this secluded cove. We hadn't seen another person for miles, and so the two of us lay down on the sand to watch the sunset. Kyle wanted to capture the moment forever, but I couldn't keep my hands off him.

"His father intercepted most of his letters, but I found this one in the garbage, and kept it hidden. He looks so happy here with you." She stares at the faded photograph with so much tenderness.

"Did you love him? My boy?" she asks, clutching the photo to her heart.

"I've never stopped loving him."

She looks fondly at the picture of us again, her emotions oscillating from happiness to sadness.

"He was my baby. He was such a sweet boy. So kind and gentle. I was so afraid that he was … you know …"

"A homosexual?"

"I knew before he did. I spent so many hours praying. I thought it might make a difference. And then he grew up and started playing sports and dating girls, and I thought my son was normal again. But he came to us before he went off to college and told us he was gay. It broke my heart."

I bite my tongue so hard it hurts. "What do you want from me?"

"Can you forgive me?"

I want to tell her there's no point crying now, that she lost the right to sympathy the day she turned her back on her child. How could she abandon her own flesh and blood and cast him out like a leper? He did nothing to harm her and worked so hard to make her proud. I want her to hurt so badly, to suffer for what she did to Kyle. But as I see the tears stream down her face and watch her tremble, I can't stop myself from putting my arms around her to comfort her. She rests her forehead against my shoulder and weeps.

"I forgive you," I say.

Chapter Thirty-Two

I fly back home to my parents' house for the weekend with mixed emotions. I secretly hope that Sarah and Ols aren't going to be there. Although I love my niece and nephew with all my heart, I know that seeing Sarah's perfect family of four is going to remind me of everything that was stolen when Kyle was taken away. The kids are both teenagers now. It's as if life moved on and I got left behind.

Mom and Dad meet me at the front door. One look at my mom's sad face and my fortitude disintegrates. I rest my head on her shoulder and blink the tears away.

My mom hugs me close. "I'm so sorry, my darling."

"Glad you're home, son," says Dad, putting an arm around my shoulders.

Another set of arms wraps around my body. I turn around and see Sarah's beautiful face. She kisses me on the cheek. I couldn't possibly feel any more loved.

The following morning there's a knock on my door and my

dad walks in.

"Come on, son," says my dad in his most authoritarian tone, "we're going for a run."

I glance at the ungodly hour on the alarm clock. It's still dark outside. Though resistance is utterly futile when it comes to Dad. There's no arguing with him.

"When did you start running?" I ask, rubbing my scratchy eyes.

"Years ago. Now get out of bed. I'll meet you at the front gate in five minutes," he says on his way out the door.

I roll over and slither out of bed. With my eyes half closed I dress myself and sneak downstairs as quietly as I can.

Dad's already at the front gate, bent over and stretching his legs in a rather unflattering position.

"You ready, old man?" I say, jogging on the spot to keep warm.

My dad smiles and we set off down the street.

"I like going for a run at this time of the morning," says Dad. "When the world is just waking up. It's good for gathering your thoughts."

My parents live on your prototypical upper-middle-income street with white picket fences and cookie-cutter homes. Everything always looks so perfect from the outside.

"You much of a runner these days, Todd?"

"Not so much on the road. This is a novelty."

"I forget that you live in the city," says Dad. He hesitates a moment before adding, "You should think about moving back here."

"I can't, Dad. My whole life is back there."

Dad squints at me. "What do you mean? You've got no family there."

"I mean my work ... my friends."

Dad cuts me off. "Those things don't matter when life gets tough. That's when you need family by your side."

"You guys are only a plane ride away," I say, wiping the first drop of sweat from my brow.

My dad looks at his smart watch. "One and a half miles. Doing good time," he says, puffing a little more than before.

"Plus," I continue, "I'm happy there, Dad."

My dad gestures with his thumb to turn around. The two of us switch direction and run back the way we came. As the day breaks the streetlights switch off, one by one.

"Your mother is much better at this than I am," says Dad. "But I wanted to talk to you about what happened with Kyle."

I'm guessing this is the real reason why he dragged me out of bed at the crack of dawn to go for a run.

"I've seen what this has done to you and your relationships over the past few years. You held that boy on a pedestal, and you've never allowed anyone else a chance to replace him."

"It wasn't fair what happened," I say.

"Sometimes bad things happen to good people, Todd."

We run a few hundred feet before we make eye contact again.

"Easy to say when your own relationship is like a Hallmark card."

My dad laughs. "You think we've always had this lovey-dovey kind of romance? You don't remember how things used to be, when you were smaller?"

I shake my head.

"Can we stop for a second," he says, panting. "I don't usually have deep and meaningful conversations when I'm running."

We slow down to a brisk walk.

"I was a shit father when you and your sister were younger. I was working too hard. Your mother's and my relationship was barely hanging together. Then, in the space of six months, I started a new job, her mother died, and she found out that she was pregnant again. You don't remember any of this?"

"I don't remember grandma at all, or Mom being pregnant."

"We lost the baby. He was premature ... twenty-three weeks young," says Dad mournfully.

I get a flicker of a memory from when I was no more than two years old, of going to the hospital and seeing what I thought was a tiny purple frog in a glass box.

"It was the start of months of bitter fighting, tears, promises and broken promises—mainly my fault."

He holds his head up high. "It took a lot of hard work. Your mother and I came so close to divorcing, I don't know how many times, but we got there in the end. We're a more effective team, and more in love now than when we first met. Life isn't fair. It isn't easy either. But you make the most of the people around you and what you have to work with."

Dad nods. "You've got a lot going for you, Todd. Your mother and I are so extremely proud of you."

"Thanks, Dad," I say, trying to process everything he said.

"Okay, lecture over. Race you to the front gate?" he says, surging off ahead of me.

"You'll need as much of a head start as you can get, old man," I shout out at him, sprinting up behind.

I arrived at my parents' house a broken man, and today I head home with a fresh appetite for life. I've made a pact with myself to stop dwelling on the past. Instead I'm only going to celebrate the good times I had with Kyle—and there were so many. Life must go on, as I know he would have wanted it to.

Chapter Thirty-Three

With a sense of utter shame, I arrive at Dr. Keller's lab. When she called yesterday, I had completely forgotten about her and the memory machine. Now I'm bogged down in guilt for subjecting Kyle to this experiment in the first place. It was selfish of me. He had nothing to gain. The technology was never going to help unlock his memories or return him to being the man he was before the attack. The doctor in me so desperately wanted to heal him and know what had gone wrong. The romantic in me wanted my long-lost love back in my life. I don't know if I'll ever be able to forgive myself if my interference somehow played a part in his death.

The same pristine white walls and space age technology in the lab does little to impress me anymore. What a huge waste of resources, creating a technology to extract memories. Who benefits? It might make life easier for those left behind, knowing what happened to their loved one, but certainly not the patient. It seems so counterintuitive and selfish.

Dr. Keller's assistant greets me at the entrance to the lab.

A fleeting smile crosses her face.

"My condolences for your loss," she says.

"Thank you," I say with as much of a smile as I can summon.

I follow her down the brightly lit corridor through a set of sliding glass doors. She leads me to a changing room, where one of the body-fitting metallic suits has been laid out for me.

"If you could please change into this, and then I'll take you through to see Dr. Keller."

"Does this mean you found something?"

"We got there in the end. Dr. Keller will fill you in on the details," she says with a huge smile and sigh. "I'll leave you to get dressed."

I pick up the suit and inspect it closely. It looks like a fish's skin, but it's soft. As I run my hand over the scaly texture, I feel the sensation of static electricity. I put the suit on and it molds itself to the contours of my body, becoming indiscernible from my own skin. If I close my eyes, it feels like I'm completely naked.

Dr. Keller's assistant walks back into the room, carrying a silver tray, on top of which sits a jet injector and a small glass vial filled with a fluorescent blue liquid. The name of the drug written on the side of the vial doesn't ring any bells. It must be experimental too.

"This will raise your seizure threshold and help your mind to relax," she says as she attaches the vial to the jet injector. "If you wouldn't mind tilting your head to the side, please."

I turn my head and she places the injector against my

neck. "Sharp scratch," she says. It stings for a second as the chemical penetrates my skin, and then the discomfort passes.

"Dr. Keller will be with you in a minute," she says, and leaves the room at the exact moment that the doctor herself makes an entrance.

"Welcome back, Dr. Chambers," she says very formally with a vigorous handshake. "I'm glad you could make it. I was sad to hear what happened to Kyle. I have viewed the memories, and what we extracted is something rather alarming." Her comment takes me by surprise, and I'm slightly concerned to hear that. "I realize that you had a close relationship with the subject, Kyle. Is that true?"

"He was my partner," I say, extremely apprehensive about all this.

She stops and looks down at the ground, taking a minute to think. A minute that feels like eternity.

"Do you really want to know what happened to him?" she says.

Without hesitation, I reply, "Yes."

"Very well then; let's do this."

She places her hand against a panel on the wall, which scans the imprint of her palm. A set of frosted glass doors open and we walk into a pitch-black space. Recessed LED lighting slowly illuminates the room to a brilliant white. Part of the wall slides across the doorway, hiding it from view. The room is a cube, perhaps the size of a two-car garage, and made up of hundreds of smaller cubes.

"The bad news is that the injuries he sustained to his brain were so severe that most of the memories we could extract were unintelligible or sensory in nature. As smart as this technology is, we haven't yet fully figured out how to project all the senses," continues Dr. Keller.

We stop in the center of the room and she rests the palms of her hands on my shoulders.

"Stand right here," she says. "You're going to feel as if the room is moving around you, but it's just an illusion. If you need to stop at any time, simply fold your arms across your chest and the projection will end."

She leaves me alone in this strange room, which reminds me of a padded psychiatric hospital cell. I look around and feel disoriented. Which wall is the doorway hidden behind? My head is spinning, and I wonder if it's the drug they gave me starting to kick in.

Dr. Keller's voice echoes all around me from a loudspeaker system.

"All right, Dr. Chambers, we're going to turn the lighting down. Can you put your arms across your chest for me, please?"

I do as she instructs and the lights become intensely bright for a second then fade back to normal.

"Thank you, Dr. Chambers. We're about to begin."

I stand there waiting for something to happen, looking in every direction. A minute passes, maybe two, and still nothing. Then, as if gravity has fallen away from beneath my feet, the room shifts around me. The floor drops, but I stay suspended in midair. The walls retract, and the room changes from a cube to a hexagon, and slowly into a perfectly round ball. The lighting dims so that it's only just dull enough to see around me. I feel like I'm going to throw up, so I close my eyes and wait for the wave of nausea to pass.

When I open them again, it's as if I'm staring through somebody else's eyes. A 180-degree view from side to side, and above and below, completely filling my field of vision. I can't make out what I'm looking at. There's lots of green and black, and it's moving unlike anything I've seen before. The image becomes clearer, and I can discern a footpath edged by green grass. The projection moves up the wall to the ceiling. A night sky full of bright, shimmering stars shines down upon me.

A loud male voice screams out, "FAGGOT!"

The image in front of me flips over and rolls around. The echo of the voice resounds and repeats. I wish it would stop. The green comes into focus again, and then the black night. One by one, faceless male figures appear from the darkness until they surround me. Laughter rings out from every direction and stops just as suddenly.

"Not so tough now," says one of the faceless men. My view fills with beautiful purple explosions that resemble Rorschach tests. The strange patterns dissipate to black, and dots of color slowly return.

I see a hand covered in intense, bright red blood. The colors are richer and deeper than reality. So much blood. The faceless men come at me, one by one, and the projection is sent spinning around the room. I have to look away. I look up to see one of the faceless men leaning over me. His mask-like face morphs into something more recognizable, the facial features sharpen, and I'm certain I know his face. Then he's gone.

I hear panicked wails. "You've killed him! We're all going to hell!" The voice echoes and the images begin to flow again in random order with words and sounds of laughter, fighting and gasping. I see the footpath, edged with the same green grass. Bright red blood splatters across the concrete. The concrete zooms towards me, and I pull my hands up to my face to protect myself.

As my arms cross, the projection comes to an abrupt halt and the room is instantly illuminated. I stand there shaking. The room is exactly as it was when I walked into it. What the fuck just happened?

My hands are still shaking. I probably shouldn't be driving a car in a state like this, but I had to get out of there. I can hardly think straight over the splitting headache that erupted as I left Dr. Keller's lab.

My phone starts to ring over the car audio system.

"Todd speaking."

"Dr. T, how are you? It's Douglas, your friendly neighborhood private investigator. I got something real interesting that I want to show you. Is the doctor in?"

"Can you come to my office in an hour?"

"Okie dokie, boss."

We end the call and my heart starts racing. I thought this was all over.

Douglas arrives at the office one hour later on the dot. He knocks before walking in with a brown envelope in his hands.

He reaches into the envelope and pulls out a pile of photographs, which he proceeds to spread across my desk.

"Take a look at these and tell me if you see anything out of the ordinary."

I pore over the photographs, which appear to have been taken from a traffic camera mounted outside the entrance to Kyle's old apartment building.

"How did you get these again?"

"You know the rules—don't ask, don't tell." He laughs. "You wanted to know if Kyle ever made it back to his apartment after meeting with the security guard at the zoo, so I called up my buddy in the traffic department. This one's on the house."

There's one car in particular that appears in several of the photographs—an old white station wagon. I remember it well. It's the same shitty car that almost hit me as I ran across the road outside Kyle's apartment the night we realized he was gone. Unfortunately, the photos don't show the driver's face very clearly. I can make out that he's a young man, Caucasian, but his face is always obscured or blurred. He's loading the car full of belongings. It's Kyle's stuff that he's taking. I'm certain of it. Looking at the timestamps, he came and went three times over two days. I get to the very last photograph and freeze. The face of the mysterious man with an armful of clothes is in perfect focus.

"You recognize him?"

"Fuck me ... it's Samuel Christiansen."

Douglas snatches the photo out of my hands and takes a really close look.

"I'll be damned. I knew that fucker was dirty," says Douglas.

"You know him?"

"Have you been living under a rock? That slimy asshole is on the ballot sheet."

"I haven't voted in years."

"Voter apathy is dangerous. It allows assholes like Samuel Christiansen to get into government."

"Maybe there's something we can do about that?"

Douglas nods his head and smiles. "Give that fucker what he deserves. Okay, I'm outta here. Must go break the bad news to a client that her husband is giving it to his secretary. It's been a pleasure."

I sit back in my chair and go through the photographs several more times. I can't believe what I'm seeing, but it must be true.

Chapter Thirty-Four

"He'll see you now," says the unfriendly secretary, sitting behind her solid oak desk. She's one of those officious types with her hair pulled back in a bun that gives her a look of permanent surprise. I survey the room with its exquisite furnishings, classic artwork decorating the walls, and expensive decor. It makes my blood boil. Careful not to forget the brown envelope on the seat beside me, I stand up and straighten my suit before walking into the adjoining office. I grit my teeth as I read the gold plaque on the wall: Samuel Christiansen.

Samuel greets me at the door. He's still as blonde, blue-eyed, and chiseled as I remember him, now with a few more character lines that make him appear refined and mature. Unfairly, age seems to have blessed him with the kind of looks that women swoon over and men envy, along with unimaginable financial and political success. I did some homework before paying him this visit. Discovered that he worked in finance for ten years before moving into politics, where he shot through the ranks.

"I'm Samuel," he greets me with a firm handshake and perfect smile. "I don't believe we've met before."

I squeeze his hand tighter than is comfortable before letting go and faking a smile. He doesn't have a clue who I am. Have I changed that much since college?

"Please have a seat," he points at one of the empty chairs sitting opposite his desk. The family photographs on his desk and walls don't go unnoticed by me. I bet he's got a white picket fence around his house, too. I sit down and he takes the seat opposite mine. He crosses his legs and rests his chin on one hand. This schmuck has no idea what's about to hit him.

"My secretary said that you were wanting to make a donation to my campaign," he leans forward and smiles. "A very substantial contribution."

"My hope is to take your campaign to a place that you never imagined it going," I say.

He grins like a greedy second-hand car salesman, devouring my words.

"I've brought a few documents that I want you to look through before we go any further."

"Everything needs to be approved by my people before it comes to me," he says, adopting a more defensive posture with his arms folded.

"That can be arranged," I say, placing the brown envelope on the coffee table between us and rising to my feet.

Samuel looks up at me, surprised and confused.

"Take all the time you need to consider my proposal," I

say.

With that, I leave the room. I don't look back. I know that he's inspecting the brown envelope, suspicious of the contents, but arrogantly assuming that it somehow contains the blueprint to his future success. I won't try to pretend that my heart isn't galloping at full speed. What I have just set in motion is akin to blackmail, and I was always taught as a child that two wrongs don't make a right. But there are exceptions to every rule, and this is one of them.

A small part of me had hoped that the prepaid phone I bought just for this ruse would ring before I left the building, but I'm already settled at the office when I finally get the call.

Samuel's voice trembles over the phone. "Who the fuck are you?"

"Mr. Christiansen, how we proceed from this point forward is entirely up to you," I say. "The contents of the envelope that you have no doubt just opened were collected over the course of just six short months. I have also included photographs from fifteen years ago to jog your memory. If you are unwilling to accept my offer, I will, at the very least, give you the choice of which photograph is sent to all the major national news outlets. I like the one from December 24th … when you shared your Christmas cheer with a twinky rent-boy after leaving your office Christmas party early."

"That's enough. I get the point," he sneers. I let the silence between us linger. "Why are you doing this to me? Why now?"

"You destroyed a man's life—" I begin, but he cuts me

off mid-sentence.

"What the fuck are you referring to?"

"Does the name Kyle Hansen ring any bells?"

"Oh Jesus. Oh no. You got this all wrong." I can hear him hyperventilating.

"Then convince me otherwise," I say.

"Please don't do this to me," he whimpers.

If he only knew how shit-scared I'm feeling. He could deny it. The photos of him outside the apartment probably aren't enough to bring a criminal case against him. He could call my bluff. He could even thank me for finally doing something he could never do himself—outing him to the world.

"Please … this is going to ruin everything I've worked so hard to achieve," he grovels.

I almost feel sorry for him, but this is what sociopaths like him do. They emotionally manipulate others to get what they want. He needs to be accountable for his actions, and I want to see him punished. I don't care if these photos of him cheating on his wife with other men never see the light of day. I want the people responsible for what happened to Kyle to get what they deserve.

"I'm sorry, but this is something you should have done fifteen years ago. Go to the police and tell them the truth about what happened the night that you and your friends savagely attacked a young man while he was walking through the park. If you don't, I will send every single one of those photographs to the media." I wait for his response, but he slams the phone down on me.

Chapter Thirty-Five

We're in the middle of a delicious family dinner with Felix, Georgina and the kids, when something flicks across the television screen in the background that catches my eye. I stare so intently at the screen that I don't hear Georgina calling my name. Felix flicks a pea at me with a spoon, which makes the kids giggle and Georgina punch him on the arm.

"I'm sorry, do you mind if I turn the volume up?" I ask.

She turns around and sees the scrolling text on the screen —*"Politician in assault scandal"*.

"Babe, where's the remote?" she asks Felix.

"One second," says Felix. "I think I left it on the kitchen counter."

He runs into the kitchen to find the remote control and increases the volume on the TV.

The news anchor says, "The incident took place fifteen years ago. It is unknown why Senator Christiansen decided to come forward at this time. Political commentators are astounded, given the fast approaching elections early next year.

It is believed that the men responsible for the violent assault were all in their early twenties when the attack took place."

Samuel Christiansen appears on television in front of a large crowd of reporters making a statement.

"I want to reiterate that I did not take part in this horrific event. I wish that I had had the courage to come forward and tell the police what I observed that night so many years ago, but I did not, and I will eternally be ashamed of my inaction. My heart goes out to Mr. Hansen and his family. Words cannot undo the harm that he suffered and I hope that the men responsible, who I cannot name at this time, will willingly surrender themselves to the court so that justice can be served."

The clip cuts back to the news anchor. "It may not be the end of his career, but it has tainted the pristine image that Samuel Christiansen had until now. In other news …"

Felix mutes the TV and looks at me with a stunned expression. He and Georgina exchange glances and look back at me, agog. I don't have to say a thing. My two best friends figure it out on their own.

The next day, there isn't a newspaper in town that doesn't have a headline dedicated to Kyle's case. Samuel's face is littered across the front pages. That self-righteous motherfucker is going to get exactly what he deserves. I follow the news online for the rest of the day as the story unfolds. Police have pressed charges against Samuel based on his confession, and so far, at least three other men have been brought in for questioning.

I decide that following the case would be lunacy. I just can't let it possess my every thought from now until the verdict is reached. And what if the outcome is not the one I'm hoping for? For my own sanity, I can't allow this to consume me. I turn off my computer and try to get on with real work.

But how foolish of me to think that I could lurk in the shadows. Not even an hour passes before my phone is inundated with phone calls from press wanting a statement. Vicki opens my office door and gives me this strange look.

"I'm sorry, Todd, but these gentlemen need to speak with you," she says.

Two police detectives follow Vicki into the room. The same two men who visited me after Cassie's death.

"No need for introductions, we've already met," says the one who did all the talking last time.

"Detectives ... to what do I owe the pleasure?"

"We're sorry to have to take up your time like this, but would you mind if we asked you a couple of questions?"

I'm taken aback by his shift in tone and mannerism. He's almost being respectful.

"Please take a seat," I say.

"Thank you, but no need. This is in regard to the attack on Mr. Hansen, who we understand was your partner many years ago ... and who recently became your patient. We need to ask you a few questions regarding his disappearance. And I must also apologize on behalf of the police department when I say that our predecessor's handling of Mr. Hansen's disappearance was both unprofessional and irresponsible. I'm pleased to say that he left the force many years ago."

"I appreciate that. How can I help you to nail those assholes to the wall?" I say.

"Tell us everything you know about Mr. Hansen's disappearance."

"I can do better than that, gentlemen." I flick through my drawers and pull out a file labeled "*Kyle*". I open the file on my desk for the detectives to see all the evidence that I've gathered so far.

"Do you mind if we take this?" asks the detective.

"Be my guest. I've got other copies."

The detectives smile.

The one who never seems to speak says out of nowhere, "Can we keep this confidential? You know ... doctor-patient confidential?"

"Absolutely."

"We thought you might like to know that we already got a confession out of that asshole Christiansen."

"What did he tell you?"

The detectives look at each other. The quiet detective heaves out a sigh and reaches inside his jacket pocket. He pulls out a folded letter and hands it to me.

"So it's going to court?" I say.

"Arrest warrants have been issued for everyone involved. It'll probably be on the six o'clock news."

I start reading through the document. It's a transcript of the confession from Samuel Christiansen.

Samuel Christiansen (SC): I wasn't the one who nearly killed him.

I never threw a single punch.

Detective Williams (DW): Who did it, then? Give me their names.

SC: I'll give them to you. You want to go after them, not me.

DW: I don't believe you.

SC: It wasn't planned. We were walking through the park on our way home when we crossed paths with that guy.

DW: What guy? Kyle Hansen?

SC: Who?

DW: His name was Kyle Hansen.

SC: This is going to sound really bad, but I knew Kyle. Well ... not personally, but his boyfriend was in a few of my classes at college.

DW: Continue. What happened?

SC: He ... Kyle ... must have recognized me. He smiled and waved as he walked past us in the park. I didn't know what to do. I didn't want the others to think he knew me. I called out "Faggot" and he just kept walking as if nothing ever happened. Harold had been itching for a fight all night after he got made a fool of in a frat house where he tried to spread the word. So he decided to pick a fight with Kyle.

DW: Who is Harold?

SC: He's on the list I gave you. He smacked Kyle hard across the back of the head as he walked by. Kyle fell over and when he got back up, he just exploded. He tried to throw a punch at Harold but ... I think it was Mark ... got in the way and blocked Kyle's fist. After that, it was a free-for-all. Kyle didn't stand a chance. The other guys held him down and took turns kicking and punching the shit out of him until he was a bloody pulp. I didn't know what to do.

DW: How long did this go on for?

SC: Till he stopped moving. I don't know. Maybe ten minutes? It's hard to remember. We thought he was dead. His whole body was limp.

DW: What happened then?

SC: They took his body back to my car. I was the only one with wheels, so they made me drive. I didn't want to. You've got to believe me. I wanted to take him to the hospital but Harold and the others wouldn't let me. Back at the house we moved the body from my car to Harold's. Mark went with him to bury the body somewhere out in the desert. It wasn't till late the next morning they got back, both white as sheets. That's when I started to panic. None of this was my fault and I couldn't risk raising suspicion if someone reported his disappearance to the police.

DW: So what did you do?

SC: I had this idea that if I could make it look as if Kyle had packed up and left overnight without telling anybody, that no one would ever question his disappearance. And I was right.

DW: What happened next?

SC: Harold still had the guy's wallet and keys, so I took them off him and went back to his apartment. Took me two days to empty the place out. I don't even remember how I did it. The first time I snapped back to reality was when I pulled away from his apartment building and nearly drove into a guy trying to cross the street. It was like being awake during my worst nightmare, and I've spent the rest of my life trying to make myself forget.

The detective interrupts my reading.

"We're still going to go after him for whatever we can, but he's negotiated a plea bargain, the details of which I can't divulge at this time."

"He says here they buried Kyle in the desert?" I say in astonishment.

The other detective snorts and shakes his head. "What

we've been able to establish so far is that the two men he refers to—Harold James and Mark Peters—drove all night until they were in the middle of fucking nowhere. It took them hours to pluck up the courage to start digging the grave. They got a foot deep before one of them heard a noise coming from the trunk of the car. Neither of those two could bring themselves to finish him off with the shovel. So they pulled into an empty truck stop, a run-down place with no video surveillance, and dragged his body into the filthy restroom."

"They just left him to die?"

"They didn't think he'd have a hope in hell of surviving till the next day."

I hand the transcript back to the detective.

The quiet detective pipes up again, "Personally, I hope those homophobic assholes go to prison for a very long time."

"I appreciate you sharing this with me."

"We may need to touch base again in the next few days if we have any more questions."

"My door is always open."

The men shake my hand and leave me to digest the details of Kyle's horrific attack. There's a stabbing pain in my gut that I know will last for hours. It feels like my throat is clamped in a vise that's slowly tightening. But it's a good feeling, an excited feeling. Those bastards who ruined Kyle's life are finally going to get what they deserve. I pinch myself. This is definitely not a dream.

Things escalate dramatically after that. Sure enough, several arrests are made the same afternoon. Each of the men is a pillar of society—lawyer, banker, engineer, and doctor. I switch channels on the television to a current affairs talk show and seethe at the sight of Samuel sitting on a couch surrounded by his wife and little blonde angels. At the bottom of the screen I read on a scrolling banner that the show was recorded earlier.

"If it weren't for the love and support of my darling wife and children—" Samuel splutters and bursts into tears.

His wife shows solidarity, holding his hand and dabbing her own teary eyes. His children snuggle their dad.

The talk show host curls her bottom lip and puts on a sad face. "You told us earlier how you blame the horrific events that took place that night for causing you to experience post-traumatic stress disorder."

"That's right," he says with a whimper.

I can't take much more of this drivel, so I change the channel again. The reporter on the next channel is standing outside the courthouse. In the background, police and men in suits escort five angry men, Samuel among them, inside the building.

"The case has already taken a dramatic turn with the revelation that one of the accused has been living a double life. When we come back from the break, we'll have more details of his sordid secret sex life to share with you."

I switch the television off and tidy up the living room before retiring to bed. As I walk upstairs, I think back to the night we found Samuel curled up in a ball in the back room of that gay bar. He was so angry and in denial of who he really was, such a confused young man. Would any of this have happened if he had stayed and listened to what Kyle and I had to say the next morning, instead of freaking out and running away? Look where living a lie has gotten him. You can't run from the truth forever. At some point, life catches up and makes you accountable for everything that you've done.

Epilogue

I stop what I'm doing and take out my phone. I've tried to be strong and resist this urge, but I've used up my daily quota of self-restraint. I give into temptation and dial his number. It rings straight through to voicemail, like I expected it would.

"Hey you," I say, pacing across my living room. "I know you're in meetings all afternoon, but I had to let you know how excited I am about tonight. I can't wait to see you. Hug and kiss." *Mwah.*

I'm going on a date with Simon tonight. We've been seeing each other for a few weeks now. After months of texting and talking on the phone, I finally felt ready to take things further. He's persevered with me in spite of all the drama in my life the past few months. Not many guys would have the patience to wait. I feel good when I'm around him, and although it's still early days, I can feel myself falling in love with him more each day. It's different than how I felt about Kyle, but still it's a "good" different.

I've been hunting through the storage closet for the past twenty minutes. I know what I'm searching for—a nondescript brown cardboard box labeled "*Stuff*"—but it isn't where I thought I'd put it. I start again. This time removing everything from the closet, creating a pile of junk on the living room floor. Tucked away in the farthest corner, I spot it, tattered around the edges and sunken on top. I pick up the box and carefully carry it through to the dining table. It's been years since I opened this treasure trove of memories, and I'm nervously excited just thinking about the contents.

I lay the box down beside the purchases I made this afternoon at the post office and stationary store. I open the box and peer inside at a mess of photographs and folded love letters. I tip the box over onto the carpet. My old smartphone and a trophy of a tiny bronze wrestler are the last items to fall out. I pick up the trophy and kiss it to say my goodbyes. Then I grab a sheet of bubble wrap and meticulously wrap the trophy before placing it inside a brand new box.

I go through every photograph of Kyle, choosing the happiest moments of our time together, and put them to one side. I purchased a brand new photo album today, and I start filling it with the photos, carefully captioning each captured memory with a meaningful description. I spend hours working on this project, until I reach the last page of the album.

There's a specific photo that I want to put on this page. I have another look through the pile of photographs and thank my lucky stars when I find it. I knew I had another copy of the photograph of Kyle and me tussling on the beach. I paste the photo down and close the album. On the cover of the album is an image of a hummingbird. I lay a hand on the bird, close my eyes for a moment and smile. But the smile quivers and a tear runs down my cheek. This was never going to be easy. I give myself a moment before I continue.

With a deep sigh I seal the album with bubble wrap and place it inside the new box. On the side of the box I write the name *"Louise Hansen"* followed by Kyle's parents' address.

It might seem like I'm giving away the last worldly possessions that belonged to the man I loved, but it's more than that. I'm passing on the love I had to someone who missed out. I'll still always have these precious memories locked away in my heart.

When I was younger, I dreamed that I would share my future with Kyle, that we would have a family and grow old together. But life didn't work out the way that I had planned. I still miss Kyle, but I've stopped sitting and wondering how things might have been if they had turned out differently. I like to think that he's in a better place now. I wouldn't go so far as to describe that place as Heaven, because I'm not sure he would appreciate the religious overtones, but I imagine that it's somewhere peaceful. He will always have a special place in my heart—a heart he broke the night he disappeared. He will forever be my first love and can never be replaced. I will love you always, Kyle Hansen.

I wonder if my old phone still works? I push the power button and lo and behold the screen flickers to life. The interface looks so low res and dated. No one would believe it was once the latest technology. A warning starts flashing —*"Low battery"*—but my eyes are drawn to something else, the messages icon. I tap on the screen and scroll to the bottom of the texts. The last message that Kyle ever sent to me is still there—*"Goodbye my darling. It's not the same when you're not around. I love you. I miss you. I'm coming home soon. xoxoxo"*

Dear Reader

Thank you for allowing me to share Todd and Kyle's story with you in my debut novel, Return to Me.

This novel started out as a coming of age romance, but soon into the creative process a different tale emerged with elements of mystery and sci-fi. I came up with this story while contemplating what it would be like for two people, who were made for one another in every single way, to meet while they were still quite innocent—the perfect couple, untainted by heartbreak or baggage from previous relationships. Their happiness comes to a sudden end when one of them is abruptly taken from this world. The idea both inspired and saddened me.

Todd loses Kyle through the cruel actions of others, forcing him down a road of dissociation and disappointment. In some ways he chooses a lifestyle that can never fulfill him, and this prevents Todd from coming to terms with the loss of his first love. When Kyle comes back into Todd's life, I wanted to write a story in which Kyle's memories returned and his journey with Todd continued where they left off, but I couldn't force myself to believe in that story. But there is still a glimmer of hope that appears when Todd meets Simon, who represents all the good that was stolen away.

I hope that you enjoyed reading the book as much as I enjoyed writing it, and I would appreciate tremendously if you could take the time to leave a review. Your compliments and criticisms are welcome. I would also love to hear from you personally about your thoughts and impressions of the book and its characters. Please feel free to email me at jamesofrench@gmail.com, tweet me @jamesofrench or send a message through my Facebook page at http://www.facebook.com/jamesofrench.

Yours sincerely,
James

Acknowledgements

To my editor Michelle, whose first edit of the book finally convinced me to trust the feedback I'd had from beta readers, and for working with me to meet the tight deadline that I so stupidly set for myself.

To my beta readers: Becks, Natalie, Lissa, and Matthew. Without your feedback this story would never have evolved into what it is today. I am grateful for the honest (and sometimes brutal) comments and criticisms, and the time you dedicated to reading a book from an unknown author.

Tracy, you deserve a special mention. Your eye for details and inconsistencies is astounding. Thank you for the late nights you put in proofreading.

Lastly, to my darling Jade, who doesn't want to ruin the movie by reading the book, and who put up with ten months of watching me slave over a keyboard almost every day. Thank you for your ongoing encouragement and total loving support.

James Oliver French

James grew up in South Africa and immigrated to Christchurch in Aotearoa several years ago, where he lives with his wonderful partner. He has been a writer since his early teens, and has written numerous screenplays and short stories for his own enjoyment. His professional career began with working in IT and he has since moved into healthcare. When he isn't hard at work writing, he'll either be seeking inner Zen at a Body Balance class or trying to satisfy his insatiable appetite for good film and television.

64577337R00194